BLEED THA BLOCK

Antonio Curtis

I just want to take the time and dedicate this book to my mother. I want you to know that I love you so much. You have been holding me down through this journey of life. You have been my friend, my motivator and have been encouraging and inspiring me to continue to push and become the best man that I know how to be. I want to thank you for being my mother. I also want to dedicate this book to my sister and brothers; Yolanda Curtis, Odell Curtis and John Haskins. I appreciate you and love you all with everything in me.

-Curtis

Acknowledgments

First and foremost I want to think god for allowing me to be able to make this possible. For allowing me the creativeness to produce this book for you all. I want to shout out all of my family, friends and all of my day ones. I would like to send a special shout out to; my lawyer Amy Fitzgibbons and my P.I. Michelle J. Eidell also Sharon Hines, Lashonda Cotton, India Bradford, Ru Ford, Gloria Manns, Kaida Hart, Carla Carls, Ty Lee, Melanie Hargrove, Latonya Neals and Deborah Reynolds.

Shout out to all my homeboys. Frank Goodman from Hardford Road, Stanford White from Chicago, Kenneth Lightly on death row and all of my Chapel Hill homies. If I forgot anybody I apologize. Each and every one of you have had a tremendous impact on my life and have changed the way I see things. Lastly I want to thank my homegirl Charmieta Christian for not only taking a chance but also for believing in me and taking on this project with me. Thank you and I appreciate you.

Life Circumstances change and sometimes we are humble yet we can be hopeful and content knowing that there is one who has promised to never leave or forsake us. As we embrace our diversity may we also make every effort to keep our unity, faith and purpose. Yes we have different abilities and backgrounds.

We speak different languages and come from different countries, but we all have the same creator who delight in so many varieties.

"Father may we make every effort to respect and value each other and our various gifts and talents and show that we need one another in order to be what it is that you want us to be.

Chapter 1

" I want everybody in this bitch on floor... Now! " K-Dog yelled as he and Tut entered the electronic glass door.

" Nigga on the floor! " Tut ordered the tall dark-skinned man who tried to exit as the old Jewish owner buzzed him out. The doubled barrel shotgun seems to take all his resistance. He dove to the floor along with the four other customers.

" Now is everybody just cooperate and remain calm we can do this nonviolently. " K-Dog bellowed with a hand full of Mr. Gold blooms grey hair. " Keys old man. " He demanded. The .45 he shoved into Goldblooms rib was for effect. " Floor " K-Dog yelled.

" Didn't we say..." Tut football kicked the black man in the side of his ass cheek. " Don't fucking move! " Tut had to smile and was glad the Richard Nixon mask hid it from his partners.

"Ssss...sorry....Ppp...please.... I..." The frightened man stuttered profusely.

" Shut the fuck up! " Tut continued to smile behind the rubber mask. " Everything cracker! " K-Dog growled with the .45 pressed to the nape of the Jewish store owner.

" All the Rolexes... Now the safe" K-Dog whispered from beneath the Penny-Wise mask.

"There's no... " Mr. Gold bloom tried to lie until K-Dog viciously punched him the kidney.

" President Nixon will you please show this Jew I'm not playing.

" Certainly, Penny Wise " Tut laughed. " Sorry nigga! " Tut giggled and begin to stomp his hands which covered his head.

" Please... stop..." Mr. Gold bloom let out faintly. Struggling to stand " I'll open it. "

" That's more like it cracker! " K-Dog shoved him towards the rear of the jewelry store. " Floor nigga! " K-Dog yelled again turning Tut's attention to back to the frightened customers.

" White Bitch! " Tut barks as he slammed her body back to the floor. She made it almost to her knees. " Sorry nigga but every time one of these crackers try us..." Once more Tut brutally kicked the brother in his side. " You're gonna pay. " He giggled menacingly.

" I...I...I..." Goldbloom stuttered, his anger apparent.

" Hurry up! " K-Dog shouted as he pushed the gun into Mr. Goldbloom's neck. " It's open.... please take it and leave." K-Dog shoved him to the floor. " Don't move! " He shouted again. Quickly K-Dog pulled velvet bags of uncut stones and tossed them into the backpack bookbag. Then he removed thirty thousand dollars in cash. Instantly he froze as he the two-gun shots.

TWO MINUTES EARLIER

" Please No! " the tall dark-skinned man mouthed at the red headed white woman who only minutes ago got him kicked. Slowly she pulled the Detective badge from her coat pocket. She palmed it to show that she was Philly's Finest. " Stay down. " She mouthed behind the masked robbers back as he focused on the back of the jewelry store. Moving slowly, she eased the Glock .40 from her holster and stood.

" Don't move a fucking inch Bastard! "she harshly murmured with the Glock aimed at Tutt's skull. " Police mutherfucker!"

"No Don't! " The white girl to her right screamed, causing her to turn just in time to see the dark skinned black man standing with his own handgun raising it towards her face. She had no choice but to aim and fire, she felt the slug penetrate her chest while she watched his eyes go blank from the shot she fired.

" Don't move! " K-Dog yelled snatching the bag up and throwing it over his shoulder. He rushed into the showroom to find two dead bodies in the middle of the floor.

" She was a cop!" Tut screamed as he kneeled over K-Dog's partner in crime. " She killed him."

" Shit...Shit...Shit! "K-Dog turned in circles. He didn't know how much love he held for Trigger until now. " NO MAN...NO! " He cried out walking over to the still breathing officer. Without a word he fired two shots into her face. Never noticing Tut moved behind the counter until he heard him scream.

" The door Penny Wise..." Penny Wise he dead man, we gotta go! " Tut held the buzzer for the electronic door.

K-Dog glanced at the two remaining witnesses and a scene from his favorite movie flashed through his mind. One body or ten doesn't matter... Rock and roll at the drop of a dime. With that thought he raised his 1911 .45 Colt and shot both witnesses in the chest and head.

" Let's go! " He muttered taking one more look at his best friend's body. " Sorry Trigga" He said and held the door for Tut who ran from behind the counter.

TWO DAYS LATER...9:30am

" I got it Kendall. " Tandeka sighed. She felt so bad for her man's loss. He and Trigga were friends since grade school. The truth they were more like brothers. " It's Tut baby." Tandeka said. Kissing Kendall "K-Dog" Woods on his forehead. " Want me to fix ya'll something to eat? "

"Naw" K-Dog smiled sadly. Reaching under the bed he grabbed the backpack full of the take from the job. Unzipped the bag he pulled the set of matching diamond Rolexes and tossed them onto the bed. Winking with a smile for his woman he went downstairs where found Talib "Tut" Turner playing with Kendall Jr on the carpet.

K-Dog stood silently watching the two wrestle for a while and remembered when Tut was just a child himself not long ago. His father Marks had Cholten and Chow Avenue on smash when Tut was only twelve years old and he and Trigga idolized Mark's gangsta until them hating ass niggas shot him dead. Most believed it was over a drug strip, the know knew it was over that bitch Lashonda's funky ass. And just like his father Tut was also a man whore. The day after they buried Marks, Trigga and K-Dog found Burt and Lashonda in a Delaware Motel room.

K-Dog now smiled as he remembered the looks on their faces when he walked that twelve-year-old boy into that room holding their UZI in his small trembling hands. He trembled not in fear as most would want to believe, no he shook in rage. Minutes later and two clips of spent shells, Talib Tut Turner finally cried for his father.

K-Dog carried his small shaking body to the car in his large arms. Never did Trigga and K-Dog let him out of their sight from that point on. " What she say? " K-Dog smiled tossing the bag on the couch.

"Man, that Russian bitch is pissed. But she said one point six for everything. " Tut said as Kendall Jr dove at him from the couch.

" Russian Bitch! " Kendall Jr growled as Tut grabbed him in midair.

" Hey Boy! " Tandeka yelled from upstairs. " Tut Don't let him talk like that! He's only five."

"See K-2" Tut winked speaking loud enough for his mother to hear. " Apologize Nigga!"

"Sorry Mom. " Kendall Jr smiled as his father shook his head.

" Take it! We're out of this game." K-Dog said taking the half blunt from his glass ashtray. "When will it be done? " K-Dog fired up the weed.

"I'll be back by 4:30 this afternoon." Tut said slamming K-2 on the couch. " Choke slam nigga! " He laughed running to the door with the bag.

" Tut! " K-Dog called. Karen still gets Trigga share!" The look he received back said it all.

"That goes without saying. " Tut said and K-Dog knows he insulted his little brother gangster.

11:30 AM

" Detective he woke this morning. He's in a lot of pain, but surprising he has all his motor skills and his strength is there. The doctor said outside of the patient's room. "The bullet entered his skull and made its exit through his face right below the ear.

"But can he speak? " The Detective asked.

"Barely, but yes. " The doctor said softly. " And only for a moment. " This way please." The doctor lead him into the room.

" Mr. Sandavolli, this is Detective Macmillion and he wants to ask you a few questions. Do you want to speak with him? " Both men stood beside as the nurse worked with Mr. Sandavolli who answered yes.

"Do you know anything that may help find the men responsible for this?"

"Twiggaaa" He mumbled and moaned.

" Did you say Twig..."

" O...O...O... Twiggah... Twiggah...mmmm. " Mr. Sandvolli moans his pain was evident. "Detective he's saying Trigga." The nurse said emptying the bed pan.

"Es...Twiggah...is arter all I'm Twiggah. Who, one of the armed robbers?"

Detective Macmillion asked leaning in closer trying to understand. " Ae Ead Un. " He mumbled again. The detective looked to the nurse.

"The dead one, they called him Trigga." she smiled. " What? My son broke his jaw playing football " she said defensively when the doctor looked at her in awe.

12:30 PM

" What! " Karen screamed as she snatched open the front door. Tut noticed the swollen red eyes and runny nose. Karen stood in the door looking as if she was about to break as Tut held open his arms.

" Karen I..." he said softly as tears rolled down his face. Slowly she stomped into his arms with a low painful groan escaping her chest.

" Why Tut? "Whhhhy? " She groaned loudly as Tut caught Karen in his arms. Quickly he lifted her off her feet and carried her to the bedroom as she continued to wail out "WHY" in anguish.

12:45pm

" Mike, I need everything we got on a black male 6'4" that goes by the name Trigga. "

" Stop it Mac. " Mike Thomas first class Detective laughed. "The Trigga? " From Lawnwood and Ardleigh street. The same Trigga responsible for that" Detective Mike Thomas pointed at the wall with the signature of one Trigga man from Summerville in bright red letters. "I know him." Mike laughed. "Runs with K-dog. Got a jacket as thick as your wife's ankles." He joked while he pulled files from the old filing cabinet.

The mugshot on the cover page proved the fact Trigga didn't run with nobody no more and never would again. He was deceased.

"He's dead Mike! " MacMillian said. "That shooting two days ago the one where Detective Blairwood died. Well this is our man."

" I thought the jeweler said he was one of the vics one the floor? "Detective Thomas said.

"He did but he also said he was forced into the back when the shooting went down. Even the security tapes were removed from the video feed. MacMillian said studying the rap sheet. "Well Mr. Sandavolli woke this morning and I.D. the dead man as one of the perps. "

"Then you can bet your last dollar that K-Dog had something to do with it." Mike whispered reaching for his phone.

"I'll get a warrant." Detective MacMIlian continued to read the rap sheet of Fredderick "Trigga or Trigga Man Clark." One thing stood out and he smiled. Mike Thomas had been right. Trigga has thirteen arrests three as an adult and all but two involved a fella name Kendall "K-Dog" Woods.

2:30 PM

Tut slid the key into the dead bolt lock. An hour ago, he'd left Karen asleep in bed, promising to return with enough money to get her out of

Philadelphia forever. Not once did she ask were the involved, she knew. But it wouldn't have mattered anyway she also knew her man, he never followed.

" Kay. " Tut called softly closing the door and looking up the stairs. She didn't answer. " Kay it's me. " He said a little louder. Tut practically lived here as well with K-Dog so he had no qualms about moving around. But he never expected what he found as he pushed open the door to the bedroom. "I..." He wanted to protest as she held out her hands. Their eyes locked.

"Shhhhh." Karen cooed standing next to the bed.

 Tut watched with excitement of a boy seeing his older sister naked for the first time. He felt sort of an animalistic incestuous lust building inside, but he still managed to voice his objections. "Karen please..." He cold heartedly pulled away from her. Tut could feel the heat of her longing for some affection in her time of need. " Look Damnit! " She slapped him across the face.

It seems as his eyes were opened at that moment. Karen has always been an older sister, just like Tandeka but now standing in front of him completely naked and wanting, her beauty roared to his manhood. " Take me."

Karen stood five-five and one hundred twenty pounds. Her breast was full and heavy her hips round and inviting. But it was her beautiful thick pussy lips that sat closed with a thin strip of peach fuzz above the slit that turned a no into a yes. " Take me Tut. " she moaned running a finger into the thick meaty lips. She immediately sucked in air as the pleasure of her own finger began to arouse her. Tut expected her finger to pass his lips and onto his tongue, but they didn't. Karen slid them into her own mouth. " Mmmm Boy " she moaned. " Taste me Tut " she wooed.

Slowly Karen backed to the bed and turned so that he could see her flower from behind, while she crawled onto the bed. " I need you Tut. I'm so ... Please... Taste me. Show me I'm still alive... Oh God! " she screamed in agonizing pain. " I want to live...Show me I am able to feel Tut...Please...Tut... "

She screamed driving her face into the bed with such force Tut feared she'd break her own neck.

" Karen! " Tut cried as he spread her ass with his large hands. He knew she had no more left as his mouth found her pussy lips.

"Show me I'm alive Tut..." she cried while he ate her pussy from behind. " Show me... Uhh...Show...Ssss...Mmmmph! " She moaned as his tongue filled the inside of her soaked pussy. Tut tried to take her pain away.

2:55 PM

" This is K-Dog people. " Detective MacMillian said standing in the police briefing room. " We think he was involved in the death of off duty Detective Blairwood two days ago. The dead man at the scene was a known crime partner of a Mr. K-Dog and we believe he was one of the other perps who got away after killing one of ours. We got a signed warrant from Judge Adams and she wants him alive. " He spoke with a low voice looking up at the ceiling. " But if he sneezes... " There was no need for him to finish the statement.

The Captain put the arrest team for one reason, they were all aggressive shooters. " Captain. Like my lead Detective said, better him than another one of us. " We'll be making breach at 4:00 pm sharp. I have eyes on the house as we speak. " Be safe and let's all come home tonight. "

3:00 PM

"OOhhh...OOhhh...OOhhh." Karen moaned loudly as Tut slid half of his ten inches inside of her moistened tight walls. He could feel she was unable to take everything he had to give, but her hands urged him deeper with every thrust. " More Tut oh God... Deep Ahhh..." She cried as two more inches sank into her pussy. " Ahhh...Ouuu Shit... More Tut... Fuck...Mo... " She begged as her hands pulled him deeper by his ass. She needed the feel of physical pain instead of emotional.

"I don't want to hurt you Kay." Tut murmured softly. Tut Seven inches deep " Cum for me Ma. " He almost begged as she pulled another inch inside.

"Ahhhh Fuck Me... Make me feel it. " She cried out slamming up into his every thrust. No longer did Karen care for pleasure. She wanted to hurt in another way besides sadness. "Ouchhh! " She bellowed and bit into Tuts chest. That did it, the lust took over his small frame. " Urrrghhh! Urrrghhh! Urrrghhh! " she cried out only to hear Tut's animalistic beast grunts while he drove into her with everything he had.

"Mmmph! Mmmph! Mmmph!"

3:40

Tut pulled on his black and gray Timberland hiking boots. He smiled as Karen's hand rubbed the small of his back under his hoodie. " You alright Kay? " Tut asked with a low tone unable to look into her dark almond shaped eyes.

"Fuck no..." The giggle that came from her mouth sounded sad and unsure. " I lost my world Tut..." She sniffed as she softly began to cry. "You must think a bitch is crazy huh?" Turning Tut took her hand.

"No Beautiful." He raised her hand to his lips.

"Look at what I just did..." She buried her face into the pillow. Tut understood she now feels guilt he also had to live with. Was it a betrayal or was it just an emotional break down that made both parties need each other to deal with it.

" Kay we..." He stopped to choose his words carefully. " Kay, I love you..." Tut spoke with an undertone. "I loved Trigga too." Standing he turned and stared down at the naked woman spread across the bed sobbing.

" That's over five hundred thousand Kay..." He bent to kiss her shaking slender back. "Leave this god forsaken city beautiful. Live for Trigga because he loved you too." Tut rushed from the home of his dead friend leaving a broken woman and a secret of sure betrayal behind. Jumping into his 1994 Capris Classic Tut cried to himself as he drove to the three city blocks to K-Dog's to drop off his cut from the robbery.

" Maybe K-Dog is right..." Tut wiped the tears from his eyes as he listened to the tribute song to Biggie Smalls Puffy had made. "...We need to get out of the game for good. " But life is no game he would soon realize.

3:59 PM

" Baby. " Tandeka yelled up the stairs. " We going to the chinks for some smokes. " She made one last adjustment to Kendall's Ralph Lauren button up short sleeve shirt. " Want something? " She pulled on Kendall's Polo coat.

"Naw Ma." K-Dog yelled from the toilet. " I'll be back in a few minutes. " Tandeka checked herself in the mirror by the door one last time.

3:59 PM 43 seconds...

The tactical abstraction team filled the block on foot dressed in black. Their bulletproof vest read in bright yellow letters " Philadelphia Police". Two men with 870 Mossbergs lead two more Detectives up to the door with a ram drill. Holding up three fingers Detective MacMillion began his count down. Two fingers...one finger... The ram was drawn back just as the front door swung open.

" Down...Down...Down...Down..." The abstraction team ordered. They rushed Tandeka to the floor and slammed the small body Kendall Jr against the sofa with such power he fell semi-conscious into the floor. " Philadelphia Police. " McMillian barked with no regards to the child he just hurt. " Kendall Woods! Come down with your hands-on top of your head. "

" Shit! " K-Dog grumbled quietly. His hand held the Smith & Wesson .357 with the twelve-inch barrel. His eyes showing the same insanity of a wild animal trapped by a predator. They said   " Not Today. "

"My baby! " He heard Tandeka scream. " Down...Down...Down." K-dog heard another cop yell as his wife's body hit the floor again. "Y'all hurt my baby " she screamed. "Mrs. don't move." The cop ordered.

" Leave her be! MacMillian vociferated. "It's her kid for Christ sake. "

" Kendall, they hurt my baby. " Tandeka shrieked

4:10 PM

The Capris Classic pulled to the stop sign. Tut hit the right signal and froze. The panic he felt didn't match the anger in his heart. " How could they have known? " He thought to himself as he heard the shots rang out.

REWIND...

" Kendall, they hurt my baby! " Tandeka shrieked making

K-Dog drop his gun in the sink. With all caution gone he charged from the bathroom and down the stairs. He had only one thing on his mind. The safety of his family.

" Freeze Mother Fucker! " MacMillion yelled as he leveled his 9mm at K-Dog's chest. K-dog never missed a step and the warning never slowed him one bit. Looking up Kendall Jr cried out with all he had inside of him.

"NO DADDY! " The bump on his head meant little to the child as the shots rang out.

"No...No...No...No...No..." Tut cried wailed out over and over again as he heard seven gun shots open up the evening air. " Please God..." He banged on the steering wheel of his car. " Please God not K-Dog too... Nooo...Nooo...Nooo! " The tear flowed freely as he turned onto Stenton Avenue. He needed to disappear he knew, but that had to wait. He needed to see K-Dog and Trigga one last time.

Chapter 2

" Precious Lord... Take my hand... Lead me on...Help me to stand... I am tired, and I am weak..."   The soloist song with such soul Tut felt his heart split inside. The soft groan he so desperately tried to hold inside escaped his mouth without his consent. Karen screamed for Trigga to get up, but she knew, they all knew this was his final goodbye.

" Kay..." Tut called out from the balcony and with every note the heavy black woman sang, Tut lost a little more of his own humanity. The only two men besides his father he loved now laid dead. Today Trigga was going home. He still needed to find out when K-Dog would be laid to rest.

" Through the wind... Through the storm... Precious Lord... Lead me on... Take my hand... and take me home..."

That angelic voice broke him down. Tut couldn't hold it any longer as he let out a tormented moan or pure sorrow. At that very moment Kendall looked up into the balcony as if he could feel Tut's pain affliction and their eyes met. Neither knew it would be more than ten years before they saw each other face to face again.

" Tut..." K-2 susurrated and laid his head against his mother's arm. He knew he was losing a close friend.

"I'm sorry K-2." Tut wept and disappeared from the church.

" Kendall. " Tandeka spoken with a softened undertone as she drove him home from the cemetery. The tears rolling down her son's face broke her heart. It was not that he cried. God, he felt sorrow for others in this cold world. No that wasn't it. It was the fact that she couldn't take his pain away. First, he had to watch his father shot down in front of him, thank God he was still alive...

Barely. Then he had to face the loss of a friend. Tut was like the big brother her and all boys needed in their lives.

" Baby, do you want to go to Chuck E Cheese? " Kendall didn't answer as he kept his face towards the window in tears. "Baby" Tandeka whispered wiping her own tears away. " How about if I take you to see that new Disney movie?"

"Tut said he'd take me." K-2 sighed.

"Tut's gone baby. " Tandeka said "He couldn't stay..." Tandeka's tears were unstoppable.

" I just seen Tut mom..." Tut promised he'd take me to see Shrek this weekend. K-2 expressed. "He promised." Tandeka fought hard to keep from falling to pieces as she pulled onto Georgian Road in front of her home. Her heart leapt from her chest when she spotted the Capris Classic parked two cars in front of her. "See mom..." K-2 jumped around inside of the Maximum.

" He's inside waiting for us."

Tandeka had to admit, she too hoped he would be sitting in the kitchen in his favorite chair eating her damn leftovers which she always complained to stop doing. She'd give anything to see his pretty smile again. She had to admit, he was like a brother she never had, and Kendall Jr loved him.

" Come on mom! " K-2 struggled with his seatbelt that held him inside of the booster seat. "Calm down baby." Tandeka smiled seeing the joy on her son's face once again.

"He'll still be there when we get inside. "

" Two pounds of Salami. one pound of Turkey and half a pound Swiss cheese cut thin." Detective MacMillian ordered from the small Jewish man behind the counter of the Delicatessen.

"Sure thing Detective." The man smiled.

" How's the department these days Mac? "

" It's went to complete shit since you left the squad Sam. Too many college grads with that sensitivity bullshit. Last week this beat cop tried to talk a love-sick dope fiend out of a stolen car..."

"Everybody on the fucking ground! " The masked man yelled brandishing seven shot Mossberg pump.

"POLICE!" Detective MacMillian said as he tried to kneel. The blast tore his head from his shoulders. The next two were for just pure revenge.

"Oh God please don't." Samuel Witzerman cried as two blasts from the Mossberg opened his chest and stomach like a ragdoll.

"I hope K-Dog and Trigga fuck you up in Hell you pig." The masked man said and then turned and ran from the store.

" Oh baby. " Tandeka managed to say as K-2 slumped in the chair where Tut use to sit. " He'll come back when he can."

" Uh huh." K-2 responded with no feeling anymore. Tandeka looked at her five-year-old son and began to weep. Her heart prayed to God to give him some hope. Don't let this break him at such an early age. Don't allow hatred and sorrow devour his feelings and turn him into... His Father...

"Where can you go baby?" Karen asked as Tut laid on the carpet at the foot of her bed. He just did what K-Dog and told Trigga always told him to avoid. "Never kill a COP! Take the prison time!" Tut rolled over onto his back to look up into Karen's sad brown eyes as she hung off the end of her bed. He wanted to relive the one time he made love, no that wasn't what it was. The one time her fucked her again. So bodily, but she put a halt to that claiming it was a mental breakdown she had during her time of sorrow.

But now he was in turmoil and needed comforting. " I don't know... Maybe I can go back to Arizona with my mother's family. Brush up on my Spanish Señorita." Tut smiled sadly.

"Mmm Hmmm..." Karen rolled her eyes and sat up on the bed. " What? Tut asked unsure why she said it in that tone. " Ain't that where you meet that little dirty Mexican bitch? What's her name... Ummm? " Karen sounded so jealous Tut had to sit up.

"Stop it Karen..." Tut retorted in a soft voice. "What?" Tut asked unsure why she said it in that tone.

"Oh, it's Karen now? What happened to Kay?" She rolled her eyes again.

"Kay..." Tut stood from the floor. He sat on the bed next to her and took her small hands inside of his. " If you want me to stay..."

"No! You gotta go Tut. " She quickly said. " I can't lose you too." Karen replied trying to put a convincing smile. Her hands went to his face. "Besides I'll need a place to come visit after I take this money and get rich. So, you go on down there with them dirty Mexicans, and what's her name..."

"Angelita." Tut said.

"Yeah her dirty ass." Karen grinned. "And don't ever come back to this shitty city." Karen stood from the bed shuffled into the bathroom. Tut heard the shower turn on. He never realized how tired he was until he laid back on the bed. What he thought would be only a minute turned into ten as he nodded only to woken by her hands pulling his Armani slacks down.

"Karen..." Tut faintly managed to say as she dropped them to the floor.

"I'm just returning the favor boy." She uttered and tossed the Terry cloth towel across the chair. Slowly she climbed on top of him and swung her legs on the other side of his hips. "Angelita huh?" Karen smiled and slid only halfway down on his swollen dick. " Angelita huh? " she repeated herself as she bounced her ass up and down and sucked on Tut's nipples.

So bad he tried to push more into Karen's pussy, but she would only allow the half inside as her ass jack hammered up and down. " Angelita huh? " She sang out as she came. Tut only screamed one name...

"KAREN"

" Hey Girl! " Karen said into the phone. " I did it."

" Is he gone? Tandeka said softly looking towards her son's room. " He doesn't know, right? " "Yeah! He left this morning. I drove him over to Delaware and put his ass on the bus."

" I love that boy. " Tandeka began to cry. " So, does Kendall... He's the one who wanted him to believe he's dead. "

"Well did you see the news? " Karen asked.

" The deli up in Frankford. " The line went silent for a moment and Karen knew the news was a shock to Tandeka and neither women wanted him to do that. " By the way, he said he left you his car."

"He did. It's out front." Tandeka replied.

"Well did you look in the trunk bitch?"

"The trunk?" Tandeka questioned. "What's in the trunk?"

"Bitch just go look in the trunk." Karen said and hung up.

NINE MONTHS LATER...

The room was full of women and young children running around and screaming. The nurse was very irritated and had Tandeka pissed. She looked down at K-2 who played with his Gameboy quietly. Somehow, he made a friend. He also sat quietly beside her small son. " Ms. Woods come to the desk and sign for your visit. "The female guard shouted over the racket of the loud talking women and screaming children.

" Come on Kendall. " She smiled. Kendall stood and looked up seeming much older than four years old. She had to remind herself his birthday just passed, and her baby was becoming a child going to first grade.

"Mom!" He huffed looking at his friend "My name is K-2 remember?"

"Oh yeah, right! Come on K-2" She smiled

"Here... You can have this Sirus." K-2 said. Tandeka looked in silence when her son gave away his favorite toy. She was proud and thanked God he was developing kindness towards the less fortunate.

" That was nice Ken... I mean K-2."

"What?" K-2 said proudly. After signing in they went through the motions of being searched and humiliated. Then they were escorted into the visiting area of the detention center.

"Hey beautiful." K-Dog kissed Tandeka long and hard while K-2 watched and smiling.

"Ken... I mean K-2." K-Dog snatched him up into his arms.

"How's my little man? K-Dog kissed his son.

" I'm doing what you told me dad. I make sure moms not sad anymore and I got my right-hand man. "

" What? " Tandeka laughed.

"Oh yeah?" K-Dog laughed. "What's his name K-2? " He was proud at how intelligent Kendall Jr was becoming.

"Sirus." He smiled.

Tandeka was just glad to see her baby happy again. For months he sulked around the house. Even his daycare teacher Ms. Henry said she was beginning to worry about his emotional well-being. But it seemed that as soon as the state allowed them visits with his father Kendall cheered up and was as bright as always.

" That's him right their Dad. "Both parents looked up to see the little kid with the million-dollar smile walked into the visiting room with the woman wearing the bright red hair, tight coochie cutting jeans and tee shirt, no bra. The bright red lip stick on her full lips screamed look at me I suck dick and the large tattoo on her shoulder look stupid.

" You better never..." K-Dog whispered.

"Hell no! Tandeka smiled. Twenty minutes into the visit Sirus came and interrupted their visit crying.

"My dad said I can't take this." He said in tears.

"But I gave it to you." K-2 said firmly. Both K-Dog and Tandeka saw the tears welling up in his eyes, K-2 was hurt.

"My dad said it's too expensive..." Sirus cried handing the Gameboy back.

"Expensive." K-2 wrapped his arm around Sirus's small body. " My mom say you pronounce it Expensive. And it's mine to do as I please. Come on." Sirus's mother and father along with K-Dog and Tandeka watched K-2 cross the visiting room.

"This is my Gameboy and I want my right hand to have it." K-2 said sounding so much older than six years old.

"Right hand huh?" Sirus father smiled. " What's your name my man?"

"K-2 "

"So, K-2 my son is your right-hand man?" Sirus looked up to see K-dog laughing. "Can you tell me this then? Do your mom wear lipstick like that?" He pointed out towards the red hair woman.

 "No sir." K-2 laughed. "My dad wouldn't like that."

"Thank you K-2! He can keep it." Sirus parents began to argue as the two boys walked away playing.

"That boy of yours." Tandeka giggled. "I swear he's a grown man in a child's body. Did I tell you they said he's way above average? They want me to enroll him in Chestnut Hill Academy for the Gifted."

"What did you expect? I'm smart and your...Ummm...your...ummm...Shit you look good." K-Dog laughed as Tandeka punched him in the arm. "Ouch!" He frowned.

"You still in pain baby." Tandeka cunningly asked.

"Damn right!" Eight bullets them crackers hit me with. K-Dog knew he had to spoil the visit with the news his lawyer Charles Puruto just gave him last night. But secrets were not for him and Tandeka "Baby..." He suddenly turned serious. "I got word from Chuck yesterday. They want the death penalty."

"NOPE! UH HUH! NOPE! " She said getting louder with every word.

"But if I take the plea its life without parole."

"So! I can't have no dead man. Nope!" Tandeka repeated in some sort of shock.

"Life is Life baby. I can't live thinking some other nigga got my family. I rather be..." K-Dog almost said it until Tandeka slapped the words out of his mouth.

"Kendal Woods! Do you think of me that way? Like some kind of hoe! I Do! That's what I said, and I mean it. Until I'm dead nigga!" She snapped. "now think about that shit next time before you go making decisions for me boy!"

They both sat silently a moment watching their son and his new friend play quietly together with the Gameboy. "Tan." K-Dog smiled.

"What?" she answered stiffly crossing her arms over her small breast.

"What color panties you got on?" He winked with his boyish grin.

"You make me sick." She cried into his arms. "I love you Kendall."

"Que'te ha pasado en la mano?" His grandmother asked.

"I slammed it in the car door Abuelita." Tut lied looking at the bandaged hand. His grandmother worried more about him then his own mother. "I'm fine Abuelita {Grandmother}" Tut tried to reassure her.

" Talib." His grandmother cried from her wheelchair. "Please Nieto... Por Favor Nieto."

"Grandma please." Tut gently said kneeling beside her chair. "Don't listen to Uncle Benito. He hates me because of my black father."

"Nieto, I care nothing of that." She cried. "I care only that I love you so much Nieto. I have no one else to love. Benito is no good...He steals from me and before you came he beat..."

"He what Abuelita?" Tut stood. He heard stories from neighbors but had no proof. "Benito did what Abuelita?"

"Por Favor. Nieto stay away from the trouble, I need you." She cried while resting her head on Tut's hip. He softly rubbed her dark black hair. She couldn't see the tears in his eye.

"Ser agradable ." Benito growled as he entered the room. The stare he gave his own mother rubbed Tut the wrong way.

"Benito if I even thought you hurt my grandma..."

"You'd what puta?" Benito snapped. "Beat me like you did Jose Rivera? Well let me tell you little sobrino {nephew} I won't just stand there like a burro."

"No!" His grandmother screamed holding his hand. "Get out Benito! Your mean and selfish...No Good... Get Out!"

"Si, Mama." Benito smiled. "But he'll leave one day. just like Maria did. It's what Negro's do."

"GO! Get Out!" She screamed with tears streaming down her face.

"Talisha you must sit still." Angelita laughed. "Your grandfather will be here soon, and he expects you to be beautiful."

"My grandfather says I'm beautiful no matter what mama. He said I was precious even when I fell in the hagg poop on his farm in Mexico."

"That's because Papa loves you." Angelita smiled. "Just like I do." She tickled her daughter's side.

"He's here! He's here!" Talisha ran to the door. "My Abuelo! Abuelito! Abuelito! Abuelito!" She yelled from the balcony waving as they pulled up.

"Talisha my sweet." Don Angel Monteza smiled. Twenty armed men spread out on the grounds of the ranch style home.

"Go to your Abeulo Talisha, quickly!" Angelita smiled. "Hello Papa!" She said following her daughter outside.

Tut strolled from the home in the middle-class neighborhood. He watched the block bounce with traffic up and down the once quiet mixed hood.

"King Tut." The small Mexican yelled from the porch across the street. "Nigga you gonna burn up in this heat with all that shit on." He laughed. "This ain't Philly son! You dig kid, God."

"Nigga that's New York Peludo." Tut shook his head and laughed. "Besides I need to look the part if I'm to be King Tut."

"Where we going?" Peludo asked jumping from the porch.

"The commercial. I want to buy my Abuelita some more earrings."

"Again? Nigga you just got her some last week."

"Fucking Benito stole them shits!" Tut growled. "I swear if this was Philly..."

"Fuck dat shit Tut! This is Phoenix! I'll put that bitch under a cactus in the Flats. Give me the word." Peludo snarled pulling his seven shots .45.

"I wish I could." Tut smirked. He saw Benito duck behind the truck when Peludo upped the baby 4-5. "But my grandma can't take that kind of drama. It'll kill her."

"Whatever you say Su Majestad." Peludo laughed as Tut kicked at him playfully.

"I see you puta." Tut yelled. "Cualquiendia de estos puta, any day now pussy!" He repeated in english, looking over his shoulder for his sickly grandmother.

"Bang!" Peludo laughed out loud as he pointed his fingers at Benito who still stood behind the truck.

"So, what we got left shorty?" Tut laughed pulling away in his new platinum silver Benz.

"About four and a half in twenties."

"Man Damn, this crack shit slow money. Tut complained. "Dope, that's where the money is." `"Nigga what you know about dope? Beside we moved almost a whole cake in less than a month. Come Saturday we'll be out again.

" Man, if we had a Mexican coke connect..." Tut whispered pulling up into the malls parking lot.

"Ain't none of them gonna deal with us Mestizo... Half breed!" Peludo acknowledged and Tut heard the pain in his words.

"Fuck them!" Tut retorted "I'm on bread motherfucka!" He yelled pushing the CD in.

"You been eating long enough... Now stop being greedy." DMX came blasting out of the speakers as he pulled in to a spot across from Kay's Jewelry.

"Why you always do that Tut?"

" What?"

"Wait until you park to push that bullshit CD in!"

"It's my wake-up system. When my car starts the music blast and puts me on point. It reminds me to pay attention."

"That's stupid!" Peludo laughed. Both men jumped from the car and entered the mall.

" Grand...father. " Talisha pouted still holding the silk slippers. " Por favor." She whined.

" No, they are too grown for my Sugarplum. These are more your age. "
He laughed holding up the slippers with the rabbit ears.

" I agree Papa. " Angelita also laughed.

" But mama I'm nine years old now. I'm not a baby anymore. " Talisha
moaned.

" You will always be my babe'. " Her mother laughed. Lovingly
pinching her cheek.

" Man Damn. " Peludo almost yelled out. He looked down at the with
the five-thousand-dollar price tag on his wrist.

" That shit out of your pocket range nigga. Get that one. " Tut laughed
pointing at to the case holding the Timex.

"Damn Tut Peludo sighed looking up at the young white sales clerk.
The look in his eyes said his feelings were hurt.

" Man, I'm just joking. I got you player."

" Naw I don't need this shit. " Peludo said. He took the Heuer from his
wrist. " I'm gonna wait for you outside. " He headed to the door.

" I think you pissed him off. " The slender white clerk said. " Should I
wrap up these earrings? "

" Yeah..." Tut watched his man walk out the door. " Wrap that watch
too. " He said. Ten minutes later Tut walked out into the mall smiling. " Come
on Peludo, let's get some music. "

" Whatever nigga. " Peludo frowned

" Come on dog. I didn't mean..."

" Yes, you did Tut." He snapped " You always play me broke. But now
I'm a joke for the peckerwoods too!"

Digging into the jewelry bag for the watch box Tut handed it to his man.

" Put this shit on punk." Tut laughed the look on his Peludo's face was worth more than words. He knew he had a friend for life.

Both men made their way from store to store buying small items making the last stop Footlocker, so they could get the new Jordan's.

" Man, where is all this money coming from? "

"Mind your..." Tut froze, his eyes locked on the beautiful dark haired Mexican woman. It's been almost ten years since he's seen her, but she still had the look of loudness.

" Nigga what's up? " Peludo asked seeing the lock on his face. He followed the Tut's eyes to the sexy thick woman with the old man and little girl. " What yall east coast niggas ain't never seen a bitch? " Without a word Peludo started walking towards the family. " Excuse me miss..." He started to say without warning four men rushed him to the ground only Tut and Peludo noticed the guns pressed to his head.

" Wait! " Tut yelled and towards his man. He saw a group of men coming his way from the right. " Angelita...Angelita..." Tut shouted as he flipped the first bodyguard and shoved the .45 in his face. " Please don't! Angelita please. "

" Papa NO! She screamed. " Esperar! Esperar! " Don Angel Monteza ordered as more men moved in with small arms. " Angelita, who is this? " He asked " Bring him and the small one too! "

The Don turned and headed for the mall exit with his granddaughter's hand in his. Angelita followed silently, while stealing looks at Tut who was escorted by the armed bodyguards on all sides of him and Peludo.

The corridor of Albert Einstein Medical Center was bright and full of medical personal. Tandeka smiled through the windows reading the name plates of the new born. There he was. " Karen Johnson" it read.

" He's cute." Tandeka smiled tapping the glass like so many people do when they visit the maternity ward. " What's his name? " She turned slowly towards Karen still sitting in the wheelchair.

" Tavious Johnson. "   Karen smiled sadly.

"Girl he looks just like his daddy." Tandeka giggled before baby talking through the glass window. She missed the sadness in Karen's eyes at the statement.

Chapter 3

The Come Up

The ride up I-10 went silently for Tut and Peludo as they sat surrounded in the tinted SUV. They were not allowed to ride with the Menteza family but followed closely behind them. Peludo eyes darted wildly like a trapped animal and Tut knew his man was looking for any chance to escape.

" Relax Peludo. " Tut whispered and twenty minutes later they entered the exclusive housing community of the rich and famous.

" Bring them! " Don Menteza barked. Angelita you take my granddaughter to her room and return to. "

" Si Papa " she mumbled. Quickly she smiled at Tut. " Padre Por Favor. "

" Sano y Salvo" Don Menteza growled looking at the two young men. When Angelita reached for her daughter's hand Talisha pulled away and walked up to Tut. Staring up into his eyes she smiled and took his hand.

" Papaito. " She whispered. For the first time Tut saw into his own eyes and his knees became weak. He had no idea when they gave out, but now he and his daughter were facing each other, a daughter he never knew he had.

" Angelita? " He whispered as tears filled her eyes.

" Papaito" Talisha hugged him tightly around the neck. " Papaito." She whispered into his ear.

" I did not know. " He began to cry holding his little girl. " I did not know. "

" Angelita! " Don Menteza growled.

" Talisha por favor...Come! " Angelita wiped the tears from her face. " Por favor Talisha." She pulled a weeping Talisha from a weeping father's arms. Peludo wanted to do something but had no idea what in this situation.

" No! "Don Monteza barked, and his men restrained Peludo. " Let's him feel what no man should know. For my grandchild has carried this same pain inside for years.

" I did not know..." Tut whispered again.

" But now you do! What will you do from here on? As you see she is special and deserve to be spoiled every way. I will not ask you what you do or if you can support my Nieta. " He held up the arm of Peludo. " I see the nice... Joyas you buy your friends. " He looked at Peludo sternly. " If you pull from me Mestizo I will cut this arm from your tiny body.

" Sorry Jefe. " Peludo relaxed as the Don slung his arm to his side.

" Now I understand that my Angelita never told you of this child. But also, she has told me you just up and disappeared. Why? "

" I'm from Philly. " Tut stated softly still on his knees as Angelita reappeared. Their eyes met again. " I went home where my father was buried. "

" Do you know who I am Mestizo? " For the first time Tut looked directly into the eyes of Don Monteza as he stood slowly.

" Why do you insult me and Mi amigo? " Tut asked annoying the question. " He has never wronged you and neither have I. It's no secret you consider yourself to be somebody, but I'm from the cold world of the ghetto... So, who or what you think you are don't mean shit to me. " Tut spoke frankly. " If I die today remember your talking to a fucking man. So, ask me if I give a shit! "

"Talib don't por favor! " Angelita cried. " Papa perdonar por favor. " She begged.

" Silencio mantenrse callado. " He looked to Angelita. " Now sir I ain't mean to disrespect you or your home, but I cannot be a coward for no one. No, it's none of your business what I do for a living, but if I live my daughter will need only me for support. No disrespect again but I rather care for my child from my own muscle, my own sweat..." Tut held out his arms inviting death if it was to come from one of the many bodyguards armed with weapons standing around.

The room remained silent for what seemed like hours, which really was only seconds. the bodyguards never reacted to his words Tut noticed and now know they wouldn't see unless Jefe said so. But Peludo shifted toward the tall guard closet to him.

" Papa..."

" Hush! Leave us Angelito. " Don Monteza said.

" Por favor papito. " She cried, and her father kissed her forehead.

" Go a manerado por favor. " The Don asked and Tut saw his only weakness. " His Family."

"You been eating long enough now stop being greedy... Just keep it real partner, give to the needy. " The car stereo system boomed to life as h started the car. Tut noticed Peludo jump from the instant loud blast in his ears.

" Relax dog I got you. " Tut said as he cut the music off. Both men finally looked into each other's eyes for the first time since leaving the ranch home in the Suburbs. The smiles that crossed their faces would have seemed out of place by anyone who passed by not knowing what just went down. " Where're on our way Peludo." Tut said.

" Don Monteza... Goddamn Don Monteza the fucking hand of death. " Peludo smiled.   " His daughter's baby daddy. "

" I got a daughter nigga! " Tut smiled and Peludo could see the tears in his eyes.

" Nigga we got a connect! " Peludo exclaimed with excitement. " No more cut up bullshit from leftovers from those puta's from 24th Ave and Van Buren.

FIVE YEARS LATER

Happy Birthday to you...Happy Birthday to you... Happy birthday dear Tay-Tay...Happy birthday to you. " The entire group sang as the brought the cake with five candles to the table.

" That boy is growing so fast. " Tandeka smiled.

" Poor kid. " Qwen whispered watching her son Sirus and K-2 surround Tay- Tay like he was a brother. " I cannot believe Karen did that shit."

" I know…" Tandeka waved to the three boys who smiled their way as the clowns cut the cake for the fifty kids gathering around the tables. " Fucking crack head... I swear Kendall almost cried when I told him that shit. You know Trigga was like his brother."

" That's Tay-Tay's father, right? " Qwen questioned and the look on Tandeka's face made her ask again. " Right? "

"Let's open up his presents " Tandeka tried to avoid the question that Qwen refused to let go.

"Wait Bitch..." She hissed. " Spill that shit."

" Girl..." Tandeka pulled Qwen to the far side away from the boys. " Do you remember I told you about Tut, my man's young boy he raised?" "Yeah, Yeah…" Qwen pushed for more.

" Girl look at this picture." Tandeka opened her wallet and pulled the photo of three males. Kendall, Trigga and young thirteen-year-old boy who looked just like an older Tay-Tay, curly hair and all. There was no need for words after looking at the picture, Qwen just moaned. " Mmmmph!"

MEANWHILE....

"Man, I don't give a shit!" Peludo growled holding his signature machete. " You got about ten seconds to get that cash." " You gonna do us like dat? "

" FIVE seconds mothafucker! "Peludo snapped again.

" Under the sofa... Under the sofa! " She screamed crying. She looked her son in the eyes.

"That's better. " Tut whispered standing from the bed. " Now..." He gripped the blond haired white girl by the neck. " For wasting my time..." Tut tossed her to the bed. He ripped the white panties off her slender hips. " Bitch! " Tut raised his hand when she tried to push him away. She covered her face.

" Come on King Tut..." The small white boy cried " That's my mom's man."

" Yeah well... Tut pulled his pants down and smiled at the look in the middle-aged woman's eyes. " You should've thought about that shit when you tried to steal the trap cracker."

" Ewww Weee! " Peludo laughed. " He's gonna fuck the shit out of that bitch!

" Climbing on the bed Tut noticed the way she pushed her own legs apart. The moan that escaped her lips when he rubbed the head of his dick into her already moistness of her hairy blonde pussy.

" Please man... Don't rape my mom. "

" Bobby... she moaned. " Let's get this over with so they can leave. " She reached down to guide Tut's dick inside knowing her son couldn't see her movements. Smiling Tut slid inside until she tried to halt him with her hands.

He knew she couldn't take it all, so he withdrew at that point. Her legs went to his hips on their own as Tut fucked her into an orgasmic state.

" I'mmm... gonna... Ohhh Tut. " She whispered in his ear while he sped up his pumping motion. " Ewwww....Ewwwww...Ewwww... she cried quietly as she came in explosions of pleasure. " Fuuuuuck Meeeee! "

Tut continued to fuck her with two third of dick until she shook again. Pulling free of her quivering vagina muscles, Tut grabbed her by the hair and barked " Look Bobby! "

" Please... Not..." Bobby almost cried until he noticed the gun in Peludo hand. He looked up as his mother sucked almost ten inches of dick down here throat. Closing his eyes King Tut shot his cum down her 45-year-old throat. She held it in both hands as her tongue licked around the head cleaning up every drop.

" Your mom just saved your life cracker. " Peludo laughed. He grabbed the bag of cash from under the brown sofa. " How much? "

" Thirty-eight five." Bobby mumbled. Opening the bag Peludo pulled eight thousand from the bag in thousand-dollar stacks. " That's your cut. Next time you stall us, you die! That big pussy bitch too!"

" I don't know about her Peludo..." Tut laughed " This pussy good.

" She smiled slyly not wanting Bobby to see she enjoyed the way Tut fucked her.

" Let's bounce. " King Tut winked down at Dorthy before kissing her swollen pussy lips.

" Man, they some freakish crackers. " Peludo laughed. " Mom and son... on some rape shit! I bet Bobby is fucking her fine old ass. "

" Nigga I don't give a damn..." King Tut laughed firing up the blunt. " Them two crackers worth the two birds a month. I don't mind playing games for that kind of money. "

" Well these niggas over in the projects ain't playing."

With that Tut stopped laughing. He knew about the 16th street crew pushing up on his spots over there. The two bodies inside the trap house off McDowell. The small convenient store he opened being shot up on 2nd street. He also knew about the bitch Selita they used to get inside of Pamela's apartment to rob her for the eighteen ounces of rock. Two brothers and their stupid ass cousin's Mark and Mathew Jenkins.

" Don't worry about that nigga Fat Boy and his brother Skip, I got that bitch red Maria on it. Tut laughed. " Me and you gonna take care of Mark and Mathew ourselves."

Tut pulled onto 25th avenue just as Uncle Benito came from his grandmother's home.

" What that nigga doing at Abuelito's? " He thought to himself as Benito rushed into his truck and sped off.

" Grandma! " Tut called as he and Peludo entered the front door. " Abuelito! " He called again, still there was no response. He went to the bedroom door and tapped. " Grandma. " Tut's heart leapt into his throat when he turned and saw her feet on the bathroom floor. " Peludo!" Tut screamed rushing into the bathroom to find her unconscious from a blow to her head where a lump had grown.

" Find him! Tut cried pulling his phone out. There was no need to say who, both men knew it was Benito's crab ass.

She' s suffering from a severe concussion. It's her age which has us worried." The doctor expressed as Tut sat with Talisha on his knee.

" My grandmother is strong." Tut confidently stated more to convince himself more than anyone else.

" Yes..." The doctor said and turned to leave.

" Talib...Neito..." Grandma moaned opening her eyes. "Ven nieta" She reached out as Talisha rushed to her side. The tears on Talisha's face cause Benito's death. " No don't cry Benito. " Grandma moaned closing her eyes for the last time.

" Abuelita. " Talisha cried out as her head fell to her great grandmother's chest. " I just found you. "

" Bebe." Angelita whispered from the doorway only to have her fourteen-year-old daughter rushed into her arms.

"Benito!" Peluda growled stepping into the bar. "Get away from me Mestizo." Benito shouted downing the Tequila shot. He waves for another and realize the bartender was afraid to move. There was five men holding automatic weapons on all the barley afternoon drinkers.

"Get up and come with us puta!" Peludo said smiling. "The king wants you alive, but I don't give a shit!"

"No!" Benito yelled. "Help me... Help me..." he screamed running to the back of the bar. "Por el amor de Dios! For god sake help!"

Instantly three men rushed him to the floor. Peludo walked calmly to his side. Without another word he kicked Benito in the face sending him into darkness.

The five other customers sat silently as Peludo pulled a thousand dollars from his pocket and tossed it onto the bar.

"Drinks are on the king today…" He looked at the bartender. "All day right? And tomorrow I'll be back and pay all of you a thousand. You've seen nada…right?" With that every AK47 chamber had a round. "Keep track of the five."

"Yes sir." The bartender snatched the money from the bar. "Si"

"Mmmm… Mmmm…" Benito shook his head wildly. The words he spoke went unheard by everyone there except King Tut who sat only inches from the gagged man tied to the work bench inside of the Monteza construction site.

Tut sat with tears rolling down his face as he looked into the eyes of his own soul through Benito. It was the same dark eyes his mother use to have, the same as his Abuelito's the same as his. For thirty minutes he cried openly, but never uttered a work. He sat quietly and stared as his only uncle bagged for mercy, strapped naked to the work table. Finally, King Tut stood, never wiping the tears from his face and whispered to Peludo.

"Make it hurt…Make it last…"

"Lastimore!" Peludo growled picking up the small ballpeen hammer and one penny nail.

"Hey!" He called as Tut headed for the door. "You should wait for me."

"Make it hurt!" Tut growled and kept going. Once in his car he cried even harder for his losses. Twenty minutes later he drove down 2nd street with his AR15 on his lap.

Slowly he pulled into the projects and drove to the far back. Tut know from word on the street that Mark, and Mathew hung out in the apartment of the whore Selita. The red Silverado sat parked behind the dumpster just like he was told. "A23" Tut thought climbing from the car. His eyes roamed the street for witnesses, there was none. Instantly he took off sprinting with the ski mask across his face and hit the door without hesitation.

"Mat…" Mark called running into the living room asshole naked. The three shots slammed into Mark's chest killing him on the spot. Tut wasted no time rushing into the bedroom. It was empty he thought, until he heard the whimpering in the closet. Tut smiled.

"Bitch come out!" Tut growled

"Baby…Baby." Selita cried coming from the closet crying. She stood naked with her hands over her head like she saw to many movies. "Please Tut don't kill me" she cried. "I ain't had nothing…" she never finished as the bullets slammed into her brain.

Tut sat on the queen size bed and pulled the ski mask from his head. Crying, he fell back with so many different feelings running wild inside. He wanted out for keeps. "We're out of the game!" He mumbled. "How did shit get so bad K-Dog?" He cried dropping the AR15 to the bed. "My Abuelita, my Papa and Mama. K-Dog and Trigga…" the mournful sounds came from his heart not his lungs. The next thirty minutes he laid in the dead women's bed in an emotional state of sorrow.

"Get your nut ass up!" He heard K-Dog whisper even though he was dead. "Nigga the game is still on and you're it…Move!"

"Slowly King Tut rose with the AR15 he grabbed from the bed and heads for the door. Even though he still cried the smile sadly crossed his lips when he spotted Peludo sitting on the sofa with his feet on the dead body of Mathew.

"I could of shot you Peludo."

"Then who would you push around?" He laughed. "Besides I'm your only friend."

Both men pulled on their mask before exiting the apartment of death. Still the street was empty.

"By the way…" Peludo stopped Tut in the doorway and open his phone. "Say goodbye!"

"What?" Tut mumbles as he heard Benito's screams in his ear as Peludo held the phone. "Bye you piece of shit!" Instantly he shotgun blast was heard in his ear. King Tut nodes and both men made their exit.

One Year Later…

"Mama can Blaque spend the night with us?' Talisha asked. Both girls strolled into the living room looking like a fashion magazine.

Angelita smiled while enjoying the beauty of her daughter and her best friend. At 15, both girls had developed into gorgeous young women. Talisha had her father's eyes, dark and mysterious. They sometimes made you feel uncomfortable, but her smile made them dance with light. She had inherited her mother's beauty and full body. So many times, Angelita worried that she may fall victim to a smooth talking young man, but most knew of the King and his best friend, the skinny crazy man named Peludo. Talisha has firm breast, hips and a slender waist line. Some men mistaken her for Roslyn Sanchez when they shopped in the exclusive shore store in Scottsdale, Phoenix. Her long hair fell down her back to her ass and she made sure it hung there so she could bring attention to its plumpness when she traveled alone.

"Please Ms. Angelita." Blaque smiled and Angelita instantly wished she was her daughter also, not the Mexican whores.

Blaque which is pronounced "black", who was deep dark mocha chocolate on two legs. Her eyes a bright sparkling blue which seem impossible for nature to create in such a dark child. Standing five eight. Blaque's body frame seem to belong to a much older woman, as with her soul. 38-26-38, Angelita knew it by heart, because these two were inseparable and compliments each other's weakness. It was no secret that Talisha was out going and spoiled, whereas Blaque was shy and brilliant. Together there was no stopping them. So, when it was time to shop for school or summer clothes the chore was Angelita's to handle since Blaque whore of a mother would never give her a dime for anything.

"Of course, she can. Did I tell you your father wanted to spend the weekend taking you to Florida? He promised Blaque could go to."

"Oh yeah!" Both girls high fived. "Colonial Drive!" Talisha danced as her hips swayed to imaginary, arithmetic beat in her head.

"Wait… Mama wants me to wash clothes". Blaque cries. Instantly her Spanish blood kicks in and she did what she always did, speak quickly in her native tongue.

"Ella siempre quejándose. Me temo que está en problemas.".

"No te preocupes!" Angelita smiled. "No pasará nada!" She told her not to worry.

"Si". Talisha grinned. "Abuelita ser permero".

"He's coming this weekend". Blaque smiled knowing Talisha grandfather loves to keep her mama for days locked up in his room and she would never refuse the powerful old Jefe.

"Si… yes, now come on! I need help before this math test comes.

"Why! You're gonna copy off my sheet anyway!' Blaque jokes. Both girls run up the stairs to the bed room.

Meanwhile in philly…

The 2003 BMW pulled in front of the Row home on 74th and 19th street. Tandeka, Qwen and their two sons jumps out dressed to kill.

"Bitch I need something to drink!" Qwen laughed pressing the wrinkles from her olive green form fitting J-Lo pants set. Her hair pulled back into a bun showed off her long slender neck. She sported the diamond choker Tandeka let her borrow to go see their husbands in Grateford prison. Tandeka was impressed with the change in Qwen's dressing habit since her husband caught 15 to 30 years. Even Kendell noticed the change.

"See!" Tandeka laughed. "You and this…" She went to point up at the house of Karen when she noticed Tay-Tay sitting on the step alone with his Gameboy. Both woman knew that look on the young baby's face only meant one thing. Karen was smoking that shit again. God knows Tan wished Karen had moved back to Opa-Locka Florida. She had plans to open a booth inside of the flea market in Miami. How in the hell did shit go so wrong from one bank robbery?

"K-2, Sirus why don't yall take Tay-Tay to Karen for a little while

"She's a crackhead K-2" Tay-Tay mumbles as he came down the front steps. "Yall was right"

Both women almost cried watching the small boy trying to control his emotions.

"This bitch!" Tandeka pulls her earrings from her ears. Using the hood release on her keychain, she pulls her Nike sneakers. "No more of this shit."

"Wait bitch…" Qwen said pulling the necklace off. "We gonna fight?"

"Hell no! I'm whipping this hoe ass!" Tandeka flatly said and headed up the steps following closely by Qwen. They slam the door open and freeze.

"OH HELL NO BITCH!" Qwen yelled.

Both women stood watching the crack fiend take on two teenage boys while two more wait.

"GET OUT!" Tandeka yelled, but neither boys moved except the two pumping away inside a smoked out Karen's moth and pussy.

"FUCK OUT OF HERE!" The tall one in Karen's mouth growled. "This bitch owes me fifty dollars. We getting mines, one way or another… SHIT!" He growls and shot his cum down her face. "Come on Teddy."

"Now I want that pussy!" He smiled. "You can get that head jump"

"WAIT!" Qwen yelled. "Fifty right?" She quickly pulls the small .380 and held it so that all four teenagers could see it, then she pulls two twenties, two fives and threw them at the leader. "Now you paid…" Her eyes went to his still semi hard dick. "Take that money and your little dick and get the fuck out!"

"Little?" Tandeka laughed. "That aint little bitch! He should of choked this bitch with all that dick. Would've saved me the trouble of whipping her ass."

"It is kind of nice." Qwen smiled. "But get out anyway… Boy either cum or move." She barked at the pumping youth inside Karen's pussy. Qwen held her .380 his way.

"Let's go Loom." The tall one ordered.

"Shit!" He moans pulling almost nine inches out of Karen.

"Damn, what they feeding you niggas." Tan laughed as Loom shoved his still hard dick in his pants.

"I'll eat you sexy." He whispered.

"Boy please! You got too much dick for me." She giggles rubbing his chest.

The four teens left laughing as Qwen and Tandeka pounced on Karen while she tries to dress.

K2 looks out the front window of his mother's bedroom, then ran back to his room where Sirus and Tay-Tay sat playing Mortal Combat and as usual Sirus was letting Tay-Tay win.

"Check this out." K-2 whispered closing his bedroom door. "You know Pimp who lives up the street?"

"Fuck Pimp!" Sirus laughed.

"UULLLL!" Tay covered his mouth. "He said Fuck."

"You too dumb ass!" K-2 frowned. "Just now Tay."

"You gonna tell?" Tay pouted.

"Naw! Listen!" K-2 pulled the two boys closer. "Pimp and his brother said that if we wanted to make some money we could come work for them."

"Doing what?" Tay whispered.

"Car trappin." K-2 said looking to the sky as if to say dummy.

"What's that?" Tay frowns now losing interest. He quickly turned back to the television to play the game . Sirus shook his head.

"You tripping K-2." Sirus smirked. "My dad said a worker is a chump."

"My dad said if you see it, take if! And I can see us making money."

"Man you nine and I'm only ten…" He mugged Tay from behind. "And Tay-Tay…"

"Tay!" He yelled. "Not Tay-Tay punk."

"Like I said, Tay is only six…"

"I'm almost seven punk." Tay laughed.

"Money is money." K-2 said sounding much older than he was.

"How much?"

"Twenty five dollars a day." He answered. "All we do is run the things to the cars and get the money."

"When do we do it?"

"This summer when school is out."

"I'm with it if my mom don't find out." Sirus whispered.

"I'm telling!" Tay yelled. "I'm telling on y'all."

"Telling what?" Tandeka said trying to straighten her hair out.

Both K-2 and Sirus looked at Tay who smiles and held his hand out.

"They owe me a dollar, right?" Tay laughed

"Chump…" Sirus growls digging into his pockets.

Chapter 4

The Take Over

Five Years Later…

2008

"Nigga get that blue Toyota Camry." K-2 ordered the slim young boy from the top of the mail box on the corner of 74th and Andrew. "Bat get that silver Buick coming up the Ave. Shit!" K-2 squinted as the black Lexus turned the corner. He jumped from the blue mailbox and moved away from the corner directing the Lexus to turn in the driveway.

"Kendell Woods!" Tandeka barked climbing from the car.

"Mom please."

"Mom my ass boy!" She swung the slap at his head. "Is this what all that schooling taught you? To be just your everyday street nigga? What about college? No fuck that…" She stopped and stared at K-2. "Boy if you duck my hand one more time… stand still!" Tandeka slapped him twice in the head. "Now like I was saying. You want to be just another sucker on the street who could have been somebody huh?"

"No mom it's not like that…I'm…"

"Like what Kendell? It's not like what boy?" Tandeka swung again. "Is this what I got to look forward to Kendell? Visiting my son in prison too…just like your daddy?"

"Mom that's not fair. My father did what he had to for you and me."

"And what you think that shit meant to him when that cracker took him away from us for lie...Forever! My husband would rather be dead then to have to hear this bullshit...what? No what Kendell... Mr. K-2 you think I'll hid this from my husband...Your father." Tandeka move closer to the parked Tahoe XL.

"Oh hi Ms. Woods." The young red bone smiled up from the floor.

"Hey Gale. You hanging with those no goods." Tandeka yelled staring Sirus in the eyes. "Don't hid boy! Get out here!"

"Hey mom." Sirus smiled climbing from the Tahoe.

"Don't hey mom me!" Tandeka slapped Sirus in the head. "You part of this bullshit to, huh?" She slapped him again. "Don't you dare laugh."

"Sorry."

"Where is Tay-Tay?" Tandeka growled. "He better not be involved in this shit. Kendell, Tay is only 12 years old. Don't you dare! Move boy!" She shoved Sirus away from her car. "Wait until I tell K-Dog this shit!"

Tandeka pulled to the hilltop and turns left.

"Man mom busted y'all ass!" Tay laughed sliding from under the Tahoe. "She's gonna tell your pops."

"Fuck it !" K-2 said grinding his teeth and tightening his jaw muscles. "What?" K-2 barked.

"He's scared." Both boys laughed seeing K-2 face.

"Never that nigga!" K-2 turned away to head back to the block.

"Scared!" Sirus laughed taking Gale's hand.

"Terrified!" Tay yelled following them around the strip.

"What up?" Pay 4 yelled crossing the street.

"Shit!" Tay dapped him.

"I'm out nigga." Pay 4 said passing the seven hundred over to Tay.

"Quarter of fifties?" Tay asked. They both looked up as K-2 directed traffic.

"Both nigga! My hustle don't stop!" Pay 4 said.

"Get that bitch out of here slick!" K-2 yelled. "This aint no hoe stroll."

"Here comes Man Down." Sirus smiles.

"I'm out!" Gale frowned. She still had a problem with Man6 Down and the way he killed her best friend's brother last summer.

"Let it go bitch!" Man Down laughed climbing from his Chevy.

"Fuck you punk ass nigga!" Gale rolled her eyes.

"You only get to talk like that because of them niggas BITCH!" He laughed as she switched away.

"What up Man Down?" Tay laughed dapping the teenage killer.

"Shit diaper boy." He head locked Tay. "Who let this baby outside?"

"Your sister punk!" Tay struggled to free himself.

"Man I said get that bitch the fuck off the block." K-2 barked "Sirus move that bitch!"

"Man leave Joanna alone." Man Down laughed.

"What up man?" K-2 dapped his homie. "I heard about yesterday."

"Fuck them niggas on Forrest Avenue!" Man Down growled. "Let's hit the Greek tomorrow."

"Can't!" Tay said jumping on Man Down's back.

"Sirus get your punk ass kid brother." Man Down laughed as the Escalade truck pulled up. Tay jumped down instantly.

"Yo K-2." Pimp yelled from the window of the passenger side. "What we got?"

"Five in quarters, three in fifties."

"Let me get that." Pimp said. "Any trouble?"

"Nope!" K-2 heads for the driveway with Man Down. As they turned the corner Man Down pulls the .45 from his belt. "Nigga!" K-2 yelled as Willie Johnson leaned inside of the Tahoe.

"Man I wasn't…" He tried to say as Man Down shot him twice in the chest.

"Shit Down!" K-2 barked jumping into the Tahoe. "Is it anybody you don't kill?"

Man Down laughed as K-2 phone rung. "Yeah." Man Down answered threw the dash board cellular. He looked back and said, "Yall niggas."

"What was that?" Tay yelled

"Shut it down!" K-2 yelled back at the dash board. "Tell pimp to meet us at the bar." The phone went dead.

"Who is it?" Tandeka asked Qwen from the kitchen.

"Who you think?" He said standing in the doorway. Tandeka screamed running into the living room. Without a word she leapt into his arms. Her tears flowing from joy instantly.

"Tat." She held on to him for dear life. "Tut."

"Tandy." Tut also cried. They held each other for ten minutes before Tandeka noticed he brought a beautiful young woman with him. Slowly she let go of Tut and held her hand out.

"Hello." Tandeka eyes parted from Tut to Talisha. "I'm Tandeka."

Without warning Talisha hugged Tandeka tightly.

"Aunt Tandy." Talisha cried. She held on for a while as Tandeka cries. After a while they all sat.

"Where is my little man?" Tut asked. Tandeka notice the Spanish accent he developed in the ten years away from home.

"Little?" Qwen laughed. "That boy is as grown as they come."

"Qwen Robinson." She shook. "Want me to call him?"

"No! Come on." Tandeka said. When Tut stood his eyes fell on the pictures over the mantel piece.

The tears rolled down his face and words could not explain why this had been kept from him. One thing for sure he was deceived and separated from his family by force once again.

"Oh no Tut... He wanted..."

"No!" Tut snapped. "How could you?" without warning Tut ran from the home he almost grew up in. "How could you let me suffer like that?"

"Papa." Talisha shouted, she knew he was gone and she was alone. Walking to the photo of the man she could see was obviously in prison from his clothes she asked. "Who is this?"

"My husband..."

"K-Dog? But he is... Oh no Papa" She turned to the door expecting to see Tut. "You have no idea what he's been through over the loss of this man he loves more than..." She instantly stopped speaking and picks up another photo. "Papa?"

"Shit!" Tandeka began to cry

K-2 turned into the driveway of the cul-de-sac of homes in West Morland Township. TO him it felt like the day before he took the young entrepreneur entry exam for Saint Joe's precollege students. His father had been so proud of his fifteen year old son. Now look what he has become, over the summer months a corner controller.

"This is the home my papa has purchased for us while we visit." Talisha smiled seeing the impressed look on K-2's face. "It is nothing... In Phoenix we own a ranch home with six bedrooms and seven bathrooms.

"No Shit?"

"And Abuelito is a man of influence."

"So is your papi" K-2 smiled "From the looks of it."

"Papaitoo is a business man also, es." Talisha touched his head. "I want you to meet someone. She's very smart and very beautiful, but she's family so no hanky panky." Talisha smiled and K-2 thought of the Spanish actress Sanchez something....

"Blaque... Blaque... I'm back, where are you?" She and K-2 looked towards the stairs waiting but no one came down. "Blaque!" Talisha called again. Still no answer.

"Maybe she took a walk." K-2 said looking around the newly furnished home in the suburbs.

"Yeah, maybe..." Talisha frowns and thought to herself. "This is twice she and papa has disappeared on trips at the same time.

"Shhh." Blaque cooed holding him in her tiny hands, her full dark lips sat inches from his mouth. "El teimpo lo cura todo...Tata (daddy)" with that said, she engulfs him into her mouth.

Usually Tut would have closed his and enjoyed the blow job while sucking on a young pussy, but Blaque was different, she had beauty. Even her vagina seemed gorgeous with the pinkness adding substance to her dark flesh.

"Yes time will heal..." Tut stared up as he pulled her pussy to his mouth. Today was suppose to be his happy home coming. To his second family, no more like his real family. Besides Talisha he had only K-2, Tandeka and if he could find her, Karen. It hurt to find out that his brother still lived all these years... In prison... Alone...

Even though the blow job was mind blowing Tut could not stop the tears that rolled down his face while she came in his mouth. Even as he explodes deep inside Blaque's mouth he silently cried.

"Tata?..." Blaque turned when she heard him sniffling. Never before has she let Tut enter her body, but the sadness in his dark haunting eyes cried out for her. Blaque reached out for him. "Tata... Por favor... Take me?"

Tut needed this very badly. Maybe it was how Karen felt inside the day he came to her. Slowly he turned to lay Blaque on her stomach with a pillow under her body for lift. Tut knew she was unable to take him deeply, but his mind was not on tenderness. He was hurt and needed to release the feeling to someone else. So he did.

"Ewww..." Blaque moaned softly at first as he slowly but fully enters her small pussy. "Ewwwww... Ewwwww..." Her moans grew louder with each ten inch stroke. "Ohhhhh tata...Ewwww papaito... Papaito..." Her nails dug into his back as he desperately slammed every inch into her small womb. "Ohhhh Dios... Por favor papi.. ewwww... Paaaa... pi..." She now screamed and Tut showed no mercy. He fucked black with all the pain he felt inside.

"So is he?" Talisha whispered.

"I don't know... I mean Aunt Karen said his father is dead. His name was..."

"Trigga right?" She sat beside K-2 on the piano bench. "My father told me about him. He was like his brother." K-2 notices something in her stare, it made him smile.

"I was very young when he died." K-2 touched the keys of the mini grand piano. "But that's the same time I lost my dad too. Mom said they had to trick Tut to leave Philly because the press was on the killers of a cop in robbery. She said my dad said to let him believe he was dead so he would not try to stay for him." K-2 looked up. "Tut was my best friend ... shidd he was my only friend." K-2 laughed slightly. "It was like I was losing everybody that year. Every man in my life gone in one week." There was that look again.

Talisha huffed K-2 around his shoulders and kissed his cheek. "Well now I'm your family, and with me who need friends?' She laughed and instantly began to play Stevie Wonder, Ribbon in the Sky.

Meanwhile in Phoenix...

"Listen sexy, life can be so much better if you'll understand that love only has purpose on these streets." K.O. whispered, leaning against the wall as she pinned the blushing young native Indian girl to the side of the old hotel wall. "You see if love was what he told you it was why would he allow so many dicks to invade your precious flower? No love isn't what you believe it to be. Love hurts, love is suffering the bitterness and the sweet. But pretty boy won't let you in to his real world of fantasy and make believe like me. Pay attention Starflower." K.O. smirked looking across the hoe stroll as pretty boy strutted up the block in his silk Prada. She waited until the bitch Chunky pointed them out.

"Kiss me Starflower and free yourself of this false hood. Kiss me and equality of life will develop in this threshold of happiness."

"But..." Starflower moaned so sexually aroused. She shook, not from fear of the angry pimp heading their way but of the wanting of K.O.'s taste.

"But shit bitch." K.O. rubbed her neck with her lips. "Kiss a bitch and get in my pocket Bitch!"

"Oh K.O. .." Starflower lips found the touch of K.O . lips to ne like fire in her soul.

"Starflower you low down half dike bitch! Break yourself hoe!" Pretty Boy roared wile snatching the pretty native Indian girl by her hair away from K.O.

"Pretty Boy... Pretty... Boy!" K.O. grinned with sarcasm on her every word. "I'm only gonna ask you to take your hands off my lover one time."

Slamming Starflower to the wall with his left, he spun on K.O. with fury in his eyes.

"So a whore wants to be a pimp. Bitch this is a Big... man's game. I'm more of a gorilla bitch, and pimpin is my game of choice not need to feed. Now I will excuse you once, but next time...Bitch ask yourself if you can take this dick, because dike or not I'm fucking you four ways. Long, hard, and deep!"

"Damn, pretty and dumb!" K.O. laughed. "By the way pretty dumb boy, that's only three ways."

"No it aint dike. The first is I'm fucking you up! So get the..." Pretty Boy's words stuck in his throat as K.O. hit him with the first of two upper cuts followed by a left hook and straight right hand down the middle. It was her signature MMA move and finished a many fights.

"Oh hell no!" chunky screamed pulling a straight razor. "Get up daddy." She ran across the street. The Mercedes Benz door flew open just as she reached the pavement.

"It's not hard to die bitch!" Cash screamed wile pointing the .44 Bulldog her way. Chunky stopped instantly.

"Bitch don't shoot me." Chunky squiled.

"Then drop that shit!" Money giggled holding the same mode .44 Bulldog. "You need to get with bass blood bitches bitch and stop playing with this greedy selfish big dick nigga."

"Starflower get in her girl." Cash smiled.

"Y'all gonna teach me how to fight like that? Starflower smiled.

"Nope!" Money laughed. "We gonna teach you how to eat pussy." She looked a Chunky. "Coming" Looking down at the unconscious Pretty Boy, Chunky ran to his side and dropped the razor. "You need this more than me." She giggled. She bent and removed his diamond bracelet, necklace and watch. "All that dick and you still can't fuck."

Standing 5'3 with a body like a stripper. Chunky ran to K.O side and handed her the fifty thousand worth of jewelry. "Mommy?"

"No bitch... Lover. K.O. kissed Chunky's lips. "Let's go have sexy y'all" K.O. smiled.

Cash and her twin sister quickly tagged the side of the hotel while Chunky and Star Flower admired the two five-foot five brave Pilipino twins. Neither Cash or Money had the ass of Chunky or the titties of Starflower, but their beauty was exceptional, and their small frames were sexy as hell.

"What's B.B.B.?" Starflower asked.

"Boss Blood Bitches." Both twins said in sync. Climbing back into the Benz, "Where to lover?"

"Blaque..." Tut whispered while she looked out the window of the rental. "Come on beautiful, don't do me like that." Tut tried to touch her leg.

"Lastimor papi...You hurt me!" Blaque wiped a tear from her face. "All I wanted to do is take away some of your sorrow Tata and you tried to make me suffer."

"Nooo, Nooo, Nooo!" Tut pulled over and grabbed a struggling Blaque. He pulled her into his arms. "I'm sorry my little sexy lover. You know I never meant to hurt you." He held her until she relaxed in his arms. "I needed you...All of you." He whispered. "Look at me Blaque. I needed comforting and I turned to you... No one else, You! I need you in my life. I want you for myself Blaque, for me only."

"For real Tata?" she looked up into his eyes. "Do you love me?"

"I do Blaque... But Talisha." Tut whispered

"She'll never know... I won't tell her Tata, and I'll learn to take it no matter how deep it goes."

"instantly Blaque leaned into his lap and unzipped his pants. "And if I choke, I die in love papi." She began to deep throat him on the side of the highway.

"Blaque no ." Tut slammed his head back. "I can't cum anymore today."

"I don't care." She giggled like the little girl she was. "I'm practicing...Drive Tata." She sucked him back deeply into her mouth.

Twenty minutes later Tut pulled onto Jenkinstown Road. "Oh god..." He groaned as he exploded in her mouth.

"See daddy..." Blaque licked the cum from his head. "Time heals everything. even this..." She sucked around his dick head making Tut's body jump and convulse.

"What is it?" Tut asked.

"I'm gonna need to leave that Tahoe here for a while." He mumbled and turned his attention back to Tay. "I'll be home in a few. Does mom and Qwen know?"

"Hell no!" Tay growled. "I ain't telling them two women shit!" He laughed.

"Count up and stay shut down!" K-2 said looking to see if Tut paid him any mind. Tut sat back smiling.

"What about pimp and his asshole brother?" Tay asked.

"Fuck em! Stay shut down until get there."

"Is there a problem baller?" Tut asked again.

"I got it Tut." He closed his cell. " Now what's up with life in Phoenix? You look like money!"

"Nigga you sound like money!" Tut replied. "Come clean… before I choke slam your ass." He smirked.

"Man it's a long story." K-2 whispered.

"It's a short ride, so get started nigga!"

"Tut what's the root of all evil?"

"Being broke with dreams of a better life." Tut laughed, but K-2 sat serious. He begin to explain his plight, school and all.

The Benz pulled up in front of Simons playground and K-2 realized he hadn't warned neither Tay or Tut.

"Tut maybe you should bounce I can handle this myself." K-2 smiled falsely trying to save some of the hurt for later.

"Naw nigga! I want to talk to you and this Tay kid about some shit I got for y'all. Check this out. Do y'all remember the story about my dad?" King Tut asked. "Well I drove through there this morning and that shit wide open."

"What those chow Avenue niggas?

"Yeah. I'm gonna buy the Manor and take over that strip or coke for that matter. Man you may have forgotten this is Philly. Death before disrespect."

"Nigga I grew up and as far as product..." King Tut laughed. "In Phoenix I'm known as King Tut. I can flood the city in hours nigga."

"Yeah right!" K-2 laughed. "Man let me handle the streets, you go back to playing business man in Arizona."

K- pulled his phone and called Tay. "I'm coming in." All that talk about the takeover K-2 forgot until they reached the playground.

Tay and Tut stole looks at each other in recognition but neither spoke on it.

"Shit!" K-2 thought as he made the introduction.

"This my little brother Tay, this Pimp and his brother Flex, We control the corner for them. My other brother Sirus is looked up for some shit that happened this morning."

"Wait a minute nigga!" Flex barked. "Don't be putting our shit in the air like that. Who is this motha fucka?"

"He's right little brother!" King Tut smiled. "I'm your new connect. The name's King Tut." He offered his hand to pimp first.

"I see you recognize." Pimp smiled. "Shut up nigga!" He looked Flex up and down. "You and Tay go get us a beer from the truck."

"Come on Pimp…" Flex complained until Pimp's jaws tighten which everybody know meant danger.

"Now let's talk business." King Tut smiled. "First of all you'll need another controller. This one is mine now and that kid too. I can do eighteen per up to five, then seventeen from there."

"Wait!" Pimp laughed. "I'm only doing three a month in quarters and fifties."

"Then you only deal with my little brother. But still I give them to at eighteen if you accept five or better." King Tut smiled. "Come now Pimp, open up your mind. There is limitless bounties we can travel here."

"May I?" K-2 asked and Tut nodded. "Pimp think whole sale. Take six at eighteen, Sell three whole at nineteen five, still three below price and flip while building up weight clientele. I'll even find some buyers for the first three."

"See why I need my little brother? Smart!" King Tut winked.

"How soon?"

"Two maybe three days tops! Deal?" Tut offered his hand as Flex and Tay came up the walk with the Buds.

"Damn right… Boss! Pimp smiled.

"Boss? What the fuck is up Pimp?" Flex frowned.

"Flex! Shut the fuck up!" Pimp barked. K-2 watched Tay stealing peeks at Tut from the corner of his eyes.

"Man this nigga looks like Tay." Flex giggled.

"Shit nigga Karen might have been creeping on your pops."

"Man fuck you retard." Tay shot back, but Tay noticed the look that was on Tut face at mention of his mom's name.

"At least I know my mom's retard boy." Tay shot back.

"Watch it Tay!" Pimp growled.

"Or what?" The voice growled back from behind them. They turned around to see Man Down creeping as usual. Tay smiled knowing if they made the mistake of jumping they'd land on their backs.

"Tut my other brother, Man Down." K-2 smiled.

"What's up boss?" Man Down smirked. "How much I get paid?"

Tut laughed and the boys followed him of the playground.

"Damn she fine!" Tay smiled like a love sick puppy. Talisha couldn't help but blush.

"Stop it boy!" She giggled trying to look away from her little brother. She knew it in her heart and so did everyone else, but Tut and Tay seemed to not want to acknowledge the plain truth.

"Wait until you see…" Just as Talisha said the word Blaque waltzes into the living room and Tay never saw Talisha again. He winked at Blaque and from that moment he knew she was his.

Talisha was in love with K-2 from the start and no matter what she promised she'd make her, K-2, and her bother bosses. But Kendell would also be her man.

"Come on y'all, mom is cooking her famous chicken and greens." K-2 announced.

"No shit?" Tut smiled. "It's been years since I stole that chicken out the fridge."

Twenty minutes later they all piled into the living room hungry and happy.

"Tut." Tandeka whispered as he stood by the mantel staring at the photos. "K-Dog called today. He wanted to see you now." She whispered sadly.

"Tan listen…" Tut slyly wiped a tear away. "I understand why y'all did it but…"

"Baby if we told you Kendell was still alive…" Tandeka paused. "Tell the truth, you would've died here."

With that they both hugged and cried together and everybody else was irrelevant.

"So you single or what?" Tay smiled into Blaque dark eyes.

"Boy please!" She blushed again. "We familia but you're cute and I got some Bad Blood Bitches for you to hit." But she was just testing hit maturity.

"I bet they not fine like you." Tay pressed. "What? Is it because I'm young? Mommy age ain't nothing. My pockets are deep." He joked trying to open Blaque's heart.

"Not yet little brother, but I got you." Talisha promised. "Come here cutie." She took his hand. "Look at papatio." She pulled him away from Blaque.

"Who?" Tay frowned.

"Sorry… Daddy. Who do you see?"

"I see you beautiful." Tay kissed her hand.

"This boy!" Talisha turned almost red with joy. "Come here." She pulled him to the mirror. "Look at us together. My eyes, your lips, out hair color. Now who do you see?"

Tay was shocked. He stood and traced her lips with his hand. He then traced his. Their eyes locked in the mirror and he let a tear slide down his soft face which Talisha quickly wiped away with her own cheek.

"No little brother our love will go deeper than lovers. We are familia by blood." Talisha said and Tay was in her arms crying. Only K-2 noticed the rest of the night. Talisha and Tay were inseparable. Blaque watched as Qwen flaunted herself around Tut sexually. And K-2 sat talking to Man Down. Tandeka felt she finally put old bones to rest, until the doorbell rang.

"I got it!" Man Down yelled looking out the peephole. "Shit!" He whispered and slid out of the door.

"Where's Tay – Tay Manuel? I'm hungry and I ain't got no money." Karen pouted. "I went up to the corner. Aint nobody out there."

"Tell my sister I'm hungry. Move boy!" Karen growled pushing Man Down out the way. "Tan… Hey Tan girl…" She yelled her way into the house and froze dead solid. The teenager Tay sat with what could be his twin, just older. "Who…"

"Karen?... Kay?" Tut almost cried out when he came into the living room.

"Shit!" Tandeka whispered.

"No, No, No, No!" Tut hand found the wall

"Hey Tut baby." She cooed in her crack fiend hoe voice. "Can't a bitch get a hug?"

There was no hesitation in Tut, for his love for her was deep, maybe deeper than Tandeka. They both found comfort in a time of need in each other's arms. Tut embraced Karen and for the third time today he cried like a baby, while Tay and Talisha watched. There was no more to be said.

"Familia." Talisha cried on Tay's shoulders.

Chapter 5

The Pusher Man

Phoenix Arizona

The caravan pulled to a halt inside of the ranch home of the gated community. Like always Don Angel Monteza's men spread out to all sides.

Standing at the top of the stairs Tut smiled at his Jefe and daughter's Abuelito.

"Don Monteza." Tut hold out his hand coming down to greet him The two had formed sort of a father, son relationship.

"Tut." He smiled It was no secret he was pleased with the ambitious kid who took a pinch and ran with it and he appreciated the way Talisha was taken care of . He wished Tut would have married Angelita instead of letting her live in sin. "Why haven't you married my daughter?" He asked.

"She loves me, but she wanted her freedom. You've raised a boss Jefe." Tut laughed

"Tell me about it. Her mama…" Don Monteza bit his hand. "She was the same way. Always No, No, No, No. That was her last words when I caught her and her bull fighter. No!"

Both men stared in aww until Don Monteza laughed. "Just joking. She's fat in Mexico eating up my money. But I did kill her bull fighter!"

"He's not joking about the bull fighter." Angelita said from the door. "Papa." She smiled rushing into his arms. They had a true and honest love for each other.

"Where's my flower?" He looked around. "Talisha co to Abuelo."

"She is shopping for your birthday present." Angelita said. "Come papa sit. I have fresh melons for you."

"One moment my sweet." Don Monteza kissed his daughter. "Let me talk to my son-in-law." He smiled. "Come walk with me Tut What's this move you are making on the east coast. I'm getting a lot of flak from the Cortez brothers." He waved his men back as they began to walk the grounds.

"It's my hometown and I need closure Jefe."

"That mess with your papa huh?" The Don asked.

"Si. Besides I got a foot hold inside already. That is why I need the extra twenty. Philly is wide open and I don't see why the Cortez would have a problem, they don't operate there anyway." Tut said confidently.

"But the Kings do and it's a long food chain son. Most people will never know the ones who pull the strings. Now! What about your Phoenix investments? Who will look over them? Have you thought about that?"

"Peludo of course. He has always done so?"

"But can he make decisions?" The Don asked. They stopped

"I will still make the calls, he will only see over the daily operations. Once Philly is up and running I will be back." Tut reassured him.

"And your son?" The Don smiled knowingly.

"I have no son." Tut frowned.

"I heard it said once. God punishes the man who abandons a son. Be careful Talib!" Don Monteza crossed his heart, kissing it up to god. "Be careful."

Tut saw the face of Tay's flash through his minds eyes It was the face of his at that age. The dark eyes , the curly hair, the strong chin. Tut was in peril, how could he except such a boy from a women with weak character. A goddamn crack head. "How could she so this to me!" He whispered unaware he spoke out loud.

"She didn't do it alone son…" Don Monteza crossed his heart again. "See god knows!." He looked up towards heaven. "It's in your heart. Now the twenty I have waiting for you at the same, plus your regular shipment. Tut you must understand my hands can only reach so far up the food chain. I am really just a small farmer compared to the other families. But I am one of the last of a dying breed. You must realize I only hold power because of political ties and prison politics and the others fear the death of so many of their familia inside. But day by day they grew stronger and I older. So make your move now while I can still hold my place at the table."

"Gracia Jefe." Tut bowed to kiss his hand.

Philadelphia…

"Yo K-2." Man Down nodded towards the black Mercedes cargo van pulling up to the suburban home.

"Remember y'all this is family. Don't go pointing those things at nobody… Unless…" K-2 said looking at Man Down especially.

"These are kids Peludo!" The slim black died whispered as they pulled into the driveway of the upper middle class home.

"Well those AR-15s in their hands will argue that point with you if you like. Look at that one on the treehouse." Peludo nodded. "His eyes scream killer."

"Boss." The black dude nodded towards Tay."

"Familia." Peludo whispered. "He must be Tay." Both men climbed from the van smiling as K-2 approached with Tay-Tay at his side.

"You must be Peludo?" K-2 extended his hand.

"And you must be Kendell. K-2 right?"

"That's me and this is my brother…"

"Ah yes Tay…Right?" Peludo embraced him with a loving familia hug. "Jefe"

"What's that?" Tay asked.

"Boss nigga!" Man Down yelled from the treehouse.

"And that must be Man Down." Peludo smiled waving only to receive a head bob from Man. "Alright I have ten piece for you inside the van and King Tut says there is twenty coming next week."

"How's Talisha?" Tay smiled.

"She sends her love to you little brother." Peludo grinned. "And there is a box for you in the van also from her."

"Tay unload…" K-2 started but was cut off.

"No…" Peludo smiled. "Smiley!" He snapped his fingers. "And give the Jefe his box."

"So y'all staying?" K-2 asked.

"Only for a week and I need you to show me who this Pimp and Flex is. There is a point we must discuss."

Phoenix, Arizona…

The snow white CLK Mercedes Benz pulled into the condominium. Neither women wanted to raise the navy blue top on the ride over. The weather was beautiful for this time of year.

"College!" Blaque squilled excitingly. "We made it bitch.

"Yeah." Talisha half-heartedly smirked. "Wow!"

"Wait! Talisha you're not totally stoked about going to Spellman next year?... Come on girl… Really?" Blaque frowned disappointed. "This is what we've been working for, for years."

"See… No…" Talisha barked. "This is what you, momma and Albuelito have been working on for years. No one asked me what I want to do with my life."

"Talisha what can be better than having a chance to rule the world. I want to be C.E.O of something, anything."

"I want to be Jefe of my own cartel." Talisha whispered. "And you could be my C.E.O."

"Whatever crazy woman." Blaque climbed from the z "Maybe you could turn the B.B.B. into a Cartel." Blaque laughed.

But little did she realize for years she had just such a plan. And now she had Philadelphia and her little brother Tay. Phoenix would soon be history for the Boss Blood Bitches. But first she need to lock down Peluda's heart.

"What, you think it's impossible for you… Jefe!" Blaque hugged Talisha around the waist. Moments later they were banging on the door of K.0

"Who the fuck…" Cash snatched the door open wearing only a strap on. Her small B cups sat firmly with thick beige nipples.

"Damn!" Talisha giggled. "Who the fuck taking all of that?"

"Bitch I call this one John Holmes." Cash giggled "And we got two new bitches." She stepped to the side so that Talisha and Blaque could both come in.

"What up blood?" K.O. stood from the couch in all her 6'5 glory. She too was naked, but to the contrast of the twins. K.O. has long dreads dyed blond, her breast were large and firm from years of weight training and boxing. Her thighs were muscular and sat open giving her an inch wide gap between her legs. Her waist was only a mere 28 inches but her firm hips were 38 inches. Talisha was always in awe of her beauty. Like Blaque she beyond pretty.

"That fuckin money bitch!." Talisha laughed. "Who is that?" She smiled slinging her purse to the table.

"Who her?" K.O. grinned flopping back to the couch and spreading her legs. Instantly Starflower had her mouth back on K.O.'s pussy. "Ssss… This is… Ohhh damn… This is Star… Flower"

"Damn! that pussy bitch." Blaque giggled pulling her clothes off. "I'm next Starflower."

"Wait your turn bitch… I saw her first." Talisha laughed.

"Look at them!" Blaque smiled when she realized the twins had a thick dark skin women in the floor. Money had her riding a ten inch dildo in cowgirl, while Cash was pushing another ten inches in her ass.

"Oh… Her…" K.O. tried to say as her body was hit with another orgasm. Thhhhhaatttt's Chun…"

"Oh this bitch got to eat this pussy!" Talisha said standing back naked. They watched Starflower suck K.O. into fits, and that was hard to do.

"I'm cumming! Oh shit I'mmmm cummming!" Chunky bucked wildly as the twins fucked her almost crazy.

"Try that out." Talisha playfully pushed Blaque towards the double dicking.

"Hell to the no… Ouch!" Blaque laughed as Chunky collapsed to the floor.

Tay slammed his room door. Karen suddenly burst it open. "Boy I asked you what was in the box!"

"Nothing mom. It's Man Downs!" He lied knowing that even his crack head mom didn't want to be on the wrong side of Man Down crazy ass.

"Oh…" She paused. "You get any…"

"Mom you know better than to ask me for that shit."

"Watch your mouth Tay!" Karen yelled. "You still only eleven years old no matter how much crack you sell. Besides all I was asking for was a few dollars to pay the phone bill."

"What happened to the two hundred I gave you for the same bill last week?"

"You know how it is Tay-Tay. I'm not good with money baby." Karen whined as if she was the child.

"I'll pay the phone bill mom… Here!" Tay gave Karen a hundred dollars. "This is the money I was saving for college."

Karen had tears in her eyes as she took the money. "Sorry Tay-Tay." She whispered and hurried away. She never noticed the tears on his young face also.

Closing his room door Tay opened the box. Inside he found a cellular phone with a number programmed onto it. On the back it had a message taped to it. It Read. "Call me every day at ten in the morning Philly time, little brother." Tay smiled and pulled a stack of pictures from the box. They were of Talisha when she was his age. Some with Blaque and a women. Tay read the back to find out it was Talisha's mother. But the last picture in the sack was of King Tut when he was only twelve. He stood with K-2's dad on his right and the man his mom said was his father on his left. But it was plain to see that King Tut was his real father. Tay turned the picture over and read. "Papa." Tay cried like a baby. So long he had to play the adult, but with one word Talisha mad him a child again. Twenty minutes later he pulled the last two things from the box. One was a stack of twenty dollar bills and the last was a ticket to Phoenix, Arizona first class for next week.

"Tay! Yo Tay come on!" K-2 yelled from the driveway behind the house.

Closing the box and stashing the money and ticket inside of the large teddy bear he and Karen won at the fair. Tay rushed out the back door to meet his brothers.

"Where we going?" Tay asked jumping into the SUV.

"To see Pimp." Peludo grinned as Tay looked around at the Lincoln Navigator. "Then to see a lawyer Jefe. Never leave one of your own inside without help."

"What?" Tay looked towards K-2

"A lawyer for Sirus."

"Oh yeah, that's right." Tay grinned. His hand unconsciously touched the cellular.

"This is Simon's playground. It's sort of like the Ruckers in NYC.."

"What the fuck is the Ruckers?" Peludo laughed.

"Never mind." K-2 laughed leading both men up into the basketball court. "Yo Pimp."

"Man please tell me you got something for me?" Pimp dapped K-2 but watched the strange looking white dude.

"Yeah I do but you need to talk to someone about terms."

"Terms!" Flex snapped. "Fuck dat Pimp! Slap this faggot as nig… Fuck! Flex tried to scream as smiley hand gripped his balls.

"See I wanted to be barbaric first and K-2 convinced me not to because you were supposed to be friends." Peludo tighten his grip.

"Fuck… Urrggghhh." Flex screamed going to his knees.

I hope he bust them for your stupid ass." Pimp smiled. "Now the terms. He turned away from his brother. "Let's talk." Pimp said.

"Yes the terms are simple." Peludo looked at Tay and nodded towards Flex. Tay shook his head no, and Smiley held on tighter.

"FUCK!"

"The terms are simple. We deliver, you pay! If for any unseen reason you have a problem we are to know in advance of payday." Peluda looked towards Tay again who was laughing in Flex face. "Jefe?" Tay shook his head no again. "K-2." Peluda smiled.

"Tay!" K-2 giggled enjoying Flex's pain also

"Alright!" Tay nodded his head yes and Peluda nodded. Smiley let Flex balls loose. Flex doubled over in pain.

"My Jefe will leave these two in Charge." Peludo said as he turned to leave, slowly as if he had a final thought. He turned back around. "Pimp… There is only one reason I come to Philly from this day forward." He looked down at Flex who now made it to his knees. "Jefe."

"Yulp!" Tay giggled and Smiley punched Flex in the side of the head so hard Flex body went into lock mode. His arms stiffened and his left leg kicked.

"That is or not getting Sirus a lawyer!" Peludo smiled. They all turned left.

"Get your bitch ass up!" Pimp barked and sat on the bleachers.

"I am his mother your honor." Qwen said wiping the tears from her eyes.

"I am god-mother your honor. Ms. Woods." Tandeka stood. The lawyer the state has provided for his bail hearing stood quietly and idle.

"I see the state has declined to persecute for the murder but has instead charged Sirus with carrying two loaded fire arms and two ounces of crack in a school zone. I'm inclined to push this issue on to adult court and out of Juvenile Court. This is a very serious matter son.

"Oh no… Not my baby." Qwen yelled and Tandeka had to restrain her. The lawyer still stood quietly fumbling with his pencil.

"Your honor please!" The hard confident voice roared from the doorway. "Mr. Puruto for the defendant." He smiled. "May I have a side bar your honor?"

"Of course Mr. Puruto." The judge smug attitude seem to have disappeared completely.

Fifteen minutes later Sirus was heading home with his momma and Tandeka and the Judge was heading out the back door of the court house with five thousand dollars in his brief case. K-2 and Tay was headed to the top.

The CLK pulled into the open bay garage of the ranch house. Blaque was the first to notice as the sun went down the numerous bodyguards standing in the darkest spots on the grounds.

"Albuelito is here." She whispered to Talisha.

"Shit! I forgot it's his Cumpleaños." Talisha said reaching over into the glove compartment. She grabbed the gift wrapped box and card. "Let's go."

"I have nothing for the man that's sending me to college for free." Blaque whispered.

"You have pussy." Talisha giggled.

"Momma would kill me." Blaque also giggled.

"Then sign the card…Quickly."

Both girls entered the house just as dinner was served.

"Feliz Cumpleaños Abuelito." Both girls smothered him with kisses where he sat. Don Monteza was a happy man.

Chapter 6

Philadelphia 2009

"Man I ain't counting shit!" K-2 barked dapping pimp.

"Flex would you please shut the fuck up? Please just once you dumb bastard." Pimp yelled. "So K-2 can I?" Pimp turned back to their conversation.

"Melina what's up?" K-2 smiled into the back seat where the thick sister played with herself with the dildo.

"Let me see it first." She giggled sitting forward. Quickly Pimp pulled is dick out and pressed it to the back window of the new Volvo Wagon. "Goddamn that's big... Shit no K-2, that nigga gone hurt my stomach." She slid away from the window laughing.

"Stop it girl." K-2 laughed. "Sorry Pimp."

"Girl that's fucked up." Pimp laughed. "One nigga."

"One Pimp... Flex!"

"Fuck you!" Flex frowned.

"Pimp one day he's gonna fuck this whole thing up." K-2 growled. His eyes was locked with Flex's.

"Brother or not I'll kill him first!" Pimp said seriously. "Bye sexy." He waved to Mclinda who looked down at his bulge and licked her lips.

"One day Pimp when I'm bigger." She giggled. Turning to his brother Pimp snapped again as K-2 drove off laughing

"Nigga what I tell your soft ass! Keep your dumb ass mouth closed..."

K-2 watched in the rearview as both brothers began to tussle in the street. The box with the kilo sat unattended on the car.

"Damn Kendell why you all the time got me acting like a whore? Them two dumb niggas fall for the same dog and pony shit every week."

"Because that's what I pay you for. To play a role. Sometimes it's to be eye candy and sometimes it's to be a distraction."

"So what was last night?" Melinda climbed up front.

"That was strictly personal sexy." K-2 winked.

"Well your mom knows. I saw it in her eyes this morning when she left for school. She ain't stupid. She probably heard us."

"Shiddd, heard you, you mean. Oh god K-2, oh lord daddy. Fuck me K-2." He laughed

"That's what I get paid for." She laughed and he stopped.

"What?" All the laughter left his body.

"Mmm Hmm see?" Melinda smiled. "You don't like it when you're made the joke. Take a bitch home." She pouted.

"Nope! We going shopping." He reaches for her hand. Melinda snatches away.

"I ain't playing boy... Take me home!."

"But what about those Timberland stilettos you keep begging for? I found them downtown!"

Melinda kept her arms folded across her nice firm breast. At 17 she was fine as shit and K-2 knew she was his. The shit she did was for him and he knew she wasn't fucking nobody else, no matter what image she portrayed for the game.

"I ain't doing that no more!" she whispered. "And he did have a giant dick...Now!"

"So we going shopping?" He smiled.

"I wear a size six and a half boy! Now take me home" she barked. "And they better be new!"

"Was his dick bigger than mine?"

"God damn right...At least by a half inch." She smiled and they both laughed.

"K-2 dropped Melinda off on Chelten Avenue and Chew so she could run into the Rite Aid. He planned on hitting the express way downtown to 3rd and Chestnut. That's where he'd found the boots online for his chick. He sat and watched the nigga moving so obvious that it was impossible for the cop on the corner not to be involved. Just as he thought, K-2 watched Monk come from the Royal Crown chicken spot and push an envelope through the passenger side window.

"Son of a bitch." He mumbled loss in thought.

"Boy!" Melinda barked. "You slipping! You know these niggas be hating on y'all. You better wake up. This pussy ain't that good."

"Shidd! Yes it is... Please go with me" he fake bagged.

"Alright boy." She giggled. "Just let me drop my son's medicine off."

All day his mind was on what he saw Monk doing. The envelope had to have money in it and them cops had to be Monks protection and prewarning system against raids. This hostile takeover king Tut was talking about was gonna be more risky than a few dead bodies. He knew this was gonna be big boy shit.

"How was the flight?" K-2 asked as he grabbed Tut's bags from the porters carry all.

"I slept why?"

"Because they got cops." K-2 whispered slinging the large Louis Vuitton into the Volvo.

"So!" King Tut smiled. "We can buy cops too!" He stepped back. "What is this shit?" A Volvo?

"Volvo Turbo all terrain. Good for all kinds of weather and shit. Zero to sixty fin in 2.2 seconds. Top speed 15 and hydraulics in special places." K-2 smiled

"A baby seat? Shit nigga, I'm a boss not a stay at home dad." Tut laughed. "Boss up Kendell."

"Man I ain't no king pen. I'm a hood nigga with dreams. Do me a favor..." K-2 smiled. "Do you remember WDAS FM?"

"Yeah 150.3 nigga?

"Turn to it using the push button going backwards."

"What?" King Tut frowned.

"Indulge me Tut please..." K-2 watched him do it. "Now turn the radio off then on twice...That small red button. Now find WDAS again forward." Tut followed instructions. Instantly a hum was heard in the back. Tut turned to find the back seat lifting.

"What the fuck man?"

"Stash spot!" K-2 smiled. "Look inside."

Tut leaned over the seat to see two AR-15s with extended clips and two rolls of money.

"The money for emergency exits." K-2 laughed. "You remember those right?"

""Damn boss! K-dog would be proud of you." King Tut smiled.

"So when you gonna go see my pops?"

"I can't..." Tut looked out the side window. K-2 did something to fast for him to catch and he heard the seat in the back decline close.

"Let me show you what this bitch can do." K-2 grinned and Tut slammed back into the seat.

"K-2... the goddamn truck K... 2..." Tut yelled s the Volvo shot around the eighteen wheeler. "Don't try... K-2... don't you... Ahhh!" Tut screamed as the darted between two school buses and came out in lane three. "Nigga stop this shit." Tut laughed checking his seat belt.

"North Philly or uptown?... Hurry... never mind!" K-2 smiled and Tut screamed.

"NOOOO DON'T!"

But K-2 shot onto the off ramp doing close to a hundred.

"Hold on Jefe." K-2 giggled as Tut screamed obsanities in Spanish

"Puta... Cabron... Mot... Stop!"

"Stay at home dad huh?" K-2 shouted as they spun onto Giruad Avenue in front of the zoo.

"Alright this shit is fire! Now stop!" Tut ordered more scared then he wanted to admit.

Twenty minutes later the Volvo pulled into the suburbs of Westmorland Township, and a hour later Tay, Sirus, and Man Down pulled p. It was time to put their plans into action.

The Isley Brothers played softly on the stereo and the chardonnay chilled in the ice bucket.

"What's that?" Cletis asked as the twins seductively kissed and passed the pill between their lips. "Ex boy... You so crazy." Money giggled in her best fake Asian voice. This was a job she and her sister Cash would enjoy. When Peludo came to them with the idea they jumped at the chance just like Talisha instructed them to do. Peludo had no idea that they weren't college students trying to earn so extra cash other than dancing. Talisha had said she overheard her father say he needed some girls to help trap a nigga. If Tut knew she was sucking Peluda's dick at the time he called, poor Peludo would of been pig food in Mexico by now.

"He so big.. Buku... Buku dang!" Cash held her hands a foot apart. "Me frighten... buku black." She shoved her tongue into Money's mouth. Money swallowed the pill. "AIGN NANG... AIGGN NANG... WOO SHUE GAYA DANG!" Cash laughed.

"What she say?" Cletis smiled with his tight silk robe on.

"She happy. I swallowed pill first...I take buku dang in ass. She scared." Money smiled. "Don't kill...too buku."

"How about some head first." Cletis grinned. Money had to admit. For a man his age he was fit with a nice smile. His cock was average but he seem to think Asians never saw big dicks before.

"Buku dang... buku dang,,, buku dang..." Cash and Money said sliding his dick between their two pair of lips

"Mmmm yes... this is worth six months free rent." Cletis knee began to buckle as cash deep throats him and Money sucked his balls. "Yessss... Buuuukuuuu... Dang is cummmming!" Cletis shot loads of cum in Cash mouth as the door apartment slammed open.

"Stay still Buku Dang!" Man Down laughed. In his hand he held the .45 semi-automatic aimed at his head.

"What the fuck is this bullshit?" Cletis yelped.

"Your lucky day nigga." K-2 yelled

"Or the last day of your life." King Tut growled coming through the door. "It's up to you...Buku Dang." And all three men laughed while Cash and Money continued to suck on his average buku dang.

Thirty minutes later Cletis was four hundred thousand dollars richer from a building work two eighty, which he paid one sixty from the sheriff sale.

everybody won and he got to fuck a screaming Asian and her sister. The best part was he and his wife got to stay in their apartment rent free for a year.

"Is there drugs involved?" Cletis stopped and asked on his way out the door.

"Do you like drugs?" King Tut smiled.

"No but that Monk fella got a spot on the second floor where he keeps a stash."

All three men smiled. "Don't worry about that.' Tut said pulling Cash to the bed. "Now if you'll excuse us. I want to show this one what buku dang really is."

"I don't know what that chink shit means." Man down dropped his pants. "But this is a big dick!" H gripped his own dick.

"Shit!" K-2 smiled looking at Cletis as he was leaving. "Where's the wifey?"

"Hey boy!" Cletis put up his middle finger.

Meanwhile...

Phoenix, Arizona

"Perludo." Talisha cooed from the swimming pool. "Mama is in Mexico with Abuelito, and papito is in Philly with his precious other familia. I'm bored." She stepped from the pool wearing nothing but her birthday suit. "Come swimming with us."

"Us?" Peludo turned just in time to see Blaque, K.O., Chunky and Starflower step from the cabana stalk naked.

"Let us play with you Peludo... take those off." Talisha tugged on his swimming trunks until they hit the cement. "See I don't lie. He's colgado... muy colgado." Talisha grinned as the women surrounded him. Each taking turns rubbing his dick.

"Mmm! Muy colgado." Blaque smiled squeezing his ass cheeks.

"I tell you what Peludo. If you can catch it..." Talisha walked to the pool. "you can fuck it!" She dove in, so did Blaque and K.O. followed.

"Oops!" Chunky almost fell into his arms. "Oh no , looks like I'm caught." she giggled.

"Me to." Starflower moaned from the cushioned pool lounge chair. Her legs spread wide open for easy access.

"Talisha?" Peludo looked at her for the o.k.

"Feliz Cumpleaños sexy." She smiled from the water. "You did not think I forgot your birthday did you?"

Two days later

Back in Philly...

"Hey Zahir." Melinda cooed stepping from the cherry red Nissan Altima with white leather interior.

"Damn sis..." Zahir looked inside of the fully loaded car. "Who shit you done jacked?"

"Nigga please! You see all this ass I'm bouncing around with?" She made it shake. "How Ezel say it? Nigga I kill I don't steal." She giggled. "Zah what it's hitting for out here? I see you still riding low key in that hooptie."

"Girl stop it!" He laughed watching the traffic move up and down the avenue. "Aint shit wrong with my cutlass."

"No Bullshit!" Melinda moved closer. "That shit don't fit a player. This Altima is your flavor boo." Melinda pulled the key pad from her pocket and hit the trunk release. "You heard that new Kanye West?" She hit the volume control from where they stood. The three ten and two mids roared to life causing heads to turn. "Come here Zah." She smirked. "You ever watched porn before?"

Quickly Zahir stepped to the trunk and saw the 19inch screen automatically tilt down.

"Watch this bitch play with that pussy." Melinda giggled. The screen lit up with a hairy pussy being finger fucked by a small hand. "Guess who she is?" Melinda licked her lips.

Zahir kept watching as the view widen and the woman's face appeared. She was some kind of Asian chick.

"That bitch fine ain't she?" She laughed. "Only one thing can make that shit better..." She was saying just as the twin's face appeared and started sliding a fat long dildo into the other one.

"Girl you too much!" Zahir laughed.

"You see them screens in the headrest?"

Zahir peeped in through the rear windshield. "Damn!"

"And PlayStation and Gameboy balled." Melinda laughed. "Here catch!" She tossed him the keys. "It's a number in the ash tray if you like the way it rides."

Stepping into the street a money green Mercedes pulled up with tinted windows. "Zahir." Melinda smiled. "Call by tonight or just leave the keys in the trunk."

The back door opened and the two Asian chicks from the DVD stepped out to embrace Melinda. She kissed the both on the mouth.

"we can be friends dude," Cash whispered

"That bitch is a whore and loves dick." Money laughed. "Bye Zahir cutie." Money coed. Melinda winked and they were gone.

"Who is it?" Cletis yelled as he snatched the front door open.

"What's this?" Monk barked holding up a form that read at the top in red letters Notice of Rent Increase.

"Don't know!" Cletis said.

"You the one renting me the apartment right?" Monk barked.

"Nope!" Cletis said and noticed Monk's eyes shoot over his shoulder. He turned just in time to see Marla waltz into the bathroom.

"Marla... Yo Marla!"

"She can't do nothing. They brought the place legally. So the rent is on them."

"Wait, you don't own this spot no more?" Monk asked.

"That is correct my man." King Tut said opening the apartment door across the hall. "This my shit now."

"Who the fuck is you? And what is this shit? Thirty five hundred a month, man fuck out of here!" Monk snapped.

"Then move... man..." Tut smiled.

"Nigga I'll..." Monk growled as Tut stepped back and Man down appeared holding the AR-15 aimed at Monk's head.

"You'll what nigga?"

"So it's like that?" Monk looked back at Cletis. "Are you sure y'all want to play these games with..." Monk suddenly lost two teeth from the butt of the AR-15 sending him to the floor.

"Sorry Boy! But my young... ummm... killers don't like talking. By the way don't even bother to stop downstairs for your shit. I gave it all to them. Man Down show this has been out!"

"My pleasure Jefe!"

With that Man Down kicked Monk in the ribs, then the head. Without missing a beat Man Down slammed the butt of the AR-15 into the base of Monk's skull.

"Lights out nigga?" Man Down laughed.

"He's gonna kill y'all" She smiled.

Tut and Man Down looked up into the eyes of a female she devil.

"Marla get in here!" Cletis whispered. "These men know what they're doing. Excuse her."

"No it's perfectly cool." King Tut said eye fucking Cletis wife.

There she stood, 5'3 a hundred and ten pounds of fire. She reminded Tut of an older version of his fantasy form the movie, Set it Off... Jada Pinkett. She wore a see through bath robe and slippers. They both could see her firm naked body with the light behind her from the window.

"Damn!" Man Down grunted as he kicked Monk in the face for show.

"Hi, I'm King Tut..." He extended his hand. "And you are?"

"A beat up bitch if I take your hand." She winked and turned towards her husband. "What you want for dinner nigga?'"

"Pussy!" Cletis giggled looking at Tut. He shut the door.

"Get this nigga out of here. Leave his ass on the sidewalk so they all can see him." Tut ordered and for the first time Sirus came from the upper stairs holding the H.K. 708.

"Dead?" He asked.

"Naw... Not yet." Tut nodded toward the peep hole. "Just naked and beat!." He laughed. Both teens began to stomp the unconscious Monk everywhere Brutally Sirus and Man Down took a foot and dragged the savagely beaten Monk two flights of stairs and out onto the busy Chew Avenue.

The money green Benz had just bent the corner when Zahir heard the Manor doors fly open. He was still grinning at the way the three women had made a scene for him. He wondered if he could hit Melinda, always prancing up and down Chelten and Chew like that ass don't stink. Quickly he turned expecting Monk to appear. He did, but on his back bloody and being dragged by the nigga Man Down from the clang and that punk ass Sirus. He realized if those two were her then...

"Come on Zahir..." K-2 laughed coming from the Volvo with limo tint. In his hand he held a Mossberg pump with a 12 shot extended clip. "You know we aint playing. Tell me you're not thinking crazy." K-2 chambered a round. "Besides we need you to make introductions. By the way..." K-2 laid the barrel of the Mossberg on Monk's forehead. "Who's gonna run the strip if you die right... Now!" It wasn't a question.

"What you gonna kill him?" Zahir nodded down at Monk.

"Not yet! Maybe tomorrow, maybe next week, maybe next year." K-2 smiled. "By the way did my bitches show you the glove compartment? Take a look nigga. And Zah called the number... Please."

Zahir and Man Down's eyes locked one final time. Both knew each other's passion for the kill and they both really wanted to prove who was the baddest. Them word meant everything.

"Zahir!" Man Down growled. Zahir just nodded with the same look of menace he just received.

"Call the number team." Tay giggled stepping from behind the mail truck holding two Glock .35.

Instantly the Manor doors opened again and out walked the man who would change Zahir life forever. In his hand he held the days' work from the apartment.

"This belongs to you Zahir Quddous." Tut smiled handing him the bag with ten grand in dimes of crack. "Tell Zanee I said Salaama Alaikum. An Zahir..." Tut took his arm pulling him towards the still unconscious Monk. "When the time comes..." King Tut kicked Monk in the balls. There was no more words.

King Tut raised his hand and the money green Benz pulled up. Tut winked and walked to the car.

"Call that number nigga... Just say yes of no!" K-2 climbed into his Volvo with Tay and Sirus. Zahir never noticed when Man Down had left. It wasn't until later that Zahir realized King Tut had mentioned his mother's name as if he knew her. Zahir took the phone from Monk's waist and dialed Freddrick and Taum. The he dialed 911 and walked away.

Both men sat facing the door as the waitress served them their dinner.

"Drinks?" The pretty black girl looked down at the two.

"Scotch" Taum winked up.

"Same." Freddrick smiled as she walked away. He looked as his partner. "So what do you think about this new development?"

"Could be the FEDs." Taum whispered.

"Naw, too violent!" Freddrick whispered. "This is a new player. FEDs no... violent yes."

"So where we stand on this. Monk's down and most likely soon to be out. I needed that grand every month." Taum leaned forward. "Besides Monk knows too much . He can really hurt us."

"Not if we..." Freddrick almost said.

"I'll handle Monk gentlemen." The voice whispered from the booth behind them. Both men turned to see Tut smiling and alone. He stood from his booth and carried his cup of tea over into their booth. "The only reason I left him alive was to get some leverage. And you're right he'll talk if you don't at least kill me." Tut smiled.

"And what makes you so confident we won't?" Taum growled taking a mouth full of mash potatoes.

"Look around fellas." Tut continued to smile. Both men looked around slyly and saw nothing but two Philippian waitresses and the pretty black girl who served them.

"What, they gonna call the cops?" Taum laughed. "You's a scumbag who pulled this 25 automatic on two off duty police officers.

"Highly decorated don't forget." King Tut smiled. "Now look again. Please." The smile left his face as he touched his nose.

"Shit!" Taum whispered as Cash lifted her dish towel to reveal the sub compact AR pistol and Money flipped her tray to reveal the same. Melinda quickly came to the table and smiled down while lifting her apron to reveal two .40 glocks.

"Two twenty one south third street. A Mary Taum. School teacher at Rowan Elementary. Beautiful. Eighty six thirty two Thouron Street. Two boys, one girl and a wife name Carol Freddrick. Gentlemen at this moment they are all safe. Unless we have a misjudgment of power. Now I'll save you the time and effort. My name is Talib Turner born and raised on the very same strip I just acquired. But you can call me Tut. I am only a businessman who lives like a gangster." Tut laughed. "Now can we stop measuring dicks since we all can see mine is longer and fatter! And get some pussy together. First I'm upping that small shit to my league. Let's say three grand, No, four grand a month cash for the job you did for the soon to be late Mr. Monk."

"Shit make it five and I'll kill him and whoever for you whenever!" Freddrick smiled.

"See we are gonna have fun fucking all this pussy together." Tut smiled. "Let's go."

Twenty minutes later the three men were inside of Cash and Money, and the three spoke no more of the done deal.

Three weeks later...

"Boy you lucky." The nurse smiled rolling him to the front door of Willow Crest. "They thought you were gonna lose that eye until that specialist came in!"

"It didn't matter... Somebody's gonna lose an eye anyway!" Monk smirked.

This morning Taum called and promised to pick him up and take him to the now captured nigga who punished him. Monk was happy when Zahir came upstairs to his room to let him know the crew had the bosses back.

"I'll take him from here nurse." Zahir smiled "Let's go Mr. tough guy. One thing I can say about you Monk, you a tough nigga."

"That's right nigga!" Monk laughed. "Now where is this dude ummm..."

"Jefe… we call him Jefe now." Zahir smiled as they approached the red Altima.

"Well I'm gonna make his ass dead!" Monk growled.

"Check this out Monk." Zahir opened the door of the new car.

"Monk my man." Taum smiled from the other side of the back seat.

"Fellas." Monk moaned as Zahir helped him in the back seat.

"Damn!" Monk smiled watching the porno on the five-inch screen on the headrest. The two Philippians were fucking Taum and Freddrick like porn stars. "Who's the freaks?"

"Oh, they belong to Jefe." Zahir laughed slamming the car door.

"The nigga who did this." Monk meant his eye.

"Yup! That's who you're gonna go see right now. And you gotta handle your shit!" Taum smiled. "Ready?"

"Damn right! Where's my gun?"

"Bats!" Zahir said turning up the music.

"Watch this part."

Monk stared at the Philippian girls fuck Taum in the ass as a nigga walked into the frame with ten inches of more bouncing in front of him. With one easy stroke he entered her throat without even a gag. Five minutes later he shot a load all over her face.

"We're here!" Freddrick said pulling into an old abandon warehouse.

Monk noticed the man he hated the most sitting in a chair in the middle of the open bay warehouse, his hands behind his back. Monk smiled.

"My turn!" He shouted climbing from the car. "Where's my bat?"

"Right here." King Tut shouted as he stood. "You can run if you like."

"Taum… Freddrick?" He turned "Come on Zahir… We like family man."

"Shiddd nigga you better run." Zahir laughed. "I like my new Jefe. By the way that means boss negro."

Freddrick popped the trunk of Zahir's car and all three men pulled Louieville sluggers. Monk ran for the door only to be met by Man Down standing in his way with another bat.

"I got a hundred, fuck it three hundred grand if you let me go…" He turned towards King Tut.

"Where?" Tut held up his hand to halt the advancing men.

"In my bitch closet." Monk began to cry. "Please I'll leave Philly I swear."

"Who Ronda whorey ass?" Zahir laughed.

"Yea Zah… Man tell them I ain't lying. It's there in a box under some clothes"

"For real?" Zahir frowned.

"Man go check… I swear… Please, please, please!"

"Man, I believe you Monk." Zahir smiled and swung with all his might splitting Monk's head like a watermelon. Instantly all the men started beating the life from Monk's body. With every sickening thud of a bat Zahir and Man Down seem to compete until Taum, Freddrick and Tut stood back and watched in awe at how unhappy both teens seemed.

"Enough! Goddamn!" Tut shook his head as he roared. "You two niggas need to chill with this who's the coldest nigga uptown shit! From here on out you two stick together like glue, learn to like each other."

"I agree." Man Down smiled. "Let's go Zahir we finished here!"

"Fuck No!" Taum barked. "We're going with y'all. That's a four-way split."

"So I don't get none?" King Tut laughed.

"Get your own... Jefe" Man Down laughed and Zahir knew he could like Man Down.

Chapter 7

Philadelphia 2011

The white Nissan NV200 pulled to the urn on the West Oak Lane neighborhood. The tinted window of the cargo van made it almost impossible to spy inside unless you placed your hand on the wind to shield your eyes. And even then the navy-blue interior made it hard to see inside.

The logo on the NV200's side read "Wayward Children." Which was a charity organization in the Tri State area. Tay smiled as the side door slammed open, and out stepped Blaque followed by Talisha.

"Bebe hermano." Talisha hugged Tay, "K-2" she blushed.

"Sexy" K-2 winked.

"Stop it boy or I might get ideas." She flirted. "Where's papito?"

"Inside with my moms." K-2 laughed, "What kind of shit y'all driving? And you better not say what I think!"

"Is you crazy? Papa... No Abuelito would kill a bitch if I trans a joint." Talisha laughed. "Look for yourself." She smiled. "I'm gonna go see aunt Tandy and Papa."

"Wait for me..." Blaque laughed as Tay tried to grab her ass. "Stop nasty."

"Goddamn!" K-2 barked as he looked into a moving pornographic studio. Tay watched from the steps as two hands grabbed K-2 inside.

"What the fuck?" Tay smiled rushing to see who hands grabbed his brother.

"Boy you a baby… GET OUT!" Chunky yelled unzipping K-2 jeans.

"Bitch please!" Starflower laughed. "That's the next Jefe. You better recognize. Tay-Tay right?" She snatched him inside and slammed the door.

"Who's paying for this?" K.O> barked from behind the camera.

"Shit!" Tay moaned as Starflower's mouth swallowed him whole. "I get it… Ewwww Shit."

"Bitch he ain't twelve either." Chunky laughed looking at Starflower give Tay her specialty. "That's a man dick." She giggled handling K-2 herself.

"Aunt Tandy." Talisha kissed Tandeka on the lips. "Papa."

"Talisha I swear…" Tandy hugged her tightly. "You just keep getting more beautiful. You and this goddess."

"Hello auntie.' Blaque smiled. "Ta… papa." She quickly corrected herself.

"Papa where is my classmate?" Talisha asked.

"Yeah right! Them bitches ain't ever seen a college classroom. We'll talk about that later, but how is my daughters." Tut smiled. "And what brings y'all to Philly?"

"Spring break." They both shouted. "The freak picnic is this weekend." Blaque continued.

"She needs a man Papa." Talisha laughed and caught the stern look in Tut's eyes, so did Tandeka.

"Where in the hell did that son of mine go to?" Tandeka barked. Both Blaque and Talisha laughed. "What?" Tandeka smiled not knowing.

"What it be Pay4?" Sirus shadow boxed with his long-lost hustling friend. "See you still getting this money out here?'

"I got to nigga! You all dumped a real hustler." Pay4 shielded away from the physical contact. Fighting wasn't his thing, hustling was. He had one philosophy... (Get money and But it). Hence the name Pay4 it. But the crew just called him Pay4. He was a phlegmatic type of person. You could shit a monkey bread pudding and he would never bat an eye. Naw, the only thing that excited Pay4 It was money.

"Nigga don't miss the matinee looking at the cartoon." Sirus groaned. "You gonna be a boss one day my man. Just be on point when the time comes and get these little niggas in line." Sirus pointed down the block.. "We never let you niggas do that shit, not here!"

"That's because y'all have violence in your system. I'm all about the biscuts." Pay4 It laughed nervously.

"Come on nigga! You gotta be excited for this cash. Follow me." Sirus growled and lead Pay4 down the block. "What up Jo-Jo?"

"Damn! What up Sirus...ummm." He pulled his dick from the piper's mouth sitting inside the car as he stood in the back door. "man this ain't... ummm I ain't even working the sack yet. Not until... Come on Pay4 tell him..."

"I still want my ten dollars." The crackhead whined.

"Pay this bitch JoJo!" Sirus continued to stare into Jo-Jo's fearful eyes.

"But..."

Instantly Sirus punched him in the side of the head. "Pay this bitch... Jo-Jo." He watched him pull a five and three wrinkled ones from his pocket.

"Let me get a dime Pay..." He never got to finish his statement until he woke up five minutes later.

"Here Joanna." Sirus handed her twenty dollars as she scrambled to pick up the eight Jo-Jo still held in his hand. "What's our role Joanna?" Sirus growled.

"No tricking on the strip." She flinched expecting at least a slap. But none came, instead Sirus dug into his pocket once again.

"Try this shit here." He handed her two dimes the size of twenties. "This is next week's product."

"Thanks baby... Do you want..." She tried to hand him the money she held.

"Naw, that's for Pay4." Sirus laughed as she ran off. Both men looked down at a waking Jo-Jo. "Get up nigga!" Sirus stooped down and lifted the still dazed man. Without warning he slammed two more vicious punches into his body, making Pay4 flinch. "This is business motha fucka! Now Pleasure?" He landed a heavy hook to Jo-Jo's chin putting his lights out again. "Yo Pay 4 keep the strip right nigga and you'll have it to yourself and these niggas gonna love you when we finish"

Both men lifted the unconscious Jo-Jo and tossed him into the abandoned car. The Sirus lead Pay4 to his new truck.

"Pass this out to the workers. That two stacks of hundred packs, Pay4..." Sirus looked him in the eyes. "Twenty workers, ten a shift!... everybody gets one, even Joe with his tricking ass, And this my man is yours." Sirus tossed him the keys to the Silverado. "One more thing... this ain't got shit to do with pimp and is sissy brother. So shut the fuck up... Boss!"

The music was heard two blocks away and Zahir shook his head knowing exactly who it was playing that loud shit. As the Terrain Subaru pulled up the candy paint glistened in the sun.

"Man Down." Zahir smiled.

"Zahir you boss you." Man Down laughed. "Its work time nigga... Time to make the donuts."

"Man that damn Sirus got a nigga on froze." Zahir pointed to the strip. "Gotta watch the money."

"Well we got the o.k. on them Temple Road cats. The King wanted that yesterday. Taum and Freddrick is waiting on our call"

"Shit!" Zahir jumped up from the mailbox. "Benny... yo Benny..." He flagged the heavyset slow moving man with the face of a grizzly bear. "Hold this shit down and watch that skinny ass punk Russia. If he comes around the strip again fire his ass up."

"With what? My finger? Yall don't allow us to carry."

"My bad!" Zahir laughed, "Here! Money straight." He hands Benny the semi-automatic desert eagle. He and Man Down smiled knowing Benny would only shoot in the air, but the sound would scare a nigga to death. "We got five on five Benny. The stash is ten over six."

"Ain't money always straight Zah? I got this." Benny smiles "And by the way I'm out so it five on four and ten over seven."

"That nigga gone take over count one day." Man Down joked.

"Good because I'm muscle niggg... gggah." Zahir smacked Man Down in the head and ran.

"Up against the car bitch! If any of you no good bitches move I'll shoot to kill." Taum growled as Freddrick searched the hustlers on the corner of Sharpneck and Temple Rd.

"Gun partner!" Freddrick barked snatching his .40 glock from its holster. "Down, Down, Down, Down!"

"Fuck Black!" The pretty boy whispered.

"You, Up!" Taum ordered. "What's your name?"

"Jen." She said. Both men realized this one was a girl.

"Ain't this a bitch!" Freddrick growled snatching the bucked hat from her head. "Pretty mother fucker."

He wasn't lying. She was caramel complexion with a haircut like a boy, low cut ceaser with spinning waves. The very baggie clothes she wore hid the fact that she was female.

:It seems like the only dirty one is black here. That was what you called him , right?... Black. Well Black this ain't about locking y'all asses up. This about a talk and an offer of sorts. First of all, we know you work for the Mayor. Second of all we know he's looking at us right now from that bedroom window right there." Taum waved and the curtains in the window closed. "Anyway I need you to tell him that if he don't call this number by tonight. The shits that's about to happen to his house will happen every single day. Me and a few of my buddies will clean the corners up of all guns then leave. So if he wants to operate tell him to call."

"Yo!" Freddrick pointed. "Jenifer, Jenny or whatever. When we leave run, I like you so listen to me... Run for your life." He laughed.

Both detectives climbed back into their car and pulled away. In the rear view mirror Taum spotted Jen slip into the driveway and smiled.

"Man don't kill nobody!" Zahir laughed as they turned the corner.

"I know, I know. The house!" Man Down smiled. Both held AR 15 modified to automatics.

"Call that number Sean Mayor!" Zahir yelled unleashing a barrage of .223 into the front of 8102 Temple Rd.

"Uh - Uh... look at these two hoes." Chunky giggled. "Living the high life while us honest hoes making a living the old fashion way. Sucking dicks."

"No bitch." Cash went into her fake Chinese accent.

"Confusion say, only suck right dick. Rest you fuck." All the girls fell out laughing.

"How much lovers?" K.O. smiled.

"Twenty eight plus..." Money smiled holding up a bag full of jewelry.

"Bitch twenty eight hundred. That's it?" Chunky growled. "Mommy gonna kick y'all ass."

"Twenty-eight grand girl." Starflower elbowed her in the ribs softly "Shhhh."

"Talisha." Cash smiled devilishly. "Girl your daddy got a big fucking dick!"

"Bitch!" Talisha laughed.

"And can fuck too!" Money whispered in a joking manner. "Made me cum for real, No acting bitch!"

"No shit?" K.O. grinned. "Z might..."

"No you ain't whore!" Talisha laughed.

"You won right girl." Money smiled. "Philly is where the future is. Bad Blood Bitches forever."

"Bitches stay true to the game." Talisha said. "I got two from Peludo and Tay can move them shits for us. Peludo wants ten apiece."

"Talisha, why us?" K.O. asked seriously.

"Because bitch. It's time for a queen and her bitches to run shit."

"Bitch this pussy money is good." Chunky smiled

"And it can't last either." Blaque said. "Cash and Money made twenty eight grand and only fucked when they needed to."

"How much you make women?" Talisha asked. "What two thousand, three at the most? That ain't no money," She continued. "Now like I explained to K.O., pussy rules the world and dollars buy it. We already got the pussy!"

"Alright listen..." Blaque took over the spill. "We got the ultimate connect, and at ten flat we can bust into the game on our own. I did the numbers..."

"Beautiful smart bitch." K.O. slapped Blaque's ass.

"That's five dollars bitch!" Blaque giggled. "But seriously at ten grand a bird we stand to profit close to twenty three grand a bird. In weight we profit ten grand a bird. This the plan..." Blaque and Talisha laid the game down for the BBB's rise to cartel status.

The NV200 pulled into the Belmont Plateau bumping Pony Ride from the interior speakers. This was the Greek picnic so the music was expected, but no one expected what came next. The doors slammed open and Blaque and Talisha stepped out into the sun with booty shorts and wife beaters on. They were soon followed by Cash and Money in thongs and bras holding a small kiddie pool. K.O. stepped down looking like a goddess in a pair of satin boy shorts and bra. She pulled her dreds back into a ponytail and wore diamond stud earrings.

The park was full of fraternity frat brothers and sisters most who passed the Nissan 200 stopped to watch the two Philippian girls do freaky shit with rubber toys inside of the pool of baby oil.

"I bet he got a big dick." Blaque smiled at the big dark skin man standing close.

"Let's see it dog!" Talisha turned and bent at the waist; "You a "Q" right? They say you guys hung papi. Let's see!" She swayed in such a self and seductive way the men with the Q dog all began to hoot and holler. "Let me see it Q Dog. If it's big I make a movie with you. Ten minutes for fifty dollars... whatever you want."

"Shidd nigga move." The young kid growled. " I got a big dick bitch!" Tay barked pulling fifty dollars. "But I want that one." He points, and the men looked up to see Chunky in the door of the Nissan 200. Her thighs oiled up and dark, thick as buffy everywhere.

"She too much for you little man." The Q Dogg said licking his lips.

"Boy please! What you working with son?" Talisha toyed with Tay.

"Let's see!" Chunky whispered sexily and Tay revealed himself in front of the crowd of men and women.

"Damn shorty holding." A female whispered from the crowd.

Ten minutes later Tay came from the cargo van smiling with a tape in his hand.

"I want her." The tall light skin man pointed as Cash who was now sucking on the dildo attached to Money's waist.

"Nigga take both for a hundred and twenty. This shit the freak picnic, let's do Greek!" K.O. yelled grinding her hips into Blaque's ass.

"Bet that ma!" He said with his Brooklyn accent, peeling two fifties and a twenty.

For the next five hours the NV 200 became a mobile pornographic studio with Blaque and Talisha flaunting sexually while Chunky, Starflower and the twins fucked, and sucked orgasmic explosions on film with all comers, men and women.

The sun was fading when they started clearing the park. But the Greek never stopped and the crowed headed to south Philly to south street to party. The mobile was on its way also. Since this was in the heart of the city the game had to change. Pussy was still the merchandise, but movies were out and photos were in. Blow jobs, anal or puss for ten minutes only still shots, same price.

"Bitch its two thirty," Blaque whispered. "Time to go" she yarned.

"Yeah shit!" Talisha agreed.

"Bitch this a hoe's life!" K.O. growled. "It's money to be made out here."

"Not no more. Let's go!" Talisha said. "Them bitches got to be soar."

"Not me..." Chunky giggled kissing the slim pizza store owner as he left. "This pussy is the real deal."

"Whatever... Let's go!" Blaque yarned again.

"She aint no hoe mommy." Chunky laughed.

"That's right bitch... She's a boss!" Talisha giggled.

The Greek picnic week went that way for them for three days each night ending three in the morning in front of some club or bar. The women were tired, but with the money they made they had enough for three more birds besides the two they already had.

Talisha gave the two to Tay and promised when Peludo made the drop next month, he would have three more. Tay promised his sister to get rid of them quickly in weight so they could build up their stash.

"Listen my man... First of all this is not a negative. I'm offering you a deal that's untouchable in the city... No fuck that in this state!" K-2 barked. " I know for a fact that the brothers are selling you two kilos at twenty three apiece. My boss wants that business. He's willing to give them to you at twenty for the first three and nineteen for the next two."

Sean Mayer sat staring at the two men K-2 had with him, both smiling knowing he'd recognize them.

"First... They owe me twelve hundred for my Coyle fish, and two grand for my entertainment center Another five grand for my wall to wall mirrors. Second of all how can I know you can be trusted." The Mayor frowned at the two killers.

"You don't!" K-2 smirked. "But I see you do recognize my two associates, so you understand that this deal I offer dies..." He paused and smiled. "Well id dies with you and your answer. And from my calculations we owe you eighty two hundred." K-2 tossed two five thousand dollar rolls of hundreds on the table. "That's ten... I need and answer now."

Sean Mayer looked up to see Zahir smiling. In his eyes he could tell Zahir wanted him to say no.

"And pimp and his retarded brother flex?" Sean Mayer asked.

"Not your problem anymore. Answer please!"

"Deal!" The Mayor smiled. "How soon?"

"First Wednesday of every month, both ways. This month is on the cuff." K-2 said as he stood. The beautiful black waitress tossed her towel onto the table over Sean Mayor's head. As he turned she was tucking the small .22 dillenger in her pocket. Melinda smiled down into his eyes.

"Good choice" she whispered.

Sean Mayor sat stunned that he never thought she was one of them. He expected death from the two gun men from his house. Reaching for his glass of beer he noticed his hand trembling badly.

The private jet landed and taxied in, after being chalked the doors opened and the stairs lowered. Tut rushed on board.

"Don Monteza." Tut hugged his Jefe. "Angelita." He smiled as she stepped into his arms.

"I'm horny Tata." Angelita whispered in his left ear away from her father.

"So am I" Tut lied.

"Come sit" the Don ordered. "You are becoming famous my boy. The Corteza brothers has ordered you to slow down operations in the east coast. They say you are pushing too hard. I'm sorry but I agree."

"But Don I build for us all. For my Angelita, for my Talisha and for the familia, you Don Monteza." Tut said taking his daughter's mother hand. The Don watched in pleasure.

"Yes, Yes I see... So tell me how can you move fifty pieces in Philly so easily? Not to mention the extra ten in Phoenix."

Tut did not show his surprise about the extra ten he had no idea about in Phoenix. Peludo never mentioned the increase or shown the profit.

"I use the Blacks." Tut whispered.

"Good, Good, don't worry about the Corteza brothers. I'm no push over. But now I must fly into Miami to meet with the black widow herself."

"Papa!" Angelita scolded. "Don't say that about mama."

"A hundred kilos a month! She's killing me!" Don Monteza laughed. "It's better than money I guess." He laughed. "You're lucky she's not the one you're dealing with son."

Again Tut showed no surprise, but his mind was working. "Angelita." He whispered. "Please." He kissed her hand.

"Sorry papa I will see you in Phoenix." She stood and was led off the plane.

"No more children without God!" Monteza yelled. "Pilot, let's go!" He ordered

The sky seemed darker for some reason as K-2 pulled into his normal parking spot. Everything inside said things weren't right, He looked towards the parked cars up and down the street.

"Nigga you tripping." He laughed shutting off the engine. His eyed darted towards his mother's home. Stepping from the car he thumbed the .40 smith and wesson in his belt. K-2 couldn't shake the feeling of something was wrong. Slamming the car door he set the alarm and crossed the small one way street.

"Shit!" he thought. "The street lights." K-2 instantly realized the street lights had been shot out. It was the sound of the crumbled glass under his feet as he walked, Instinctively he reached for the gun in his belt holster a second too late.

"Don't!" Pimp growled. "What you thought I wouldn't realize the move being made against me came from you and that half breed Mexican. Man I played fair. Why?"

"Why what Pimp? Why we had to help you build that corner from two hundred a day to ten grand a day? Or why I had to force you to except almost free dope and push you to move into the weight game? Listen slim you're out of your league and in the open. Man you so green to the game, you don't even realize that if I wanted to I could have everybody you love deaded in a whispered word. What you think if you kill me it's over?" K-2 laughed taking a step closer to Pimp. That's when he noticed the retard holding the double barrel. "Let me explain this to you like I always done. The King Tut organization will kill any and everybody you love if something happens to me. Ms. carol, your daughter Casey, even that old lady on green street you think we don't know about. Who is she your grandmom?" K-2 laughed. "Move nigga!" K-2 pushed pass Pimp. "And get that shit out my face puta!" He snapped on Flex. Half way up the stairs K-2 froze and turned. "By the way Pimp we had bigger plans for your dumb ass, but now..." He continued his walk inside

"Shit!" Pimp thought. "I fucked up."

"We should of killed him!" Flex growled.

"And what... let grandmom and Casey die? What about mommy you dumb bastard?

"Oh yeah...right." Flex whispered.

The bubbles in the tub smelled of jasmine and vanilla and reflected the candle light.

"Tut what do you always ask me to marry you when you know you're a free spirited man" Angelita asked rubbing his nipple while he leaned back into her arms. "I mean I know you love me or love the thought of loving me. Truth is you're a man with an unsatisfying sex drive and no one women can please you and that monster" she giggled.

"I asked you Angelita because it keeps me honest." Tut took her hand and kissed it. "If by chance you ever said yes... then I would quit this life for good."

"Even if you're not rich yet?"

"For you I'll live broke!"

"Liar!" She giggled. "But you keep me happy, so go head and lie. But tonight is far from over. By the way..." Angelita kissed the top of Tut's head. "I saw that look when father mentioned the extra ten kilos. You didn't know!"

"No I didn't! Peludo?" Tut moaned and Angelita heard the pain in his heart.

"Well tonight I'm gonna do what they did for you by myself." She giggled.

"What who did?" Tut sat up.

"Those two Asian girls on that DVD in the player I watched while you fixed dinner...No! It's alright." She laid him back to her heavy breast. "I can take what they cannot mister big dick." She laughed.

That night Angelita took everything Tut could give and made him surrender. Tut fell asleep with these words on his lips.

"I love you Angelita." He cried openly.

"I Know Talib." She cried with him.

"What it be Zahir?" Tut smiled stepping from the Benz. I see you got this shit up and running."

"24-7 Jefe" Zahir smiled. "What's up?"

"Nothing... Just need a place to chill out for a while. Zahir get someone to move that shit for me I ain't here you dig, especially for Cletis begging ass."

"Mmm hmm! That bitch fine, but she's trouble. Tut believe me, Cletis loves that bitch. You gonna have to bust his ass one day. Trust me nigga, early."

"Man I ain't..." Tut just laughed. "Did everyone know he was a hoe?" He thought feeling his dick get hard.

Marla was fine and her body was tight, but she was no Angelita. After last night Tut was surprised he wanted more pussy. Maybe it was the way Marla always begged and tried to run from the dick. He still hadn't gotten all the way inside of her yet, but this morning...

"Man I ain't here!" Tut laughed.

"Benny... Yo Benny!" Zahir called down the strip.

Tut smelled the fish and home fries as he climbed the stairs. he knew it could only be coming from two placed since the other four apartments were occupied by his team of hustlers who Zahir hand-picked. He was right, as soon as he opened the door to the two bedroom flat, Marla stood at the bedroom door in the purple see threw teddy he paid two hundred dollars for from Freddrick of Hollywood.

"First I'm gone feed you nigga, then I'm gone take every inch this time... I promise! Even if it's in my stomach." Marla said with her legs slightly parted.

"Cletis might notice I stretched it." Tut licked his lips.

"So... my two fingers can stretch it more than his five inch dick."

"What up Zah?" Cletis smiled as he walked up. "You see Marla this morning?"

"Naw nigga I aint no babysitter!"

"She'll be hot as a firecracker. A nigga ain't come home last night. Out here fucking some no good stripper bitch." Cletis laughed and danced in place. "Know what I mean?" He tried to dap Zahire who just turned away. "Whatever nigga." Cletis entered the building he once owned and now paid rent in but Tut only charged him two fifty for what he could have gotten at least seven for. Not to mention giving them the first year free already.

"You see Marla I was at my brother Gary's house right and we got to drinking that yak and...' Cletis went over his story again climbing up the stairs to the second floor. He froze solid in front of apartment 2a and frowned. Suddenly he shook his head no as she screamed out in ecstasy and pain. "Naw!" He giggled and opened his door across the hallway.

"Marla I know you mad but first let me explain." He said closing the door. "I was at Gary's house right..." Cletis stopped when he noticed the place was silent. So silent he could hear the moans of a woman across the hall again. "Marla baby." He called out heading into the bathroom. "Listen Marla I..." He froze and heard the screams again.

"Ohhhh godddd, Lord Jeeesus stop Tut!" Marla begged with each deep thrust Tut slammed into her small 110 pound body. Tut had her legs on his shoulders drilling with a furious stroke of pure lust to open up her womb.

"Take this dick... mmmph mmmph..yea Marla take mmmph...mmmph...mmmph...this dick..." He growled with long drawn out words.

"Somebody... ohhh goddd... please Tut... baaabby please I'mmmm about to pass... urrgghhh... arrrgh.." She cried in pure shock of a man going so deep in her body.

I was no longer about busting a nut. Tut had came five minutes ago when she cried out his name. No it was now about showing Marla he was King Tut. She would pass out from the dick if he continued to beast fuck her like this.

"Say it bitch!" Tut grunted. Without warning he rolled her onto her stomach. She was helpless to fight his strength. "Say it!" He grunted again as he slid deeply back into her pussy.

"Tuuuuuuut" she screamed clawing at the pillow.

"Say it bitch!"

Using the pass key he kept since he use to won the place and Tut never changed the locks. Cletis froze in the living room with doubts now. The woman no longer sounded like Marla . Her screams, her begging and pleading sounded more animalistic and Marla would never let someone treat her like that. But he continued to move towards the bedroom.

"Say it bitch!" He heard Tut growl as she screamed for god.

"Oh god my stomach...Tut yooooou gooonnna kill meeee! Take it ouuuuutttt!"

"Say it and I'll cum." Tut grunted with each deep stroke as Cletis reached the door. His heart made a sound in his chest only he could hear, it felt a pain no one else could describe as he saw from the back ten inches being slammed into his wife as she begged. Slowly his hand found the old .38 smith and wesson in his back pocket.

"Say it Marla, say it now while I cum." Tut moaned

"Your dick is bigger than..." She tried to scream.

Boom! Boom! Boom! Boom! Boom! The shots ended her statement as King Tut fell over dead and shot his cum into the air.

"Fuck both of y'all" Cletis cried. His eyes seem to only focus on the way Marla pussy lips looked now. For years he barley looked at her pussy, now they looked alien to him. Turning he walked into the living room just as the door was kicked in.

"Fuck you Zahir!" Cletis barked as the .38 reached his temple. "Kingdom my ass. The King is dead!"

Boom!

Chapter 8

The King is Dead, Long Live the King

The limousines lined the block, twenty in all. Talisha had insisted Tay ride with her, Blaque and Angelita in the first limo with grandfather. K-2 and Tandeka rode in the second limo with Karen and Peludo. Sirus, Man Down, and Zahir rode in the third, and the rest were filled with the team.

The cemetery was the same one that Trouble was laid to rest in only feet away from the deep cold hole Tut would soon be dropped into like warm food.

For the second time K-2 lost Tut and again Tandeka saw the little scared, lonely, hurt boy she knew as Kendell Jr.

"I'm done..." Karen whispered "Stop this god damn car" she cried. "Stop this car I said." She began to scream. "No... Uh Uh... Stop!" She slung open the door. They had no chance so they stopped and Karen sprinted up Cheltenham Avenue screaming. "Noooo!"

Tay watched in tears as Talisha held him still in her arms. "Mommy" he whispered as Karen disappeared down the avenue. Her pain and shame came to light.

"Damn it!" Man Down growled from the third limo. "Not now auntie Kay. Think about Tavious."

K--2 still cried silently alone refusing any kind of comfort from anybody. It happened again.

The burial was nice and quick and ended with the solo being sung by Melinda who cried all the way through.

The King was dead and they all new times of turmoil was to come. All but one. He was not afraid to be who he was. Yes the King was dead. Long live the King!

Two Weeks Later...

"What we got left?" K-2 asked sitting at the table in the manor. It now belong to Talisha who gave them the run of the place. She left Philly the night of the burial.

"We got ten whole and twelve bagged." Tay said. "K-2 if we're gonna survive this we need a connect."

"Peludo!" Sirus suggested.

"He won't answer my calls" K-2 frowned.

"Mine either" Tay said. "Jefe my ass!"

"We could hit Puerto Rican Mike for a few" Zahir said.

"That Rican ain't giving us shit! This his chance to drive us out of business. He knows he can muscle us so this is his only shot!" Sirus said. "We should plant his ass!"

"Fuck it! We going to Phoenix!" K-2 said. "But first we need to get some help down there."

"I know just who." Tay smiled.

"Hello little brother." Talisha voice held a smile as they spoke. "I thought you'd never call."

"Talisha I need you."

"No! That is forbidden in gods eyes." She laughed. "But you can have Blaque. She's a whore."

"Fuck you bitch!" Blaque yelled in the back round.

"Hey Blaque!" Sirus yelled.

"Am I on speaker phone? take me off!" She snapped. "Tay you know better!"

"Talisha we all need to..." K-2 tried to explain only to be scolded.

"Kendell you are the smart one. Explain that if I say something it's for the person I speak with. When I speak to you it is for you no one else. If I order a death who is to know but who I give the order."

All the men looked towards K-2, Sirus frowned and mouthed the word "Order?"

"Tay give the phone to K-2" she continued. Holding up his finger K-2 took the phone and the struggle began.

"Listen ma! This aint what you think." He stopped and smiled as all looked on. "That's the reason we're calling. First of all every word we speak, my team will hear... Yes from me and only me... Well that's not what Tut wanted and we, yes we are gonna respect that. You'll finish school, we'll finish business... No! Then so be it, we'll just find..." K-2 smiled. "Now you're thinking little sister. We'll fly in this weekend...sure..." He handed the phone to Tay but spoke loudly so Talisha could hear him through the phone.

"It seems that Talisha can help us. Me, Tay and Man Down will fly into Phoenix this weekend. I will not discuss how much either way over the phone." K-2 smiled because Tay covered the mouth piece to giggle. "Zahir you and Sirus keep business straight and watch the snakes. Kill all snakes!" He said more as a warning to Talisha than as an order.

They all heard Talisha on the phone yell "PUTA!"

"He's my brother!" Tay snapped. "And was Tut's brother too..." He continued and the four boys watched as the youngest of the team check his sister.

Zahire and Sirus boarded the plan in Philadelphia alone with the first class ticket. Neither of the men had been to Phoenix, Arizona before and was anxious about the trip. Is wasn't they why because they both killed before. But now they killed on unfamiliar grounds. Six hours later American Airways landed in Phoenix on time.

'Hey baby." Chunky slung her thick ass everywhere in the new Prada dress the team paid for. K-2 had told her to dress the part and wired her five grand for the dress and other things.

Kissing her juicy Megan Good lips Sirus had no chance but to palm that fat smooth ass. He soon found out she wore no panties. "Damn Chunky baby."

"Fuck that." Zahir mumbled. "Did you get them?"

"Of course nigga! I'm a real bitch. Let's go" she winked. "Listen I had to improvise on one little detail."

"Shit!" Zahire whispered. "What?" He continued as they exited the terminal of the sky harbor airport.

"The car... I know y'all said low key but Hertz only had that!" She pointed. There in the arrival area of American Airways sat the vanilla white Escalade SUV with snow white interior.

"Goddamn!" Zahir smiled. "I'll drive!"

"Good!" Sirus barked and gripped Chunky's ass again as the white folks looked on in discuss.

"Boy I sell pussy! Ain't shit for free" she giggled running away and jumping in the back of the SUV

"Bitch when we finish you gone have to pay me!"

"Y'all get a room." The white woman rolled her eyes as Sirus and Zahir climbed into the SUV.

"Push that button Za." Chunky giggled as Sirus tried successfully to lift her dress. "Mmm boy..." She inhaled as his wet tongue found her clit. "The Four Seasons hotel on 1st Avenue and Washington."

"Destination entered proceed south on interstate 10 to..." The voice said cheerfully from the speakers.

"Nasty ass nigga!" Zahir laughed putting the car in gear.

"Oh god Sirus..." Chunky screamed as Sirus ate her chocolate ass up.

Thirty two minutes later Zahir pulled into the Valet parking station while Chunky rode Sirus crazy in the backseat.

"Damn y'all! We got a suite upstairs."

"Shit!" chunky whispered "I was almost there again." She kissed his neck. "I owe you fifty dollars." She giggled in his ear.

"You don't sell pussy no more... Right!"

"Boy please. You can't turn no hoe into a housewife." Chunky slowly stood and let his dick pop out of her thick hairless lips. "That's them right there." She pointed. "He'll get there around 11:30 tonight and most likely leave around 4:00 in the morning... Sirus!"

She stared into his eyes "I wish you was fareal." Her lips softly touches his.

"I was ma." He touched her cheek and grabbed the bags. "Come on up."

"I can't..." Chunky said and Sirus saw in her eyes the last tears of sadness he ever wanted her to feel. "I... I... can't." She jumped from the SUV just as valet was climbing in to take the Escalade.

"Man Down said you was feeling ma!" Zahir smirked "Always taking her away from the party. Nigga she a hoe remember that shit!"

"Yeah I know." Sirus followed Zah up to the front desk.

K-2 and Tay eased into the house talking and laughing. They both was surprised to see Tandeka and Qwen sitting on the sectional smoking weed. Beside the women set two thick wooden mop handles.

"Tay lock my doors... no boy the screen door too!" Tandeka barked loudly. "Now go upstairs to your room."

"What's wrong?" Tay asked out of concern. Everyone in the uptown area knew Tandeka, Qwen and even Karen his moms was not to be played with and not only because of them "Who..."

"Tay!" Qwen shouted.

"Yes ma'am." He said now knowing this was about K-2. He disappeared up the stairs but stopped to lay on the floor at the top of the stairs to watch and listen.

"The Dean called me today Kendell." Tandeka started to whisper as the grayish smoke left her lungs. "Said you missed the last three days and a very important test." She pressed the rolled up weed to Qwen who red eyes showed the same anger as his mothers. "Why Kendell?"

"Mom I..."

"Don't mom us! Why boy?" Qwen yelled. Instantly K-2 was Kendell the sixteen year old school student not K-2 the mid-level pusher.

"I'm gonna take the make-up this weekend." He lied

"You lying!" Tandeka stood. "The Dean said there is no make-up. Straight A's boy! And now you fucked that up for what? The streets? What about Harvard. The promise to my husband, your fath..." She swung the stick at his leg and K-2 easily dodged the wack. "If you move one more..." Tandeka hissed as she and Qwen stood.

"Come on mom... y'all can't..." He tried to object to a whipping but got no further as both women beat his ass with the wooden sticks.

"Now get upstairs... and don't come down until you remember what's important!" Qwen yelled. "And Tay!" She yelled! "Get your ass down here."

"They fucked you up!" He laughed as K-2 growled at him coming up the stairs. Instantly Tay began to cry like a baby and K-2 froze as the smile left Tay - Tay's face.

"You some shit Tay!" K-2 whispered.

"But I won't get beat!" He instantly slammed himself against the railing and both women only saw K-2 push by him. Tay grabbed the banister as if to stop his fall. "What I do?" He looked back at K-2 crying and winked.

"Mom I didn't... shit!" K-2 frowned into a crying Tay's face. "Boy!"

"Boy what?" Tandeka yelled. "Boy what?" She charged pass Tay to wack K-2 on his hip as he ran to his room on fire.

"You alright Tay?" Qwen asked pulling him into the middle of the living room. "He hurt you baby?"

"Nooo." Tay fake cried and sniffed.

"Good!" Tandeka yelled from behind him. "Why you ain't been to school?" Both women whipped his ass the same way they did K-2.

"Ahh-haaa!" K-2 yelled from his room Sirus only got away because he was in Phoenix.

"Hurry up nigga." Zahir kept watch on the apartment complex.

"You want to do this." Sirus whispered as the window lock slipped open from the slim jim. "Got it." He dicked behind the bushes as the Lincoln Town car cruised by.

"Man get inside and open the fuckin door." Zahir said looking at his watch. "It's already 9:20. Shit!"

"Zah relax." Sirus giggled sliding into the first-floor window landing on top of a small wooded coffee table. Shit!"

"Shhhh!" Zahir whispered walking out of the bushes and up to the front door.

"I can't" Chunky whispered as Starflower pulled her by the hand.

"Please! He scares me!" She pouted.

"Please? Bitch get up and get my bread!" K.O growled while Peluda headed their way. "This ain't Burger King, ain't no your way bitch, it's your way hoe. Get my money!"

"Let's go!" Peluda smiled as he bent to grab a beer. He pushed two pills into his mouth and drank. "X-pill and Viagra" he smiled. "Ladies, tonight I am a stallion." He humped Starflower's hip. "You sure K.O.? Not even two grand?" He almost begged.

"Naw! But if you ever grow a pussy..." She winked up as Cash and Money both leaned into her arms. "I'll be the first bitch to make you call your momma confessing your love for me."

"To bad..." He dropped the envelope on the club table. "Try these." He handed K.O. the triple stacks. "on me this time." He walked out of Pimps Paradise with the two fines hoes in the place.

"Look at this shit!" Zahir whispered standing over the dark dresser in the dark bedroom. "Rolex, Raymond Weil a goddamn Tudor and Peugeot. Shit this one is mine." He shoved it in his pocket.

"This safe is open nigga." Sirus pulled the door open. "Motha fucka!"

"What?" Zahir rushed to see the contents of the safe. What he saw made him smile.

"That's gotta be twenty or thirty stacks."

"Whatever it is nigga..." Zahir snatched the pillow from the bed. "It's ours now!" He loaded the jewelry, the cash and a few ounces of weed in the pillow case.

"Shit!" Sirus pointed to the living room as Chunky said out loud. "Home sweet home daddy."

"I'm gone want you to do that thing again Peludo." Starflower laughed. "It makes my toes tighten."

"After we shower bonito."

"What about me Peludo?" Chunky said loudly again.

"You will taste delicioso sitting on my face." He laughed. "Come here!"

Both Zahir and Sirus now stood in the walk-in closet with the safe.

"Dammit Zah!" Sirus pointed to the full pillow case on the bed. Zahir just hunched his shoulders and smiled.

The light suddenly came to life and both Starflower and Chunky danced into the room naked followed by Peludo.

Zahir first thought was of how hairy the half breed was. His second thought was... "No wonder Sirus is fucked up about this bitch Chunky."

"What the fuck!" Peludo shouted, His eyes held the sight of the pillow case on his king size bed,

The closet door opened and both men stepped out to bring a nightmare alive for the soon to be deceases trader.

"Shit!" Peludo yelled diving for the nightstand.

"Sorry nigga." Sirus laughed holding up the .357 magnum. "Get up!" They both noticed Peludo's eyes dart towards the Armoire.

"What... this?" Zahir held up the .45 colt 1911. "Yeah we got them all, even the one under the safe, so stop."

"So, what is this then? Did you come to rob me or is there more to it?" He spoke to Sirus directly. "The day I came to get you from prison I knew you didn't have any loyalty..."

"See you're wrong... Zah..." He nodded towards Starflower. She had eased closer towards the door.

"Bitch!" Zah growled. "You already know us." She froze next to Chunky.

"Peludo my loyalty was and will always be to the King's team. Not you, not Zahir or Tay... Nigga the King's team. Not one but all. But I do respect one thing." Sirus smiled and without a word shot Peludo in the heart once. "You gangsta!"

"Hmmm!" Starflower slapped her hand over her mouth.

"Shhhh!" Chunky whispered. "Don't." But Zahir had already turned towards them.

"No!" Sirus shouted. "Chunky." He held out his hand and she quickly took it.

"Please... I won't tell... please..." Starflower cried.

"I know!" Zahir smiled holding out his hand. Starflower took it trembling and afraid. "Do you like small dicks?" Zahir laughed bringing a smile to her face. "To bad because my dick is huge!"

"Stop it!" She giggled as he led them out to the white Escalade.

"Talisha, Blaque." K-2 hugged both women as he entered the Dave &
Busters

"Kendell Jr." Talisha flatly said. "Tay"

"O.K. wait!" K-2 sat. "Let's cut the bullshit and get the dumb shit out of
the way. First thing is, and you must understand this is only out of respect and
love for Tut. You will never be allowed to dig too deep in the business Second
is the name is K-2 and I only sit as a figure head of the King's team. The word is
team that I need you to notice. Tay, Man Down, Sirus, Zahir and myself sit as
equals only under King's team rules. Now this is how you can fit in your spot.
We need introductions.

"No! He will not meet with negros." Talisha smirked.

"Tut was half black."

"Yes, and the other half was Mexican. This may be a big ego check for
you Ken... K-2, but this world you play in still sees colors." Talisha said with
malice.

"Of course,... green!" K-2 smiled. "And if some old has been..." He
hesitated to let the insult sink in. "Wants to be racist, then fuck it and him. We'll
go to the Corteza brothers." He smiled. "Oh, I see you had no idea how deep I
play in... How you put it? This world" K-2 stood. "Let's go Tay... Man Down!"
He nodded towards the door.

"Wait!" Blaque quickly whispered taking Talisha by the arm.

"Pene en ridículo... Hacer el negocio. Now!'

Talisha rolled her eyes and looked up into K-2's eyes.

"She's right Talisha... don't be rediculous! Hacer el negocio... make the deal ma" K-2 winked. "Si hablas un idioma extranjero."

"Bastardo... cabron..." Talisha smiled. "Alright how much?"

"Thirty at ten five plus transportation cost" K-2 whispered sitting back down.

"We can do twelve no less and that's for familia" Blaque said. "Trans is one grand per."

"And quality?" Tay asked.

"The best of course little brother." Talisha smiled.

"How soon?" K-2 asked.

"That is my question to you?" Talisha said right back.

"Tay?'" K-2 looked at him.

"Three sixty in two hours." Tay smiled.

"Delivery next Wednesday afternoon. Same method. Cash and Money only." Blaque said.

"Let's go Blaque." Tay said. "Man Down"

"It seems the queen is born for the king." K-2 grinned looking into Talisha's fiery eyes.

As Tay, Blaque and Man Down left the King and Queen sat silently until Talisha whispered.

"Why Peludo? You almost sealed your fate."

"He crossed Tut... ask Angelita and the Don." K-2 said she knew more than she said and K-2 knew it. But he knew not to expose his hand to such a woman who showed no respect for her dead father's wishes. Maybe she was behind Peludo's transgressions. "Maybe" he thought.

Chapter 9

Say Hello to the Boss... Blood... Bitch

Delivery...

"We got company." KO. Whispered. "Two cars back, to the right… The white escalade." She said pulling into the far lane of 76 east.

"That is them." Talisha rolled her eyes. "Keep going."

"Out of their league huh?" K.O. frowned. "Seems to me they're on top of their game. And thot Man Down is creepy. Not once did he put his gun down even when Cash and Money put it on his ass."

"They are most definitely in the league." Blaque whispered. "Each has a part, and each does it to the end. Even little brother five times he made me count until we agreed it was not short. I added two thousand to the count and he actually told me to keep the extra, but when I said earlier for him to keep the shit, he refused. No, they are not out of their league. And to underestimate them is to lose the game."

"My Abuelito said to fuck a cat, you must first tie its claws… All of them!" Talisha giggled. "Come off on Broad. Let's take the long route."

"That's not Cash or Money." Man Down said into the phone." Yeah Delaware like you said."

"That's Blaque in the passenger seat." Zahir said "And it's somebody else in the back. I can't who." He looked over at Zahir "Is the bitch playing him or what?"

"She acts like she's for real and Sirus thinks she's the truth, and he's team."

"I say we down that bitch. He don't have to know!"

"She's his man! She's team nigga!" Zahir growled. "No!"

"I still don't trust the bitch. Besides he brought the bitch a car already. Two weeks... Fuck that!" Man Down barked.

"Man listen the bitch played her part in Phoenix. She is good nigga, Drop it."

"Whatever!" Man Down said. He followed for the next ten minutes in complete silence. "Shit!" He smiled.

"What?" Zahir asked.

"The bitch just waved at me" he laughed. "I guess that's that." Man Down sped up beside the NV 200. Rolling down the window he yelled to Blaque "hey sexy."

"Caposa hermano. Can a bitch get some dinner?" She winked

"Sure... I'd love to eat out with you." Man Down flirted.

"Nasty ass" she flirted back

They rode Broad street side by side uptown and into west Oak Lane and across to east Germantown.

"That's forty-five." Tay said coming into the living room of the same apartment King Tut died in. Both Talisha and K-2 sat staring at each other. Not one word passed from their mouths only the unsaid words in their eyes.

"Count again!" K-2 whispered keeping his eyes locked with hers.

"There is no need, it's forty-five" she said locked into K-2's soul.

"We paid for…"

"Thirty! I know… but things happen and my shit stinks too. So fifteen at eleven because I need you now." Talisha whispered. "I must ask for this favor…Ummm Por favor papi"

she smiled beautifully.

"Sure, Why not." Tay said and K-2 flinched before he thought.

"I thought it was equality on the King's team" she pushed.

"It's Tay's call…" K-2 looked at his little brother. "We take them I need two hours to get your money."

"That can wait! Tay can you go get Blaque hoe ass away from that boy?"

"Yulp!" Tay walked off and no sooner than he stepped away from the apartment Talisha walked into K-2's face. Her lips found his, her tongue tasted his mouth and her lips pressed into his hard. Her breathing grew rapid.

Finally, he reacted and kissed her back. His hands found her waist and pushed away softly.

"You are my only match." She breathed heavily.

"No one can be your match. You're…" K-2 pulled her into him once more and they forgot the world and all in it.

"Goddamn!" Man Down barked. "Can y'all even breath?"

Slowly they pulled apart, but their eyes remained locked as was their hearts.

"I'm what Kendell?" Talisha seductively asked in her tone, in her stance and on her mind.

"Ahhh hemm!" Blaque cleared her throat. "Anyway, why don't y'all just fuck already!"

"Blaque that's fifteen at eleven… not twelve."

"Wait! What? No!"

"Blaque!" Talisha barked. "Eleven I said!"

"Shit bitch!" Blaque mumbled "Queen Talisha! Alright… that will be one sixty-five… shit! Tay can you handle this or do I gotta wait until K-2 puts his dick magic on my sister and we don't get shit."

"Let's wait until they fuck then" Tay laughed.

"Nobody is fucking." Talisha took a step back from K-2. "Not yet at least."

"Tay take Blaque and pay her twelve on each…"

"But…" Tay yelped.

"Dammit Tay! Twelve!" K-2 turned away.

"Shit… maybe we should wait until they fuck" Blaque smiled. Now it was Talisha's turn to interrupt.

"I said eleven Kendell."

"I know, and my name is K-2! First of all, this is business, so the team will not be obligated or in debt. Twelve Tay"

"Come on Blaque before this nigga gives away my PlayStation." Tay laughed.

"Man Down!" Zahir nodded towards the corner light

"Aww shit." Man Down whispered. His eyes quickly darted towards he NV 200. K.O., Cash and Money all sat eating the cheese steaks while Starflower danced around listening to the Beans CD Zahir had booming from his trunk.

The red Camry pulled up playing the new Jill Scott with Chunky behind the wheel. No one took notice except K.O., who stepped away fast moving toward Chunky who sheepishly climbed from the car.

"How much bitch?" K.O. barked, without warning she had Chunky by the short Halle Berry cut.

"Ouch mommy!" Chunky cried. "Stop… Sirus!"

"Let her go K.O." Sirus said calmly. "She's mine now."

"This hoe is BBB. Not a housewife." K.O. growled. "How much bitch?" She asked again.

"Let her go!" Sirus now shouted. No one saw him move but he now had K.O. by the throat.

"Mistake Bitch!" K.O. barked shooting an uppercut that Sirus saw coming but barely was able to slip. The hook flew next over his head. The body shots land solidly to K.O.'s body and she never flinched as she spun with a back fist to the side of Sirus's head. Quickly she tried to bring a forward knee thrust to his solar plex which never landed as she stumbled backwards from two quick left jabs. K.O. smiled

"Alright let's get serious."

"K.O. don't do it." Man Down warned.

"Stop it K.O. I chose Sirus. You know the rules, I came, and I left. Money is the only thing we keep."

"Bitch shut up!" Cash yelled stepping towards Chunky with malice in her voice and her gun in hand.

"Don't do it whore!" Man Down pulled his .40 Glock. "Drop it!" He shoved the gun in her face.

Money reached only to feel the Heckler and Kock .7808 against her head.

"Drop it Cash… Please! I like you, but I'll blow your goddamn head off!" Man Down almost screamed "Please!"

"Mommy please don't let this go down." Chunky begged. "I finally got a chance to be happy. Please!"

"We don't want to do this y'all." Blaque said coming from the door of the manor holding her .380.

"No you don't!" Tay smiled holding his .45 1911 colt behind Blaque. "When we kill… we kill everybody!"

Blaque turned around to find Tay with dead aim in her head. "hermano?" She looked surprised.

"Familia Blaque!" He growled and Man Down, Zahir and Sirus all smiled.

"K.O.?" Sirus asked. "Friends?"

"Punk!" She smiled kissing chunky. "You can fight." She winked.

"Ouch!" Sirus rubbed his head. "Bitch you punch like a man. Can you fuck because I'll take you instead" he laughed.

"Boy!" Chunky yelled rushing into his arms.

"Man Down?" Zahir whispered. "Come on man."

"No!" Man Down growled. "Not until she promised me some pussy!" He slowly smiled. "Please… I'm broke."

"Sorry." Cash laughed. "Buku Dang!" Everybody relaxed accept Blaque. Quickly she strolled to Tay's car. "No more games" she yelled. "Let's go Tay" she rolled her eyes

"Fuck it!" Tay shrugged his shoulders. Crossing the street Tay climb into his Mustang GT Shelby. "What?" He asked looking into Blaque's eyes.

"You would of shot me little brother?" She asked.

"Would you shoot my brothers?"

"No… I just wanted to make a point!"

"Point was well made then!' Tay laughed and Blaque saw a man, not a thirteen-year-old boy.

"Yes… mmmm… yes…" She moaned holding the top of his head as he ate her pussy. "You learn very fast… Ohhh god little… brrrooothhhher!" Blaque screamed grinding up into his mouth. Her legs squeezed his head tightly between her thighs. "Stttoooppp." She tried to push his mouth from her clitoris, but Tay was in love with her taste. "Stop! Stop! Stop... por favor... por favor" Blaque shook uncontrollably finally able to free her smooth dark pussy from his greedy mouth.

"What you stop me for?" He kissed her plumped ass cheek as she laid on her stomach still enjoying the glow of an orgasm.

"Tay... Tay..." she stuttered. "A woman can only take so much."

"Not me. I can take it forever. It feels so good when I bust a nut." He licked the small of her back making her tremble.

"We will see." Blaque growled. She rolled Tay to his back and licked his nipples one at a time. Slowly she worked her way down his body and slowly pulled his balls into her mouth one at a time. She smiled when she noticed his toes ball up. Gripping his thick shaft, she looked up into his eyes. "Forever?" She smiled and deep throated him until she gagged over and over. Ten minutes later Tay fingers dug into the bedspread, but Blaque slid from his dick to lick his thigh as she slightly punched the head with her fore finger and thumb.

"Oh shit!" Tay whispered. "What the..."

"Shhhh... forever remember?" Blaque said running her tongue up the length of his dick. So fat and juicy." She whispered and took the head into her mouth again only to fun her tongue around stiffly with quick jabs of her mouth up and down only two inches deep.

"OHHHH SHIT!" Tay yelled as he busted in her mouth and her tongue and lips stayed in the area of the head sucking fast and stiffly rubbing the head.

"Ohhh shit Blaque… ohhh shit stop…Urrrggghhh…" Tay laughed as his body jumped with every stroke of her tongue. Tay had to wrestle away as his stomach tighten and he came once again.

"No forever boy!" Blaque growled and slammed him back to the bed. "Tell me you love me Tay." She climbed on his still hard dick. "Say it, mean it… prove it!" Slowly she eased him inside her deep tightness. And just like his father he ran deep into her stomach. "Mean it Tay… say it baby." She moaned slowly riding up and down with a mixture of emotion and pain. "Tell me Tay… please… mmm… Tay… Tata… oh god…" Blaque nails tenderly dug into his chest. "I'm almost… tell me tata… ohhhh godddd I'mmmmm commmming Tut!" She screamed as Tay looked up at a crying Blaque face whose eyes were closed.

"I love you Blaque." He whispered as she came hard. Five minutes later Tay came inside of her stomach and pulled her onto his chest.

"Tay I'm sorry" she sniffed.

"For what Blaque?"

"You know… I loved him you know… he loved me too Tay… He was my only male lover ever until…" She paused. "You look so much like him.

"He didn't want me" Tay whispered.

"That wasn't it Tay… He was ashamed of his betrayal."

"You mean with my moms and pops?"

"Yea! He told me he felt guilty because he loved Trigga and K-Dog like fathers. When he looked at you he felt their eyes on his heart. Tut couldn't tell you that. Men are dumb." Blaque kissed Tay chin. "But now…" she kissed his chest. "You got to prove…" she kissed his stomach. "You deserve me." She engulfed his dick and brought it back to life. "When the time comes I'll prove I deserve you lover" she whispered.

Meanwhile…

"Your pops is getting suspicious." Maria whispered. "The Don is no idiota. Last week he asked me where did a whore come across such an outlet. He wants to know how I got someone to trust me with so much money?" Maria's lips found Angelita's nipple. The thickness between her lips was a desired feeling for both women since high school. Neither one a lesbian, even though sex between the two continued over the years. "But he loves me, so I used his heart for you again."

"For us amante… mmmm… for us… yes my amante… I want to cum again." Angelita moaned pushing Maria's head toward her coño. "Suck and be quiet my amante… yes suck…" Angelita began to grind into Maria's mouth, but she smiled for different reasons. She thought of her long time plan she hatched over the years.

"For so long Mema and Papito has been the figures of the Montezas, who the familias looked at as the duel Jefes, and poor Angelita was just the only spoiled child who sat around and lived off the fruits of the Don and his wife." Angelita pressed up into the mouth of her best friend. "Make me cum amante." She closed her eyes and her thoughts drifted again. "Now I have what Tut unknowingly set up for me to finish my plans. He's the man I had in place to sit at my side… But his big polla controlled his fate better than my coño, but still he left me the King team…" Her body shook as she pictured the boys. "I'm venidero… I'mmmmmm commmming amante." Angelita cried out grinding hard into Maria's mouth.

"So?" Talisha asked as they loaded into the cargo van, she took Blaque's hand and pulled her towards the back. "Do you think little brother is ours yet?"

"Soon." Blaque smirked.

"How long does it take to pussy whip a child?" Talisha barked. "Puta!"

"He is young yes, but he is no child!" Blaque insisted. "He's grown hard and daring and very, very, very dangerous."

"Bullshit!" Talisha snapped. "He's only thirteen!"

"She is right." Money said over her shoulder. "If you could see the look in his eyes. One move and we would lose one Boss Blood Bitch yesterday. Him dangerous."

"Shit!" Talisha growled. "O.K what about Chunky?"

"Now that bitch good." K.O. laughed. "She made me believe she was in love with that dick."

"But can we depend on her, will she gather the information we need?"

"Boss Blood Bitches stay true to the game." K.O. smiled pulling into traffic.

"And him?" Talisha nodded towards Man Down as they pulled off.

"Both of them must die!" Cash and Money whispered together. "We can handle them."

"Shhhh! I'm calling Mema." Talisha laughed but Blaque pushed the phone down.

"Uh huh bitch!" She held her hand still with the phone. "Spill it!" What about that shit yesterday with K-2?"

"Oh that! Momentarily a lapse in my fat pussy. He's fine and I got horny! That's it!" She lied and Blaque knew.

"Fifteen thousand dollars lapse in your... How do you say fat pussy huh?"

"Yelp! But I finger fuck myself. That's over!" She lied again to their faces.

"Trick bitch." K.O. giggled. "Wish I had a dick bitch."

"No you don't mommy... You afraid of dick!" Starflower joined in and everybody laughed.

"Si." Angelita answered. Her voice harsh and breathless.

"Mama it's done. We're coming home..." Talisha said looking around as if everybody could hear her private conversation with her mother. Angelita sounded as if she was fucking a minute ago.

"How much?" Angelita ran her tongue deep into Maria's ass

"The asking... And mama we received the payments for the extra already..." Talisha frowned as she heard Maria squill in the back round. "Mama please!"

"¡No vayas adonde no te llaman! ¡No es asunto tuyo!" Angelita barked and slapped Maria on the ass. "Shhhh!"

"Sí Mama... Sí... we are headed back to Atlanta so I can get my car..."

"No, come home! It's time to sit and talk. Bring the bitches and the money." Angelita ordered and hung up. She crawled up the bed. "We must watch those two." She kissed Maria as they laid together. For so long they have been secret lovers, every touch found the perfect spot.

Chapter 10

Time to Clean House

"Summer, summer, summer time… Time to kick back and unwind… summer time"

The music blurred as the stolen Lexus pulled beside the Escalade SUV. Both women sported tennis skirts and cotton sleeveless tee shirts.

Chunky leaned out of the passenger window and tapped on the driver's window. Pimp looked down and smiled as her skirt rose to expose her fat juicy thighs the color of Hershey chocolate. He rolled his window down.

"Damn Ma, you got a player losing all his cool air and shit."

"What, I aint worth the heat? Boy you better check that shit and recognize a boss bitch. See that's what I keep telling my cousin… you niggas in Philly ain't got no game… Anyway… Y'all got any weed up in there?" Chunky smiled and the horns behind them began to blurr

"Pull over pretty?" Pimp pointed. He followed behind the Lexus as it drove a half block up a small street off of Broad street. He and Flex watched chunky get out of the Lexus built like a sex goddess and when the driver stepped from the car Pimp's dick grew hard as still Instantly."

"Ain't that that faggot nigga's bitch… Melba?" Flex growled.

"Melinda nut! And I'm fucking that bitch today. Flex don't be yourself." Pimp whispered as they approached. "Don't I know you little girl?" He smiled from the driver's window.

"Shiddd!" She winked. "I'm bigger now!" Melinda giggled. "Girrrrllll!" She turned to Chunky and spread her hand almost a foot apart. "Fareal."

"Stop playing... Uh huh girl... you..." Chunky laughed.

"Hell no bitch... not yet..." Melinda giggled. My shit wasn't on grown women status yet."

"how about now sexy?" Pimp smiled. "Or are you still that little girl with the pretty ummm... smile?"

"I ain't no little girl." Chunky quickly said with her hands on her hips. "What you trying to gut my little cousin? I can take the dick but the can you handle the pussy is the question?"

"I can handle the dick too." Melinda pouted childishly.

"Won't y'all get in, Damn!" Flex barked as if they were bothering him.

"That's Flex girl." Melinda whispered loud enough for them to hear as they went to the back door. "He's kind of slow they say." Chunky giggled as they climbed into the back seat.

"So... ummm Pimp right? Well Pimp..." Chunky fanned her legs open and shut. Pimp could see the dark red panties she wore flashing him. Her monkey as fat as his fist. "Is it true... what she said... Is it true?"

"Bitch you think I'm lying?" Melinda barked and turned to Pimp. "Show her Pimp! Show her fast ass what a big dick looks like."

Chunky spread her thighs wide. "What? This what you want to see?" She pulled her panties to the side. "This is what a fat ass pussy looks like... Pimp."

"Oh y'all want to play games huh?" Pimp whispered pulling his dick out and climbing in the back seat. "What you gonna do with this mutha fucka?"

"Oh shit." Flex growled as Pimp's dick brushed his forehead in passing. "Nigga! Bitch mutha fucka!"

"Then move nigga." Pimp laughed sitting in the seat beside Chunky. "What you gonna do ma?"

Jerking her head towards Flex, she gave Melinda the eye as she licked her lips. "Bitch I got this one" she smiled. "Handle Mr. Grumpy up front."

With that Melinda took two thirds of Pimp into her throat and caught everybody attention, even Flex.

"Goddamn!"

"Is yours like…" Melinda whispered sounding afraid.

"Bitch I'm the big brother." He laughed pulling his pants down to his ankles.

"Come on let's get this shit over with." Man Down said. He watched as Sirus face turned dark with rage.

"Yeah! Change of plans. I'm going too!" Sirus growled.

"Naw nigga you're driving! Let's go!" Zahir said pulling on his ski mask. "Creep up quietly nigga! None of that hot red shit. Let's go!" Zahir said a little louder. Both he and Man Down know it was the sight of Chunky with that nigga in her mouth that made Sirus pissed, but K.O. told him. Hoes and housewives are two different animals. He wondered if K-2 would have reacted differently if he could see Melinda now."

"Uggghh… Uuggggh… Uuuggghh…" Melinda gagged as Flex shoved her mouth further and further down on his almost twelve inches. "Uuuggghhhh… Uuuughhh."

"Relax bitch! The dick is yours to control. Relax your throat." Chunky smiled and engulfed every inch of Pimp down the neck. Slowly she withdrew. She circled the head with her tongue.

"Goddamn I'm gonna bust in this bitch mouth." Flex laughed insidiously shoving Melinda roughly down on his abnormal size dick.

"Uughhh… Uuggggghhhh…" Melinda chocked as the stolen Dodge Charger pulled up slowly beside the Cadillac truck.

Flex just closed his eyes to cum when he heard the first blast and felt brain matter splash his face and neck.

"God No!" He screamed as jets of his cum jumped into Melinda's face. He scrambled for the .357 on the floor at his feet.

"Sorry my man!" Zahir whispered snatching Melinda from the caddy. The next three shots entered Flex's head. "Run bitch!" He pointed his gun their way. Chunky jumped from the SUV in full stride grabbing Melinda's arm.

"Run bitch." She screamed spotting the white man on the phone.

"Zahir fired over their heads as they reached the corner. "Let's go!" Man Down shouted jumping into the stolen Charger. Zahir fired two shots into Pimp's body and turned to the white man and smiled while aiming his way. Moments later the Charger turned on to 9th street and was set ablaze.

"Shit slow tonight nigga." Black said sitting on the steps of the empty house that was up for sale.

"What do you expect, it's Tuesday nigga!" Jen replied. The BIC lighter flared up and she lit the Garcia Vega full of orange Kush. "But it'll pick up around twelve, watch."

"What the…" Black almost yelled as K-2 and Tay came around the corner holding AR-15s.

"Shut up! Don't move!" Tay growled.

"Black right? And you're too cute to be anybody but Jennifer, but you rather be called Jen right?" K-2 smiled reaching on Black's hip to the .40 Glock.

"Man we ain't…" Black started to say.

"Shut up and listen." Tay smiled at a blushing Jen.

"Now listen, the Mayo is on his way home from the strip club." K-2 continued. "Tonight he dies. The question is… Do he die alone and you two take over daily operations for the King team or does he die with two stupid niggas who passed up the chance to become paid?" K-2 smiled.

"Answer the Boss!" Tay winked at Jen.

"Shiddd! Whatever you say Boss." Black answered, "my little sister scared, but she agrees too!"

"I ain't scared…" she blushed smiling at Tay. "I can answer for myself, now how much do we make boss?'

"I'll go over that with you tomorrow." Tay winked again. "Put my number in your phone." He said directly to Jen.

"I ain't got one boy! I'm only fourteen by the way." Jen continued to blush.

"So am I" Tay handed her his phone. " Go somewhere and I'll call their phone in two hours. Answer it!"

"Not you Black! When shit go down just stay still. You my next corner boss." K-2 said "Jen you bounce."

"Bye ummm…"

"Tay" he softly touched her hand.

"Bye Tay" she smiled. Quickly she disappeared into the driveway.

"Listen mami." Sean Mayor whispered turning onto Upsal street. "I just want you to feel comfortable. No pressure as all. If you feel you don't want to do anything, it's cool. We can watch television or something.

"See guys like you are always married or something" she frowned. "Be straight up Sean" she shifted in her seat. "You married right?… Maybe a girlfriend who lives somewhere else… right?"

"Nope!" Sean Mayor whispered. "I'm just lonely and want company. I don't give a damn about sex or dumb as shit unless you feel I deserve it. I just like the way you made me feel comfortable at the club." Sean Mayor was on one. The Ecstasy had him in a zone. He turned onto Thouron street and up to Sharpneck and made a left on to Temple road. Black stood behind the blue mail box as usual that late at night smoking his blunt.

"Can you cook? Never mind… I'll make us fried shrimp and onion rings.: Sean said as he parked.

Neither him or the stripper noticed the masked men until Sean Mayor's head hit the windshield in pieces. His body jerked inside the car as fifteen more .223's tore threw him seconds apart awakening the quiet Mount Airy neighborhood.

Black disappeared without a sound.

Both women came from the 9th district police station smiling. The horn blew as they looked up to see K-2 waiting on top of the hood.

"Hey baby." Melinda leaned in to kiss him. He turned away. The look on his face said pissed, hurt and betrayed. "Kendell?" Melinda almost whined.

"Get the fuck in the car." He said flatly and both women looked at each other.

The drove away silently together and it wasn't until K-2 pulled over onto East River Drive that anyone spoke.

"We told them we were call girls." Melinda whispered sadly.

"Nigga we did that shit for…" Chunky barked not liking the way he had Melinda feeling in the front seat. But his look shut her up.

"Baby… I…" Melinda whispered as a tear rolled down her cheek.

"Bastard!" Chunky mumbled and turned away.

"Bitch!" K-2 yelled. "What you think I'm made?" He turned to face both women. "I'm fucking ashamed of what I asked my woman to do. I'm fucking ashamed of asking my brother's woman to be…" He bowed his head. "I'm sorry Melinda." He reached out for her hand. "Baby never again… I swear, Never!"

"Kendell I'd be anything for you." Melinda let the tears flow. "I love…" He cut her off.

"Open the glove compartment." He whispered. Melinda swore she saw a tear in his eyes.

Inside there were two thick envelopes, both held with rubber bands, stuffed with bills.

"That's fifty thousand ma" he whispered. "If ask you to be my whore. You'll be the highest paid whore on the East Coast."

"Both these mine?" she smiled, and the tears still flowed.

"Sorry boo" he chuckled. "One is for the Bitch in the back."

"Bitch that's what I call a pimp!" Chunky danced snatching her envelope. "Want me to suck your dick?" She laughed as Melinda tried to slap her over the backseat.

"You gotta go home… My man Sirus is fucked up over what he saw." K-2 frowned. "I tried to smooth shit out last night… but I ain't got no pussy!" K-2 joked but Chunky knew Sirus was probably hurt.

"Shit! He saw me?" What he say? Is he mad?"

"They all did." K-2 frowned holding Melinda's hand. "Sorry" he spoke mostly to Melinda who now blushed in shame.

Sliding closer to K-2 Melinda laid her head on his shoulder and softly cried. "Kendell can you take me home?"

The ride to their homes were in silence with only the smallest of sniffles and the sound of the lightest of touches from Kendell lips to Melinda's crying eyes. But mostly each was lost in their own thoughts.

Melinda of love and the American Dream of family and friends and the white picket fence.

K-2 of getting out, going to Harvard or Yale rich and becoming a husband and father.

And Chunky… of how she wishes she didn't have to do it, and what life could be…

The white NV 200 pulled into Phoenix Arizona and all six women were ready to get home and into their own beds, but K.O. drove straight to the ranch home of Angelita Monteza.

"Talisha." Blaque whispered. Her eyes shifted quickly to the two men standing at the gate as they pulled in.

"Shit!" Talisha groaned. "It's grandmother."

"Tah what you want us to do?" K.O. drove to the front door as not to draw attention.

"Remember you are college roommates and friends." She looked towards Cash and Money. "I will introduce you two as exchange students from the Philippians. Cashmere and Monica, and remember she is not grandfather. She will not enjoy cuteness."

The cargo van pulled in front of the front door where two very large men stood holding mini sub machine guns behind Angelita, Maria and Selina Monteza.

"Grandmother." Talisha yelled jumping from the van. She rushed into her arms and was smothered with her kisses.

"My small bird…" Selina Monteza glowed with joy. "My how you have grown in ten years." She kissed Talisha again.

"Mama…" Angelita said "These are my Bitches." She pointed towards the surprised women stepping from the van." This is Blaque the brains. She's Maria's daughter.

"Beautiful." Selina smiled. "Absolutely beautiful" she hugged the surprised girl.

"This is K.O. the strength and courage of the Blood Bitches." Angelita winked making K.O. blush.

"Also gorgeous and big.. come… come." Selina said with open arms. As K.O. hugged her Selina whispered, "you are my granddaughter's protection… do not let me down?"

"Yes ma'am K.O. answered shyly

"And these two …" Angelita pulled Cash and Money towards her mother. "Are Cash and Money. The two I told you about. They will serve us good in the future with K.O. of course."

"They are all so beautiful and killers too.. come" Selina held her arms out for the twins. She embraced both and whispered, " to kill for love is one thing, but to kill for loyalty is worth everything."

"Jefe." Starflower nodded to everyone surprise.

"Well Lolita?" Selina asked

"Yes Jefe, they are official and can be trusted." Starflower looked every girl in the eyes. "I'm sorry for the deception, but it was so much fun. You were the best assignment my Jefe has ever given me." Starflower stepped close to

K.O. "And you…" she kissed K.O. on the mouth. "Are the best lover I ever had… EVER!

"Star…?" K.O. moaned holding her hand.

"Sorry I belong to the Cartel… Sorry amante."

"Yes mina…" Selina smiled. "Like you're the Boss Blood Bitches. Let's go Inside."

"Blaque the money" Talisha said.

"No! That is for them to split. You and Blaque will not share in that. Only K.O. and her girls."

"So." Angelita smiled. "They will not be pushed."

"No Mama… they will not" Talisha said. She took notice of Blaque and Maria having words. Blaque seemed heated while Maria seem to be soothing the issue with gentle words and touches that Blaque tried to avoid.

"They deceived us!" Blaque barked.

"No!" Talisha smiled. "They used us and made us stronger. We now have unlimited resources to build with.

"Yes, to build for them!" Blaque growled.

"No!" To build for us all. We will still be rich, and you and I are the future. Why is it so bad to know that your mama was not what she seemed? She is not the whore she led you to believe? She is a Jefe of her own ranks!"

"No but…" Blaque slammed the teddy bear to the bed. "They lied to me for years… I lived with so much pain, so much shame. So much…"

"Stop it bitch! You had everything. Now you know it was really Mama's money. That's what hurts." Talisha said picking up her teddy bear and placing it back on the shelf. "And nothing more."

"And what of the Boss Blood Bitches?" Blaque whispered.

"What about us? We are sisters… Blood is thicker then iron and Blood Bitches stick FOREVER!" Talisha smiled and all the women nodded. Even K.O. who split the up six ways She handed Blaque her bag and did likewise with Cash and Money. Talisha took hers to a small safe in the wall of her room.

"Do you want me to keep hers?" Talisha asked.

"Yeah! She's Blood." K.O. handed Talisha the other pile.

Chapter 11

Love Jones

August 2011

Two months later…

"Let me get those royal blue and black forces." Pay4 bounced to the D-Block beat inside of City Blue urban clothing store. "Those red and whites too sexy."

"Boy! You gonna get me fired talking to me like that." The shy white girl looked up at the owner's wife. "She already jealous of me" she whispered.

"Then work for me" Pay4 smiled.

"Stop it!" She laughed walking to the rear storage room to retrieve the three pair of size 11s. She came back with all three boxes. "Those run small, so I brought '11 ½ in the Pumas.

"Bet." Pay4 sat to try them on.

"Hats too, right?' She smiled.

"You remembered."

"Boy please. It's the same every week, shoes and hats. I swear you got to have fifty pair of tennis shoes."

"Seventy-three is more like it." He joked.

"Boy stop it!" She shook her head.

"But for real." Pay4 offered his hand. "They call me Pay4 and all those months I've been coming here you never told me your name." He smiled.

'Wendy." She shook his hand looking up at the wife of her boss. "Pay4 huh?"

"My real name is to funny. When I was young I use to pay my sisters not to call me by Gastepi."

"No shit!" Wendy laughed. "Gastepi? No shit."

"See there! How much?" He giggled.

"No, I think It's cute."

"Then you'll go out with me for lunch?" He asked.

"Well Gastepi…" she giggled. "I only get thirty minutes and this bitch…" She jerked her head towards the cash register.

"Chick-Fil-A is right there." He pointed "Chicken and fries on me. Let's talk and share a smoothie."

"All righty then." She giggled again. "It's a date Gastepi."

"Dammit! Here!" He handed her ten dollars. "Pay4 Please!"

She giggled again.

Pay4 paid for the three pair of shoes, the matching hats and exited the store with a promise of lunch in two hours across from City Blue.

"I see you like that vanilla bean and cream." She whispered making him turn. "Yeah I see you in there getting your mack on. I guess sisters ain't your thing…" She rolled her eyes. "What is it? A little short in places?" She looked down at his groin.

"What?" He frowned. "I ain't short nowhere and, and, and" he paused. "Don't I know you?"

"Nigga if you don't remember this…" she put her hand onto her wide hip. He could see her ass from the side. "My booty is starting to lose its size and shape. I had niggas crash watching this booty."

"Chunky, right? Yeah that's it, Chunky! Sirus bit… Sirus woman" Pay4 smiled. "What up girl?"

"Horn… I mean…" she giggled. "Hungry." Pay4 looked back at Wendy who was stacking boxes in the back near the shoes. "Come on let's go eat." He smiled. He snuck a peek at his watch and knew he had two hours.

"My car is in the back near the movies." Chunky whispered.

"Come on I'll drive you around, then I'll follow you. Where you want to eat?" He asked leading her to his Silverado truck.

"Engine Forty-Seven."

"Down on Delaware Ave."

"Yulp!" She smiled. "I can afford it if…"

"I got it, I was…"

"What the white girl? Shiddd never mind. I don't play seconds to no bitch, especially a cracked with no kind of body. See you niggas with y'all cracker fetish and chicken. Move!" Chunky pushed by him. "I'm going home to a man!" She looked back, "I wanted to play too!" She turned and left. What Pay4 didn't see was the devious smile on Chunky's face as she made her exit. His mind could only see the tight fitting capri jeans and belly shirt that exaggerated every curve of her body.

"Stupid mutha fucka!" Pay4 Whispered.

"I love you Pops." K-2 smiled as they embraced.

"Kendell you promised." K-Dog held on tight. "You made me a promise."

"I swear dad. This summer and I'm finished. I'll have Harvard money and moms can get a house up here" he lied. Not about the house for his mother, but there was no way out now. To many families depend on him to live.

"He's not being honest Kendell." Talisha cried. "The money he has now is more than enough to buy five housed and college three times."

"Mom please!"

"K-2 your word son." Kendell senior whispered as K-2 made his exit from the prison's visiting room.

"What up K-2?" Sirus father asked as he sped by with tears in his eyes.

"Mom, dad…" Sirus whispered standing. They knew he had to go. K-2 was his brother since he was six.

"Thanks for the money Sirus and the clothes. See you next month son." He smiled as his son sped up to catch K-2. He knew he would soon be home in the mix of them and he wanted in.

"K-2 wait up." Sirus called out as the desk guard buzzed them out into the exam room. "Man what's up?"

"Moms on that bullshit again. Got me lying to my pops and shit."

"You know my dad comes home next month. Nigga think he's gonna weasel in. I'm purring that nigga up Frankford projects with Howie and Fate. Away from us!" Sirus laughed. "nigga on some old gangster shit. Things changed I told him, so if he wants that old hard to hand combat shit. Them project bitches got what he likes."

"That's cold Sirus." K-2 laughed.

"Yulp! Now what about the shipment coming in? Did Tah say how much?" He asked.

"Naw, she keeps playing her bullshit games. The bitch wants to be a boss so bad. But one thing she'll never do... she will never out boss us! I told Tay to stack a half in counted and wrapped bills." K-2 grinned. "A hundred stacks per bundle. Let the bitch play. In minutes we'll take her sexy ass down a peg."

"K-2..." Sirus sounded serious now. K-2 stepped and turned his way. "Man how much is enough?"

"Ain't no such thing Sirus. You think Bill Gates or Joe Kennedy said that's enough. Warren Buffet said money is nothing but a hobby if you can count it! And my hero said I ain't rich or wealthy. I'm powerful!"

"Taum and Freddrick is still complaining again." Sirus said jumping of the subject before K-2 started his history bullshit about the billionaires who started in illegal businesses.

"Don't we get them a yearly salary?"

"Amongst other shit... cars, trips, strippers and free lancers."

"Tell them to chill until Christmas and we'll give them a bonus of half the year." K-2 growled. "One day we gotta figure out how to get new help."

Sirus checked his phone as he pulled it from the locker in the waiting area of Gratisford Prison. "Tay called and so did Man Down."

"Yeah Zahir called me." K-2 whispered. "Let's bounce."

"Damn nigga where y'all at?" Man Down asked. "They here!"

"Fuck out of here!" Sirus frowned. "They early as fuck." He spoke into the car system.

"Yeah and they got other surprises too. Tay on the shit now."

"How big is the surprise?"

"Twenty-five over at twelve plus ten over that at ten five. This bitch is pushing nigga."

"Naw man this bitch is counting." K-2 cut in. "I'm calling Tay... sit on them bitches and Man Down..."

"What up?"

"Hard if need be. Where is Zahir?" K-2 asked.

"What up dog?" Zahir has no idea K-Dog was his father's name.

"Good you're there... Don't let them bitches move y'all!" K-2 hung up. "Sirus them no good hoes think we stupid. They believe we playing games here..." K-2 paused and spoke to his car system. "Tavious." Then he turned back to Sirus. "See they're trying to see if we got the cash on hand to cover the price. If we fell for it once, they think that they can try it again. It's like sizing up your fighter... testing their power."

"Yeah." Tay answered breathing heavy.

"Tay hold all cash movement until we get back to Philly."

"Well I got Blaque here with me counting now." Tay said.

"Tay can she hear me?" K-2 mumbled.

"Naw! Why?"

"They setting us up for something. Keep that bitch there and don't let her leave. She cannot be in contact with Talisha until shit get straight. Forty-five minutes at the most."

"I got that." Tay hung up

Tay closed his phone and rolled over. "Now where was I?" he smiled.

"Let me show you Tavious" Blaque cooed. She took Tay by the head and guided him to her flower. "See Tata you remember."

"Was that Kendell?" Talisha smiled.

"Yulp! Be here in thirty minutes" Man Down said.

"Good, that gives us time to go get cheese steaks" K.O. danced in circles.

"Check this out. I'll order y'all some steaks from Pagano's. I'll send Benny Doo to pick them up. They some of the best we got uptown.' Zahir said.

"But I…"

"K.O." Talisha shook her head no. "Let them order." She quickly flipped her phone open and pressed two, two and the phone rang on Tay's dresser.

"Stop… ohhh goddd… stop… one momento por… fa… vooooor… I'mmmm cummmming." Blaque screamed as the call went to voicemail.

There was barely a pause and she never realized Tay had slid deep into her body as another orgasm hit her hard, sending her body into fits. She spoke no more English as she screamed.

"Manejar una situación bien... Por favor Tay manejor este concha amante... ewwww shit!"

"They're here!" Zahir said unlocking the door.

"Zahir" Sirus dapped him coming through the door.

"Man" he dapped Man Down. "Tah."

"Where to boss?" Talisha smiled.

You're looking at them sexy" Sirus pointed to Man Down and Zahir. "We a team, and the sooner you get that shit in your pretty ass head, you'll understand you can't out think us. Now this is the deal. We'll take…" he smiled. "The twenty over at ten. Cash up front, and the ten on the cuff at fifteen. That's it, no more negotiations. See the way we see it is you're trying us, and we're tired of these games. So, if you don't like the offer get in that shit out there and bounce!"

"Then we take our business elsewhere."

"Oops! You must ain't understand. I said we'll take not buy. So, if you refuse then…"

Zahir and Man Down both upped their AR-15s

"So, it's come to this?" Talisha whispered.

"Only if that's what you understand. See we tried to be familia to long and you continuously disrespected the honor of what your father has built. The money is there, but only with respect will you receive it… otherwise…"

"Yes, I think we will take the money" Talisha smiled. "Have Blaque deliver it to the house."

"She's with K-2 as we speak."

K-2 sat quietly on the sofa inside of Tay's mother's home listening to the Sex-4-A-Thone upstairs. He had all intentions of storming in and holding Blaque hostage while Sirus handle Talisha snake ass. But it seemed he had no need to. Over and over Blaque screamed her love for Tay and promised her loyalty in a fit of sexual passion. Not once had Tay mention love.

Smiling K-2 look at his watch. "Thirty minutes" he thought knowing he must have interrupted Tay when he called from the highway an hour ago. "Damn master dick" he laughed to himself. Little did he know Tay was sucking Blaque into submission.

Another fifteen minutes passed before he heard Tay and Blaque coming from the room. K-2 stood and slammed the front door.

"Yo Tay… Blaque… y'all here?"

"Yeah I was showing Blaque to the bathroom" Tay lied for her sake.

"Did y'all count up yet?" he know Tay wouldn't count until he gave the word, but this was for show as was the door slam.

"No, not yet. We're waiting on Talisha to call" Blaque said coming down the stairs. "I missed..." she stopped herself and blushed.

"Hold up!" K-2 smiled as his phone vibrated It was Sirus. "What up?"

"We good nigga" Sirus replied. "Is she still with y'all?"

"Safe and sound..." K-2 looked Blaque in the eyes. "Man Blaque is glowing like she just had the best day of her life. She's fine."

"Stop it" she smiled very hard as she turned. "Por favor Kendell."

"Someone wants to speak with you gorgeous" he handed her the phone.

"Hello" Blaque's facial expression changed immediately. "Si... si... the count is correct... si..." she turned to both men. "Si... cuatro y mitad mil... si... and the rest envoi a domicilio... si?" Blaque closed K-2's phone. "We have a deal then, and I am safe?"

"Tay four and a half up front, and another one-fifty in two weeks delivered by you to Phoenix" K-2 turned to Blaque.

" I need you to listen very carefully..." the hesitation was for dramatics, but he understood the Spanish culture and it meant serious to them. "Our worth is none of your business. Our ventures together have and will continue to be profitable if and only if the games stop. I've spoken to some very interested brothers over in Mexico who guarantee delivery and privately at brother prices. But our loyalty is to your Jefe. You Blaque must decide... who are your loyalties to. Talisha must stop these games of mitad mil every month goes to the Monteza's enemies."

Tay come back up from the basement carrying four expensive Ghurrka leather satchel bags.

"Four hundred and half thousand heavy ass, heavy ass bags of money" he dropped them at K-2's feet.

"My loyalty is the future of my Jefe K-2" Blaque held her stare with Tay. "My Jefe."

The three of them carried the bags out to the car and laid them on the trunk. K-2 climbed into the Volvo to wait for Blaque.

"Tay… trust me… Jefe." She kissed him softly and knew K-2 watched as her hand trailed down his chest sexually. She rushed to the car and climbed in. K-2 saw the water well up in Blaque eyes as they pulled away.

"Blaque what's real ma? Talk to me" he compassionately whispered.

"I'm in love with a kid." Instantly Blaque broke. The emotions inside came free, and there was nothing she could do to hide them any longer. "I'm in love with Tavious."

K-2 pulled over in Lynnwood Gardens complex so that she could cry in peace. Kendell stepped from the car. He also needed time alone to think. Shit in his mind was moving real fast. First Sirus with Chunky and all the mistrust Man Down had for the ex-whore. Now Blaque and Tay. Shit was spiraling out of control. Not to mention his lust for Talisha fine ass.

"Fuck it! It is what it is! Tomorrow will take care of tomorrow" he mumbled climbing car.

Blaque whispered "she wants it all Kendell… the Cartel, the streets and my soul. She cannot have Tavious!"

"She won't... we are brothers."

"Blaque?" Talisha frowned and spun on K-2 "What have you done to my familia?"

"Not a damn thing" he responded stepping back.

"Then why was she crying?"

"I'm sick Tah... the count is clear, let's go" Blaque said.

"No, we are staying until payment is fulfilled. K.O. and her hoes can deliver the cash."

"But..."

"We stay..." she looked around. "Here!"

"Hell no!" Man Down snapped. "This is my spot to crash."

"And we keep work here in this building. We cannot let you sit on dangerous ground. I'm security so I say no!" Zahir barked.

"He's right." K.O. said. "You're too important. No! You and miss thang got to get a hotel room" she winked at Zahir.

"On me" K-2 smiled. "The Ritz Carlton."

"Very well, but I need a view" Talisha smiled.

"Spoiled brattt!" K-2 laughed. "Come on K.O. help me load the money in that shit y'all call a stash."

"Oops!" Talisha laughed at the look on K-2's face. "The clerk crushed his boss image with four little words." She continued to laugh.

"Stop it Talisha!" Blaque giggled. "He has the money at least. Here!" Blaque handed him her card. "Two suites up high with a view. A private bar and large bed."

"Yes ma'am… sorry sir." The clerk turned red in the face.

"Shiddd! Don't be sorry, you just saved me…" As he almost got it out Talisha snatched the ten thousand dollars from his hand. "We're going shopping tomorrow. Pick us up around ten in the morning."

"Yes, my queen" K-2 bowed.

The following week…

This is why I'm hot… This is why I'm hot… The music blared from the red Canary that spun the corner at the top of the hill. Pay 4 It stayed on top of the blue mailbox as K-2 and Sirus use to do to watch all movement. He watched her park.

"Jo-Jo heads up! Could be the nigga from Forest Ave."

"Naw nigga. That's that bitch who drove through last week looking for Sirus."

"Oh snap!" Pay 4 know exactly who she was. He jumped from the mailbox and jogged up the hill.

"Boy what?" Chunky rolled down the window.

"That's what I was about to ask you ma" he smiled.

"Boy mind your business! And you need to spray on some cologne… smelling like weed and shit" she snapped. "Move before you give me away."

"Away to who? This my strip my workers."

"Excuse me?" she frowned. "Sirus is my man remember?" she rolled her eyes. "Besides you like those… move sellout nigga." She rolled up her window.

Pay 4 shrugged his shoulders and turned to walk away.

"Hey!" Chunky yelled from her driver side window. "Get in for a minute."

Pay 4 heard the locks click open. Quickly he climbed inside.

"Got anymore weed?" Chunky asked. She saw his eyes lock on her brown expose thighs. She slightly opened them and scooted forward just a little to expose the pink panties covering her thick pussy lips. "What boy?" she giggled following his eyes as if she hadn't noticed already. "Nasty!" she giggled look at his hard on. "Mmmm look at you Pay 4… all excited and shit" she giggled.

"Sorry I…" He stuttered knowing Sirus would whip his ass.

"No boy! I'm flattered. At least somebody finds this…" Chunky spread her legs wide so that Pay 4 could see it all fat and puffy sticking out in those hot pink laced thongs. "Sexy. God knows Sirus don't know more. Who this bitch name Gale he's been seeing Pay4 ?"

"Gale the whore…" he stopped knowing he just crossed the player's code. "Naw not Sirus. That's my bitch!" he lied.

"Stop lying Pay 4. I know already…" Chunky stopped talking and looked back at his dick. "Wow boy." She instantly reached over to massage it. "I got you like this?"

"Chunky… mmmm shit… Sirus gonna kill me, stop it!"

She could tell that he wanted her more than he showed, but he was frightened of Sirus. His penis twitched in her hand as she rubbed the length up and down.

"Why should I stop? That nigga fucking a different bitch every night, then comes home and won't even touch me." She paused her massage of his dick and grabbed his hand. Chunky pulled it onto her hot pussy. "Ssss… see Pay.. 4… it… ohhh god I'mmm… rub it boy ohhh shit…" her hand went back to his dick. "I… need… toooo… yesss boy…" she spread her legs wider. He expertly slid her lace panties to the side and rubbed her clit.

"Can you fuck me boy…" Chunky shook in a fake orgasmic shake. "Please ohhhh goddd…" she screamed. "I'mmm commmmming Pay… SHIT!" she slammed her legs shut to make it convincing. She felt him stiffen and heard his moan as his dick jerked inside his pants. Chunky knew she made him cum in his pants.

"Want to go to my crib?" Pay 4 asked.

"Nooo! Sirus will see my car. I got a hotel room downtown let's go. But can you do me a favor while I drive?" she grinned.

"Sure, what is it?"

"Eat this pussy!" She slid her panties off and Pay 4 acted like a starving artist. Chunky came for real twice by the time reached the garage of the Ritz Carlton.

"Shit I forgot to tell you Pay 4" she smiled sexually. "You gotta fuck about five times today, I already know you can eat the shit out of some pussy. But that dick is going to be put to the test upstairs."

Chunky and Pay 4 climbed on the elevator and the operator asked for the electronic key. Chunky gave him the room key to Suite 1802 two floors below Talisha and Blaque.

Stepping from the elevator Pay 4 was impressed. Not once had he been in this historic hotel. Even though he lived here all his life. He realized this was way out of his budget and lifestyle. Chunky led him down the long hallway with thick paisley carpet to the suite.

"Ready boy?" she paused at the door.

"Yeah ma of course I'm…" He lost his confidence when the door opened, and two naked Philippians stood in the sunken living room on both sides of a giant sexy black bitch, sucking on each of her titties.

"Come on and taste this nigga!" K.O. moaned as her fingers spread her thick beige pussy lips.

"Do it Pay 4 It." Talisha whispered from behind him. He had no idea when or where she came from. All he knew was that she had her arms wrapped around him unbuckling his belt. "I hope you're ready. We're gonna fuck the shit out of you."

"But first 'm gonna suck your dick crazy." Black moaned from his left and again he didn't know how or where she came from. He only thought he died and went to beautiful girl heaven by mistake.

"See Zahir!" Man Down growled. "I told you that bitch was scandalous.

"Dammit!" Zahir gritted his teeth.

"I'ma do the bitch upstairs." Man Down continued. In his hand he held a six-inch titanium navy seal knife.

"How? This place got some serious security. We can't even take a elevator without a key card. Nigga we barely made it under that fucken gate before it closed. We lucky we can push the up button to get out this bitch." Zahir stopped talking when he spotted Chunky come from the elevator. He followed her with his eyes.

"Son of a bitch!" Man Down smiled. For the first time both men recognized the white NV 200 she was climbing in. "Be right back nigga!"

"Naw wait" Zahir smiled holding Ma by the arm.

"Why? Let's kill this snake bitch!"

"I got four hundred thousand reasons why nigga." Zahir whispered as Chunky jumped out of the NV 200 with two stacks of money in her hand. Man Down smiled knowingly.

"What?" K- snapped. He looked at Sirus and Tay wrestling on the floor. "Bring it to aunt Kay's" he hung up. "Shit!" He barked making both Tay and Sirus look his way.

"What now nigga?" Sirus sat up only to get put in a sleeper hold from behind.

"You going to seep punk!" Tay laughed Sirus struggled.

"Them bitches!' K-2 growled. "Stop fucking playing Tay! That bitch Talisha just won't quit. Man Down and Zahir was on Chunky…"

"Wait! Nigga you had them following my bitch?" Sirus stood defensively from the floor.

"Naw, naw" he said lying "They was following Talisha and Chunky showed up. Guess who with? Pay 4!" He looked Sirus in the eyes. "As we speak they are all at the hotel in a suite…all them bitches."

"Talisha, Blaque and Chunky? With Pay 4?" Tay asked.

"And all the rest of them too nigga. Man and Zah found the van. It still had the money inside. They took it all and will be here in a few minutes." K-2 said.

"I'm smokin that cross artist ass nigga!" Sirus growled snatching the Glock from the table.

"Naw chill." K-2 smiled. "This is perfect. We'll skin both them fish when the grease gets hot. Now this is what's up…" K-2 explained the plan twice, once to Tay and Sirus and again to Man Down and Zahir when they got there with the leather Ghurrka satchels.

"Escalade time nigga!" Man Down high fived Zahir.

"You know it!" Zahir yelled stuffing his share back into the six-hundred-dollar satchel.

"Bay…" Chunky rushed into the living room. "Can I use the gym pass today. I want to work on my booty… Do you think it's getting flabby?"

(Ding Dong) The doorbell rang at that moment. "Naw it's fat and juicy… Just like I like it." He smiled as she opened the Chestnut Hill Village apartment door. Sirus kept his eyes on her as her face almost hit the floor. He had to admit, the bitch was good at disguising her emotions. "Who is it?" He yelled.

"It's ummm Pay 4 It…" She eye balled him with the question in her look. He just shrugged fearfully.

"Cool… I've been waiting on him. Tell him I said come to the bedroom." Sirus stood and made his way to the bedroom.

"What the fuck?" Pay 4 mouthed.

"Be quiet nigga." Chunky mouthed back and followed him inside. Before she made it to the room the bell rang again.

"Get that baby" Sirus yelled. "Come here Pay 4."

Chunky opened the door to mind Man Down and Zahir smiling holding up boxes of condoms. Only then did she notice the other twenty men coming their way, all with that look of lust.

"Party time hoe." Man Down growled and without warning Zahir grabbed her by the hair. "I always wanted some of that fat ass. Yo Sirus." He laughed slinging Chunky across the room.

"In here y'all!"

"What I do? What I do?" She cried as three other men began ripping her clothes from her body. "Help Sirus."

"Bring that bitch in here!" Sirus yelled. "Naked and ready."

"What's going on?" Pay 4 tried to smile.

"Nigga I'm going to let all y'all fuck Chunky until she tells me who she was fucking two days ago at the hotel. My man Mike is the elevator boy there. He seen my bitch with a nigga going up to a suite. He'll be here in an hour or so.

This bitch gave the nigga some money too!" Sirus grinned. "Nigga just finished setting up the goddamn digital cam, so we can film this shit! Gang bang of the fucking CENTRY!"

"Yeah nigga!" Man Down laughed. "And we got them fag boys Kool Aid and Bo Pete from Bi-Hi nightclub to fuck the nigga when she tells us who the fuck he is. I ain't no homo, but them punks got dicks the size of a pony. They gone kill some shit" he laughed.

"You first Pay 4... nigga I know you wanted some of Chunky for a while. Throw that bitch on the bed. Give this nigga one of those small condoms" Sirus laughed. "Pinky dick here."

"Naw I'll film cuz." Pay 4 said trying to get out of it.

"Wait! Man Down make that bitch sit still."

"Please Sirus... Pleeeaaassse don't baby. I love..."

"Bitch!" Man Down slapped the spit from her lying mouth to the wall. "If you move, fight or try to escape. I don't care how much Sirus love yo ass. I'm gonna cut your fucking eyes out!"

"Fuck this bitch Pay 4." Zahir grinned. Standing six foot three, two hundred and seventy pounds. Zahir was not to be played with. As was Man Down who only stood five eleven, a hundred ninety pounds.

"I'm next!" Pony Boy stepped to the front holding nine inches of a cucumber size dick. "I'ma bust that ass wide open son!" he slapped Pay on the ass.

Slowly Pay 4 It undressed and climbed between her legs. He whispered into her ear as his five-inch dick slid inside of her deep pussy. "Take it for me please... I swear I'd do anything for you... Please Chunky..."

Chunky's only response was to stare at a crying Sirus who didn't even turn the camera on. She knew then, she was not the star of this film. "Anything?" she cried.

"Yes" Pay 4 moaned as he came inside of her pussy.

"Damn nigga! Two minutes?" Pony Boy laughed. "Naw nigga!" He smashed a big right hook into Pay 4's temple as he tried to get off the bed. "I'll told you I'm next and I'm gonna bust that ass wide open.

Pay 4 tried to clear his head as he watched Sirus snatch Chunky from the bed and wrap a robe around her. She cried into his chest as he led her to the corner of the room.

"Naw! I like them to fight a little!" Pony Boy laughed flipping Pay 4 It on to his stomach. "Hand me that KY Kool Aid."

"Nooo!" Pay 4 struggled with the six foot of muscles who just did twenty in the pen.

"That's right…" Pony Boy smashed a body shot to Pay 4 ribs. "Fight me nigga!" Pony Boy grabbed his throat lifting him almost off the bed. Pay 4 watched as Kool Aid and Bo Pete kissed and masturbated each other huge dicks. "Watch me nigga!" Pony Boy hit him in the gut. As the air rushed from his body, he seemed to feel himself being turned upside down. "Houston we have lift off!" Pony Boy laughed and Gastepi Jones felt his bowels release with fire in his guts. Pony Boy was nine inches inside his asshole.

"Woe, woe, woe, woe, woe! What money and what goddamn van? Talisha I know you're not talking about the fucking four hundred grand I just paid you. Listen, first of all my team has been here in Philly with…"

"Don't play stupid Kendell!" she roared. "The can was here all along and you knew it!"

"Stupid bitch!" K-2 snapped and before he knew it Talisha leaped at hem fighting mad. Her hands pound his neck and he began to choke, her mouth found his chest before he could shove her away. "Stttoooop!" he pushed her away. She hit the floor hard but jumped back up and like lightening she was at him again. This time he was ready for her. Catching her in the air as she leaped at him, he slammed her to the bed with a belly to belly slam. He heard the air rush from her lungs.

"Arrrggghhhh, Kennnn... dell." She moaned and fell still. K-2 had no idea what did it. Was it the way she just moaned his name, was it the heaving of her underneath him or just her feisty way. He knew he had to take her now!

Standing he ripped her Ralph Lauren blouse from her round coco breast. Her eyes widened but she was lost to struggle until she could breath. Without hesitation K-2 rolled her over and unzipped her skirt and ripped it from her perfect round hips. His dick grew harder when he saw the skin tone thong made of silk. "Please Kendell... not like this babe please." She begged as he flipped her back onto her back. She was made to watch him strip standing over her. Talisha had regained her wind and was ready to fight him off until she saw the burning desire in his eyes that said he would not be denied her body again.

She watched him drop his boxers and it sprang to life inches away from her face. She sat back a little afraid of its madness and size. Peludo was nowhere near this big of wide.

"Kendell I'm afraid" she whispered.

"So am I Tah" and he pulled her into his arms. As their mouths fit perfectly together she felt him slip in between her well muscle thighs. He touched her ass cheek from his length and his thickness parted the lips of her concha on its own.

"You're gonna hurt me Kendell... please... I cannot stop you... I cannot stop me... It's up to you for god sake... Don't do this to me..." Talisha pressed her mouth back to his and slid her tongue into his mouth.

K-2 lifted her into his arms as she wrapped her legs around his waist. She felt the head of his dick touch her lower back softly.

"Do you really want this to end? Tell me now!"

"No, my Rey... los reyes." She began to cry as he laid her onto the hotel bed. He didn't want to hurt her, but he need to be inside of his queen. "No!" She stopped him as he went to suck her pussy. "I am ready for you Rey... make it deep with one final thrust... take you reina now please." She moaned into his mouth as she felt him enter her small delicate flower. Talisha arched her back and took him with two words. "I'mmmm yoooouuuuurrrrs!"

"Hmmmph... Hmmmph... Hmmmph!" Kool Aid grunted with each long slow deep penetrating eleven-inch thrusts. Unlike Pony Boy, Kool Aid made love to a whimpering pay 4. Placing kissed on his chest and face while holding his legs up on his shoulders. Somehow Bo Pete had managed to suck Pay 4 It into an erection while Kool Aid slowly fucked him. "Hmmmm shit bitch..." Kool Aid moaned. "Look!" He lifted up and held Pay 4's ankles high while he steady pumped only seven inches into his ass slowly.

"He's cummmming." Bo Pete squealed in that high homosexual voice they all use. Sirus focused in and sure enough Pay 4 It was shooting jets of cum onto his belly.

"So, bitch. It ain't like I don't make you cum to." Kool Aid giggled going deep again, bringing another hot jet of cum from a moaning Pay 4.

"But I'm gay and love dick" Bo Pete squealed.

"I wonder if…" Pony Boy smiled into the camera. "Let's see if he loves dick to." He eased up into Kool Aids face with his dick hard again. He quickly engulfed it for two minutes and pulled away.

"Feed my baby." Kool Aid bent to kiss Pay 4. Pony Boy slid his dick between their lips and Kool Aid forced it into his own mouth with his own mouth with little effort. Pay 4 sucked greedily.

"This is what they're forced to be with. When my love for you is so strong I can even forgive this shit!" Sirus lifted Chunky's chin. "Bitch I'm in love with you."

"But Sirus I'm a hoe…" Chunky cried openly.

"You were… goddamn baby!" he whispered.

"Then teach me how to be somebody else Sirus. I don't know nothing else. This is what my mom taught me. My daddy was my first pimp. I'm… I'm… oh god Sirus… please!" Chunky cried real tears for the first time in fifteen years since the age of ten when she got broken in by her own father and cousin… Pretty Boy.

"Shit I'm cumming!" Pony Boy yelled as he shot cum into both Kool Aid and Pay 4's mouths. Instantly Kool Aid came in his anal cavity with one long stroke.

"My turn bitch!" Bo Pete grinned holding almost a foot of dick.

"Please no more Sirus... pleas no... no... more... Arrrrggghhhh!" Pay 4 screamed as Bo Pete ruptured his bladder. Five minutes later Bo Pete came inside of a dead body giggling.

"See what you did!" Kool Aid frowned. " He was going to be one of us bitch!"

"Oops!" Bo Pete laughed. "They was gonna kill his ass anyway... Right?" He turned to a frowning Man Down. " Right handsome?"

"Damn uncle Pete!" Man Down shook his head.

"Boy don't act like you ain't get one too!" Bo Pete giggled. "It's a family trait!"

"Yeah that's true." He laughed grabbing his dick.

"Nigga right... Pete this nigga ain't get no shit like dat!" Zahir laughed. "Shit not even close/"

"Fuck you!" Man Down laughed.

"Hell no! I'm scared of dick!" Zahir continued to joke.

Slowly chunky walked over to Zahir with tears rolling down her face she spoke. "I'm sorry but I don't..."

"Listen." Zahir stopped her. "Sirus really loves you and you hurt him. I don't want you to take this the wrong way, but next time I'll make you disappear and he'll never know. Now give me some pussy." Zahir joked pinching her butt.

"Man Down..." she cried.

"Girl go on" Man Down flagged her. "You heard what Zahir said. It's real here in Philly. Either you are with us or you not."

"Y'all niggas get dressed!" Zahir barked opening the bedroom door. "Unless y'all want to fuck Kool Aid and them. They'll like your pretty ass Jo-Jo. By the way... Jo-Jo is the new corner boss. Pay 4 is going to Colorado for a while. Come here Jo. That truck gotta make it to Pennfield Street without your prints. Tomorrow I'll take you to get your own shit, maybe a Pinto or a Gremlin hatch back" Zahir laughed. "Y'all get the fuck out and Mike-Mike go buy a real dick... Where you borrow that from, your little nephew Nick?"

"Fuck you Zah" Mike-Mike laughed.

"You probably could, and I wouldn't feel a thing." Everybody fell out laughing.

"Yeah fuck y'all too." Mike-Mike pulled his pants up.

"Did I hurt you?" K-2 whispered as she laid in his arms. He could still feel her body trembling as he held her gently.

"K-2... " she whispered. "It's not the dick that I'm afraid of. Yes, it did hurt for a while and I'm sore. But my Corazón... I love de todo corazón... For so long have been digging into my soul. Forcing me to love you Kendell. Why?"

"For every King there is a perfect queen. So, do not ask me why because I do not know Reina... All I know is we are in destines hands now." K-2 kissed the lips of Talisha as she mounted him this time.

"Sssss... Ouch Rey!" she cried as she forced him deep into her small body. "Ouuuuuchhh my king. Ummm!" She dug her mails into his chest. All thoughts of money, power of the rules of a kingdom was gone. All Talisha wanted was to be able to take all of her King. And she did, all night long.

Chapter 12

"Y'all did what?" K-2 screamed. "Wait! Where's the body? I know y'all niggas… Sirus? Man?" K-2 frowned over at Zahir. "Come on Zah… I know you ain't have shit to do with this dumb shit?" K-2 looked out the window of Sirus's Benz wagon. "Sirus… Tell me that ain't Pay 4 It back there! Come on nigga… Say it!"

"Yulp that's Gastepi's bitch ass. The nigga was an undercover fag anyway." Man Down laughed.

"Pull this bitch over!" K-2 growled loudly. "Stupid niggas."

"We almost…"

"Sirus if you don't let me out this bitch…" The look on K-2's face finished his threat. "Assholes!" He mumbled as he slammed the Benz door. They watched as K-2 walked down the deserted road in Montgomery County talking to himself.

"That nigga pissed." Zahir grinned. "Maybe I should…"

"Naw nigga!" Man Down grabbed his arm. "You helping dig."

"Fuck him!" Sirus barked. "K-2 is starting to forget we all put this shit in motion. Sure, he had the vision, but we… all of us made sacrifices to build this shit…"

"You tripping Sirus!" Man Down said. "Drop it nigga, let's go plant this faggot."

"Yeah, whatever!" Sirus mumbled and Zahir gave Man the look. They both felt the energy was negative, but brothers always went through shit.

All three men buried Gastepi Pay 4 It in the back woods of Norristown's Camp grounds off the Blue Route. Two hours later they were headed back to Philly when the phone rang.

"Yeah." Sirus answered.

"Baby I'm sorry." Chunky cried. "Sirus I truly do love you but..." All three men listened as she cried softly.

"Don't do this Belinda... Please... We are gonna make this shit work baby..."

"Until you're tired of me... then what baby?" Chunky paused to cry louder. "Daddy I'm a hoe, what's gonna happen to me then. Oh, Sirus you don't know what this is doing to me. Who knows..." she continued to cry. "I may kill myself."

"Belinda don't do..."

"Bye Sirus." The line fell dead silent and both men looked at a broken heart Sirus crying silently.

"Pull over nigga!" Man Down whispered. "I'll drive" And drive he did. Only Zahir noticed his destination and his speeds of close to a hundred miles an hour.

"You alright girl?" Blaque cried also.

"No... I did fall..." Chunky cried loudly as K.O. loaded her bags into the NV 200.

"Fuck him bitch! It's us… triple B's forever and no man can divide that shit." Cash tried to hide the sorrow she also felt for Chunky's only true lost in life, a man to love her. But truthfully they all felt her pain and prayed for the same chance in love she just gave away.

"How much?" K.O. wiped a tear from her face. "See what you've done bitch… dammit Chunky!" She sat on the step of the van emotional.

"Money is not important right now!" Blaque cried. "Let's get out of Philly!"

The women all loaded in the van and even Talisha set silently as they pulled out of the Ritz's garage.

"Get them!" Man Down hissed darting in and out of traffic.

"Sirus do it!" Zahir leaned up off the back seat. "Sirus! Never mind!" He leaned over the seat to turn the radio on by hand, back off and back on. Then he hand turned the radio backwards to WDAS 105.3 and the back seat rose. Zahir pulled both Ar-15 modified weapons. Even though they carried Glocks he wanted more fire power to deal with them two gooks.

The NC 200 turned onto Broad Street heading north off Spruce street. The emotional pain inside the cargo van was so over powering that neither K.O. or Cash noticed the fast-moving Benz 350 behind them.

"Don't let them bitches get on the expressway!" Sirus whispered. In his hand he held his Glock 35.

"I got em!" Man Down sped passed the van and cut in front of it as it crossed Chestnut. Both he and Zahir jumped from the Benz holding AR-15s.

Man Down had K.O. and Cashin his sight before they could react. Both knew to react would mean certain death.

"Don't!" Talisha barked as Money reached for her own sub machine gun. "They'll kill us all without K-2 here to stop them."

Blaque looked at Chunky. "He really does love you."

"I know" she whispered and stood. Chunky moved to the door and stopped. "Boss Blood Bitches... Right?" she sadly smiled and opened the door.

"Want me to..." Zahir said from the sidewalk as he watched citizens scramble to escape the masked gun men.

"No... I love her!" Sirus cried. He held out his hand for Chunky to come to him. "Belinda I truly love you and will not let you leave me."

"Baby I'm a hoe. No matter how much I love you, I can't hurt you no more. I'd rather be dead then hurt you like that" she cried.

"Sirus!" Zahir yelled letting a quick burst rip down the street towards two-foot patrol coming fast. "We gotta go!"

"I love you daddy" Chunky kissed him on the lips and turned away.

"I love you too Chunky..." Sirus moaned and raised his Glock 35.

"Noooo!" Blaque screamed as her eyes locked with Chunky's through the windshield. She read her lips as did all the bitches.

"Boss Blood Bitches for life..." Chunky mouthed as tears rolled down her cheeks like water

Boom! The Glock roared, and all the women saw the smile cross Chunky's face. She was finally happy in death

"Car!" Man Down yelled letting two burst loose down Samson Street. "We gotta go!"

Sirus raised the gun once more to his head as Zahir placed a perfect right to his chin putting his lights out.

"I got this dumb nigga here!" Zahir said slinging Sirus into the front seat. Standing, he let the .223's pepper the wall over the two terrified officers head. "Go men!" he yelled driving into the backseat. "Go nigga!"

"They robbed us for our clothes we just brought on vacation from school. Belinda confronted them, and she was killed!" Talisha quickly yelled as they watched the Benz pull away. "Everything else tell the truth about. We live in Phoenix and are friends from childhood. Me and Blaque are students of Spellman. They are strangers to us." Talisha finished and jumped from the van screaming. She rushed to Chunky's dead body in screaming madness only a mournful fried could do as the police eased closer barking orders.

"Down! Down! Down! Down!" The Boss Blood Bitches only gathered around their dead lost bitch!

Chapter 13

Retribution Is sweet

New Year's Eve...

Tandeka and Qwen watched as club Destiny moved in waves of sexual dances and the D.J played all the latest hits.

"How's life now that your man is home?" Tan asked "I see you walking funny" she giggled.

"Bitch please..." Qwen looked to see who could be listening. "Uh uh girl something ain't right. He been home six months and he still slinging dick at me every night. Shit!" she grabbed her side. "I think he knocked my shit loose inside. I mean damn. If I pee, that nigga got his dick in me. I woke up last week and he still was inside me. I had to start crying to get him to take that shit out."

"Mmmm girl I wish!" Tan smiled.

"No, you don't... Ouch!" Qwen held her side. "I need a doctor girl."

"Ladies!" he ginned walking up with a beer.

"Jake the snake" Tandeka laughed.

"I see Qwen has been telling you about my high school wrestling names." He laughed. "My favorite was Slaughter Man."

"Mmm Hmm... I heard about all those late-night moves." Tan whispered so that only Qwen could hear.

"Let's dance Qwen?" Jake bounced from side to side.

"Hell no my side hurts. Baby you got to slow down on me." She finally confessed to her man. He looked relieved.

"Damn... Thank god women." He giggled. "I thought it was you who wanted it every night. All them sexy ass nightgowns."

"I wear those for you." She laughed.

"I thought you were... Thank you Jesus... One more night like last night and my back was going out. Lie or not I was going down for the count!" And they all laughed.

"Mom." K-2 smiled. "Look who I brought as a date." He smiled hiding someone behind his back.

"Hey Joe Frazier." Karen said stepping around K-2.

The scream that left Tandeka's mouth lit up the VIP area. She instantly cried and jumped up and down for joy. "Karen... Karen... Karen." She cried over and over. Tandeka was so happy to see her again. Not the smoked-out Karen, but the beautiful healthy sister, she loved and missed so bad over the years. Without warning Tandeka had Karen in her arms tightly and refuse to let her go for the next twenty minutes.

"K-2 look at this nigga." Zahir whispered nudging him to attention. K-2 looked across the dance floor as Sirus danced with two unknown women with a bottle of Moet in his hand. He poured champagne down their chest.

"I got him" Man Down said standing from the table. They both watched as Sirus pushed Man Down away and staggered away with the two women.

Man Down shrugged and K-2 flagged him back up to the VIP section. "He tripping again Zah."

"Man Down said he been taking bitches we don't even know to all the spots. Bragging and shit… saying shit that should never be talked about, shit never said out loud."

"I got him Zahir…" K-2 grimaced angrily.

The smile on her face showed she was pleased with the way Tavious looked when she opened the door. He wore the three-button wool suit by Luigi Bianchi and over his arm he carried the three-thousand-dollar winter silk coat. It was the perfect color to match her Antonio Berardi gown. They would make a striking couple tonight at the New Year's Eve party.

"You're el hombre mas apuesto… Magnifico." Blaque kissed his cheek. "They will be most jealous of me."

"I'd rather them be jealous of me… look how beautiful and sexy you are." Tay said turning Blaque in circles. "Ma this dress fits you like you fit into my heart… Perfecto."

"Do you mean it Jefe? I'm in your heart? Truly!" Blaque pressed her body into Tay's. "Say it Tavious… tell me again."

"Blaque words can't say it… I'm… ma listen…" Tay held Blaque for a quiet moment. "Baby don't get this wrong, but I thought I could never understand what Sirus felt. How could you kill the woman you love, how could a man try and take his own life moments ter. But understanding the way Sirus must fell isn't as all possible, unless you truly know… Blaque I'm young but life made me a man early. I know… I know every morning when I dial your number. Those early flights to Atlanta just to have lunch with you. I know when you walk away unhappy. Most of all... I know you know Blaque. I'm in love with you, for real ma."

Blaque eyes sparkled with moisture as she looked up into Tay's eyes. "So, you'll die with me... For me?

"Better... I'm gonna live for you... get us out rich" Tay kissed her forehead.

"You are not fourteen!" She whispered as he took her hand. They left for the party.

"Sorry my man . No I.D, no admittance. Club rules." The big burly bouncer smiled.

"But he is part owner" Blaque smiled.

"No I.D no admittance... move please."

"Wait here Tavious." Blaque frowned up at the bouncer. She quickly entered club Destiny and spotted Kendell sitting high up in a private area with Man Down, Zahir and some others she had yet to meet.

"Hey sexy thang!" Sirus roared holding two women in his arms "Don't I know you?"

"Good! Sirus that big bald man at the door will not let Tavious in."

"What?" Sirus barked drawing the attention of the team. "We'll see about that ma... go have a drink, I'll handle this." He slurred and Blaque frowned wishing she hadn't said anything to the unstable one as they now called him in Phoenix.

Her eyes locked with K-2 with a plea and she watched as all three men stood quickly and rushed her way.

"It's Tavious and the door man. I didn't mean to mention it to Sirus." Blaque whispered in his ear as he reached her.

"K-2!" Tay yelled rushing through the door. "Hurry up… It's Sirus…" Tay turned and ran back to the door, followed closely by the team.

"Nigga the Boss! Say it! The boss!" Sirus growled. He had a five short Desert Eagle under the man's chin. "Say it or die nigga!"

"Sirus what the fuck you doing?" K-2 barked, "This is a party for our little brother's surprise nigga!"

"This mutha fucka disrespected his boss!" Sirus smirked.

"I didn't know man." The bouncer whispered.

"This ain't good K-2" Taum whispered and his hand slid to his Glock.

"Don't." Man Down pressed the barrel of his Glock to Taum's skull. "This only ends our way."

"He's an officer of the law." Taum relaxed. "Stop this K-2… Now!"

With that K-2 noticed Jack barge through the crowd. His big hand gripped Sirus's wrist and twisted it up in the air. "Boy is you crazy? A cop in public?" Jack took the gun and handed it to Tay. "Y'all go inside" he looked at the boys. "I got my son."

"Chill pop!" Sirus slurred. "I was just…"

"Just what nigga! Going to the electric chair. Mutha fucker not on my watch! Come on!" He dragged Sirus inside. Neither notice the grey Mercedes Benz parked facing the club.

"We almost got lucky!" K.O. giggles.

"Luck ain't gonna work with these guys. Bitch we gotta deal with them" Talisha said bitterly. "Let's go."

Cash and Money stepped from the car in Chinese red silk designer dresses made by Louie Chang Mai. The thigh length slit up the side proved worthy of their shapely legs. The oriental hair bun with pixie bamboo shoots stuck them, gave them the exotic Asian look they strived for. Both opened the rear doors for Talisha and K.O. to exit either side, and they did. K.O. in an all-black Gucci gown with platinum sequence sparkling to match the diamond and platinum choker and bracelet she wore. The four-inch pumps seemed to elevate her to amazon stats. She wore no panties to cover her firm large ass and hips which seem to have a life of its own and K.O. knew how to move it seductively.

Talisha was another story all together. K-2 had awaken her sexuality the last time she was in Philadelphia and she, his. Even though it's been months since Angelita would allow them to return for fear of their lives. She dreamed of the moment her King would again take his Reina, his queen. She stood from the Benz now that all eyes were on them, wearing Prada winter silk and lace. The color as closely as the designer could come to her own skin. From the first look Talisha appeared naked. Her full hips and firm perfect breast seem to be exposed to the world with only a two-carat diamond pendant centered in her cleavage. But even wishful thinking had its limits. The dress was one of a kind made in Japan by hand to her body form. The Jimmy Choo open toe pumps ere studded with Swarovski crystals and in her ears she wore small studs and no make-up.

"Goddamn!" Somebody yelled as men gathered to stare.

"I forgot my purse." Talisha smiled and straight leg bent to retrieve it from the seat.

"Lord have mercy!" another yelled.

"Si… only the lord." Talisha giggled. "Because the Boss Blood Bitches have none."

As a group the women entered he club under VIP status thanks to K-2 and the king team. It seems the club had a hush ran from the dance floor to VIP when they entered.

"Kendell" Tandeka smiled. She knew this was a problem. The look on Melinda's face said it all.

"Dammit!" he kissed his woman. "Baby I'll be right back." He quickly darted a hard look at Blaque and knew she held this secret on purpose. "Tay… Man Down… naw Zahir watch over Sirus."

"Oh, it's like that now?... Poor Sirus needs a babysitter… fuck you… Jefe… patron… you selfish bastard!" Sirus slurred drunkenly. "FUCK YOU!" He growled quietly as Melinda laid her head to his shoulder.

"Please Sirus… stop, this is for Tay sake." Melinda whispered.

"Yeah Tay… the other goddamn Jefe!" He mumbled snatching a bottle of Moet.

"Boy… straighten up or I'm gonna beat that ass…" Qwen yelled snatching the bottle from his hands.

"Momma…" Sirus laughed. "Another Jefe."

"Leave it be Qwen" Tandeka whispered. "He's hurting inside."

Sirus continued to gloat over the loss of his one and only love. "Boss Blood Bitches!" he screamed down at Talisha and the bitches. "She was more boss then any of y'all!"

"He's drunk." Talisha frowned with fury in her stare. K-2 could see the want for revenge in her eyes.

"He did what no man should ever have to do" K-2 said. "Love is a strange and unpredictable emotion."

"They should've let him blow his brains out like he did that Boss Bitch Chunky!" K.O. growled

"K.O. he truly loved her and did that… I don't even like you so…" Man Down stepped up close to the amazon.

"Nigga please!" K.O. shoved him away only to be slapped hard by his right hand.

"Bitch!" Man Down smiled knowing he had hurt her with only one third of his power.

"Stop this!" Blaque yelled stepping in between them. "K-2 you'll let this happen?"

"If this is what it must be… then let's do it here and now!" He said staring into Talisha eyes.

"No, my Rey… tonight I come back to satisfy my own heart. Is there room for a Reina in your life?" she whispered

"In my life you… in my lifestyle… no!" K-2 held his stare.

"We will see…" Talisha kissed his lips softly. Leaning up she whispered in his ear. "How do I look?"

"Just like you feel to me… perfect my Reina." He whispered back. "Don't make me love you Talisha… it can only end one way." They both looked up at Sirus, who stared down in rage and beside him sat Melinda in tears.

"See he even betrayed you." Sirus grinned. "He's the boss, we don't matter no more."

The party grew out of control as the crowd danced and drank. Some smoked weed, some did pills, but everybody partied hard.

"What up baby?" K-2 pulled Melinda into his arms.

"Is it true Kendell? Did she take you from me?" Melinda whispered and K-2 felt her pain shout into his soul.

"Come here!" He stopped dancing and dragged her across the floor. They stepped into the kitchen area before K-2 spoke again "Look at me!" he demanded. "I said…" He roughly took her chin in his hand. "Melinda Jones, the future Mrs. Melinda Woods don't you ever let no bitch make you feel like they got my heart. It's us baby… you and me! I said to you I love you… Bitch don't make a nigga prove that shit like Sirus did.." He laughed as Melinda punched him in the chest. She instantly began to cry and fell in his arms.

"I rather be dead Kendell" she whispered.

"Shiddd should I call Sirus?" He joked holding his real queen. His ghetto Reina… Melinda!

Wiping her eyes with the sleeve of his pure silk tie, K-2 looked at his watch. "We got five minutes, let's get up to VIP with the family."

They made it through the crowd and notice the circle of men standing around watching Cash and Money perform sexual dance moves on K.O. while exposing peeks of their own pussy lips and ass cheeks. Inviting touches and sometimes kisses to their parts from willing men and some women.

"Them bitches is whores." Melinda giggled.

"Rich whores with Cartel money behind them." Talisha growled. "Kendell I need a word with you." She looked at Melinda. "But not around the help…please."

"Help? Bitch I'll…"

"Boss Blood Bitch ghetto piece of shit!" Talisha whirled ready to fight for her king. She knew she had no chance against Melinda but fight she would.

"No! No! No!" K-2 gripped both women's arms to separate them. "Melinda go to my mom's table and make sure Tay is ready. Go!" he whispered harshly. "And you come this way!" He pulled Talisha who sucked her teeth and rolled her eyes at Melinda.

"Trash!" Talisha yelled.

"Rich whore!" Melinda yelled back only to stop as Talisha lunged at her. K-2 picked her up into the air to stop her attack.

"Stop! Go head Melinda… Please!

"Do not beg trash… you are a king… my king, my man!" Talisha hissed at Melinda.

"Bitch you wish… you couldn't take the dick anyway"

"Did that trash… every inch all night!" Talisha smiled. "Yes, deep in this pussy and he loved it. I'm new and unused trash… not like you!"

"Melinda go!" K-2 ordered.

"Is it true baby?" Melinda cried as K-2 pulled Talisha away yelling.

"Yesss… yesss… yesss… every inch…" Finally, away from Melinda K-2 stopped and turned.

"Why this… why now Talisha?"

"I love you now." She said cupping his face. "It's not my fault. It is something you forced into my heart Kendell." Talisha slammed her head to his chest. "Tell me you don't feel it to."

K-2 couldn't lie he was feeling Talisha, but he was in love with Melinda. Always have been.

"Say it Kendell and I will leave… Now!"

"I'm in love with Malinda Talisha!" K-2 whispered and slowly she lofted her head from his chest. She looked deeply into his eyes and smiled because she saw the truth. He could love her, but the ghetto trash stood in the way, but not for long.

"Ouch my king." Softly Talisha kissed K-2 and turned to leave. She stopped two feet away. Without looking back, she spoke again. "Kendell."

"Talisha please… don't."

"Next time you will come for me my king. SUUUWUUUUU." She barked, and the Boss Blood Bitches gathered by her side, even Blaque…

"Ten, nine, eight…" The music instantly stopped, and the DJ began the count down. "Seven, six, five, four…"

K-2 watched as Talisha spun and without warning rushed into his arms.

"Three… two… one… Happy New Year's."

"Happy New Year's Kendell my love…" Talisha kissed him so passionately and their tongues met naturally in her mouth and K-2 realized she was right. He felt it too!

Talisha pulled away even when he held on. "Say it my king."

"Nooo!" He whispered and turned to leave only to find Melinda and the entire crew watching them.

"You'll come!" Talisha laughed loudly as the BBBs left.

Tay watched Blaque leaving and felt the tug on his heart. He had no idea she would just leave him like that.

"happy New Year's Tay Tay." Karen whispered from behind him.

"Mom?" He spun and the tears he held burst out of control. Once again Tavious was a child in his mother's arms crying out of control. The mother he missed for the past eight years.

"Baby." Was all she could say while crying herself. She was truly sorry for the life she forced on him, and while they cried together she thought of one man… Talib Tut Turner. Tay Tay's father. "Baby." She whispered.

"Baby you alright?" K-2 smiled.

"Boy please." Melinda helped Sirus into her car. "I know when you're lying. You love me… even though you fucked that skank bitch. How much she pay you for he dick? And where is my share?"

"I'ma give you your share tonight. First let me take these drunks home." K-2 helped Tandeka into his car while Man Down and Zahir helped Jack and Qwen into K-2's backseat.

"You coming to the apartment right?" Melinda winked. "I got that new Pinky tape. Want to try that choke me shit again?"

"Try? I chocked you ever since you were…"

"Damn y'all making a bitch horny…" Tandeka giggled.

"See boy!" Melinda blushed. "Just hurry up."

"Bye boss. Fuck you very much!" Sirus fell into the backseat of Melinda's Lexus.

"Don't you spit up in my car nigga!" she grinned. "You do, and you brought it Sirus… I'm for real nigga!" she slammed the door.

"Want me to follow them" Zahir asked.

"Zah take your drunk ass home!" Man Down smiled.

"Two beers nigga… no more… ever… I keep my wits at all times." Zahir said putting Man Down into a head lock.

"Naw Zah trail Tay and Karen for me. Man follow me. After I drop moms and them off we gonna hit the blocks and pass out bonuses. Zahir catch us on Chew in an hour."

"Yup!" Zahir yelled letting Man Down go. "You lucky punk."

They watched Melinda and Sirus drive off heading towards Chestnut Hill, then they all hit the streets.

By the time K-2 got Tandeka to Jack and Qwen's crib she was ready to get out his car with that loud as music and smoke. "I'm staying here Kendell. Send Tay of Sirus to get me tomorrow afternoon" she smiled. "Come on bitch, let me help you with this nigga."

"I can walk." Jack laughed as he fell to the ground. "Well almost." Both women laughed and so did K-2.

"Come on Sirus, you home" Melinda frowned. "And you buying me a new Lexus tomorrow." She rolled her eyes. "I got you baby." Melinda struggled to pick him up from the seat.

"Do you think she loved me? I mean like you love Kendell Jr." Sirus asked leaning on her shoulder.

"Don't do that to yourself boy. Not tonight." Melinda helped him through the breeze way and up to the door. "Where your keys?" She asked searching his pockets. "Yeah that's not a key... wow!"

"Nice right?" Sirus giggled. "Chunky us to love it."

"Stop boy! Find somebody else. She ain't love you like that If she did..." Melinda paused. "Never mind. Come on." She opened the door and took him to his bedroom. Melinda laid Sirus down and removed his shoes. "Sleep this shit off boy and be ready tomorrow. I want a new car or at least a detail job."

"How about a kiss." Sirus joked rolling onto his side and balling up a pillow.

Melinda kissed Sirus on the forehead and turned off the lights. "Bye handsome."

"Bye beautiful... thanks."

Melinda turned and walked into the living room and everything went dark.

"Wake that bitch up!" Talisha smiled and K.O. threw the pitcher of water in her face.

"Wha… wha…" Melinda tried to shake the dizziness from her head from the hard-right hand that K.O. decked her with. "What the fuck… Bitch!"

"Go ahead… He'll be dead before you blink." Talisha grinned. "Now what was that you called me tonight, ummm…"

"A whore bitch! It ain't no mystery." Melinda growled. She looked as K.O. holding the gun to his head.

"Yes, a whore… Well my dear tonight you are the whore.:

"Don't do this… Talisha he loves her." Sirus whispered. He noticed Cash with the magnum behind Melinda's head, and Money viciously sucking his dick."

"Who me?" Talisha laughed" I will do nothing it will be you or she will die, understand!" Talisha nodded to K.O. who shoved two pills into his mouth

"Swallow!" K.O. giggled pushing a glass of water to his lips.

"Don't worry… It is not poison. The blue one is Viagra and the white one is ecstasy triple stack." Talisha smiled when she saw Sirus shoot jets of cum into Money's mouth. "Don't stop… keep him hard and you Me. Ghetto Trash… open up!" Talisha reached to shove two pills in her mouth. "Swallow bitch! Yes, nice and big… Well not as big as Kendell but hard and ready." Talisha giggled. "Don't stop… move!" She snapped and dropped to her knees. "K.O. get her ready for this." Talisha whispered and took Sirus into her own mouth for the next ten minutes.

"Please don't... I..." Melinda closed her eyes as K.O.'s tongue did what no men could ever do. The way she rolled it over her clitoris, the way is dug gently inside. "Please don... Mmmm shit... god nooo... not thisssss... don't make me cummmmmm..." She screamed, and her body went into fits. Cash and Money both handed their guns to K.O. and took over with the sexual assault on Melinda's body with their mouths.

"Mmmph." Talisha jerked her mouth away as cum dripped from her mouth. Two more jets slapped her in the face before she could move. Quickly her hand wiped him clean and he was deep in her mouth again. He moaned loudly as Talisha kept him erect.

"I'm cummmmming!" Melinda screamed for mercy. Both Cash and Money shared her clitoris with tongue strokes.

"He's ready!" Talisha growled. "Sirus I will cut your hands loose now and you will either fuck her everywhere and both of you live or I will Kill both of you... Her first... Choose."

There was no need to convince either, the pills had taken over and their sexual lust had kicked in. With no resistance Melinda let her body be guided to the bed with finger strokes upon her nipples. Sirus held his own erect dick, needing to be in someone somehow.

"Take her!" Talisha smiled as Sirus drove into Melinda's waiting wet pussy lips. The thickness of his dick easily stretched her swollen pussy lips wide.

"Ohhhh goddd fuck me Sirus." Melinda screamed as her own animalistic lust drove her towards her dark side.

"Girl can you help me?" Qwen giggled. "His ass is too heavy to carry upstairs. Pull his shoes off."

"What you gonna just let him sleep on the floor down here?

"Noooo! First I'm gonna go get him a blanket and a pillow, then let him sleep on the floor down here." Qwen laughed. She staggered up the stairs leaving Tan to remove Jack's shoes. When she returned her husband laid naked on the floor while Tandeka stared at his penis. "Tan you can if you want too." Qwen smiled feeling her own juices between her legs soaking her panties.

"Oh shit I didn't mean to... I pulled his pants off so he wouldn't... Dammit I'm so sorry Qwen."

"Listen Tan." Qwen slowly walked over dropping the pillow and blanket to the floor, she knelt down beside them both and took Tandeka's hand. "Touch it baby..." She held Jack's dick between her and Tandeka's hand.

Instantly he began to get hard. "Rub it Tan, feel it getting hard."

"Oh shit, girl he's kind of..."

"I know bitch." Qwen smiled. "Why you think my goddamn side hurt. Wait until you see how long it gets." Qwen said leaning in to kiss Tandeka. Their tongues met as both women rubbed Jack into an erection.

"Qwen I..."

"Shhhh. I wanted to do that for years girl. You act like you don't know how fine your ass is."

"I never,,," Tandeka kissed Qwen again. This time both women began to fondle each other as they undressed

Jack smiled and reclosed his eyes as his wife stripped Tandeka bare.

"Kiss it" Qwen whispered.

"What?" Tandeka asked breathing heavy.

"That." Qwen placed Tan's hand back on his hard dick "Put it in your mouth Taste him, make him beg for more." Qwen took Tandeka's dark brown nipple between her lips and Tan closed her eyes and began to masturbate Jack's now swollen hick long dick.

"Girl he's so goddamn…"

"Suck him Tan, do it… let me watch." With that Tandeka bent and stretched her mouth to the limit to let his head sink into the back of her pallet.

"Urrggghhh." She gagged easing some out.

"Jack is fat, ain't he? Wait until he's in your pussy." Qwen pulled Tan to her side making sure she kept her husband deep in her mouth. "Suck that dick girl." Qwen whispered as her own mouth fond Tandeka's thick pussy lips "Mmmm."

"Mmmph! Mmmph! Mmmph! Mmmph!" Sirus grunted as he slammed into Melinda with every ounce of strength he had. He held her legs on his shoulders as his balls slapped her fat ass.

"Ohhh shit I'm cummmmming." K.O. moaned while watching Sirus beast fuck Melinda deeply. She grabbed the back of Cash's head and grinded up into her mouth. "Ssss owwwwww." She whined setting off a chain reaction starting with Melinda who screamed with a mixture of pain and pleasure.

"Fuck meeeeeee!"

First Blaque who watched fingering herself while money sucked Talisha to a screaming mad mess. "Ohhh my godddd."

"I am going to cummmm!" Talisha cried and finally Sirus grunted with his third nut of the night.

"Mmmmmmmmmph shhhhit!" Pulling from inside Melinda who still shook from a powerful orgasm as Sirus shot his cum on her chest.

"Turn her over... Now!" Talisha growled still holding her gun. Melinda rolled with little coaching. Nodding at K.O. and Money, Talisha smiled "hold her." Grabbing the bag nobody seemed to notice, she removed a jar of Vaseline and dipped a handful for Sirus dick. She rubbed it full keeping him erect with the help of the Viagra and ecstasy pills.

"So, I'm a whore..." Talisha smiled and lined Sirus dick up with the head pressed into her asshole.

"Goddd noooo!" Melinda tried to beg as the lust over took Sirus and with one deep thrust he opened Melinda's ass to its fullest.

"Ohhh... Ohhhh... Ohhhh... Ohhhh... Ohhhh... Ohhhh..." Tandeka moaned with each thrust of Jack's pelvic. It's been twelve years since she felt a man inside her body and none of her vibrators could match his girth or length. Jack seem to not want to hurt Tandeka, but each thrust opened places unused in years. "Ohhh... Ohhhh... Ohhhh... Ohhhh..."

"Shhh take that dick Tan." Qwen whispered while controlling the rhythm of her husband's hips. "Circles not Jack." She whispered.

"Mmmmm....Mmmm... Mmmm..." Tandeka's moans became squeakish and her hips began to slam up to meet all ten inches. "I'm gonnnna dieee." She wailed, and her body convulsed with orgasmic pleasure.

But Jack kept the rhythm Qwen forced him into.

"Baby that's how you fuck the shit out of a woman with this kind of dick." Qwen whispered "Anyone can hurt the pussy, but very few can make the pussy beg for more."

"I'm cummming again..." Talisha bucked wildly.

"She's passed out!" K.O. smiled.

"So! Fuck her harder... Now!" She demanded and Sirus did as told. Fifteen minutes later he came in Melinda's bleeding ass.

"Water" Sirus licked his lips. "Please!"

"Orange juice!" Talisha smirked. "Then back inside her ghetto asshole."

K.O. handed Sirus the glass of juice which he downed.

"Put it back in her asshole!" Talisha laughed and watched Sirus still hard erection began to go limp. His eyes fluttered, and he passed out on top of Melinda's naked body.

K.O. whipped the magnum clean and placed it in Sirus hand. She raised the gun to Melinda's temple.

"Do it bitch!" Talisha growled and the roar pierced the early morning of the small Chestnut Hill community.

Each woman dressed quickly and left, leaving only behind one dead, one murder and lots of vaginal secretion.

"9-1-1 how may I help you?" The voice said.

"I'd like to report a murder." Talisha smiled giving the apartment number as they drove away. "There was screaming then a gun shot."

"Who am I talking to?" The operator asked. "ma'am... who am I speaking with?" She asked again as the phone spun in circles on the cold morning asphalt.

"Yo Mel." K-2 yelled coming into her apartment. "Girl I hope you got that shit on." He stopped to listen and got no answer. "This woman sleep." He chuckled entering the bedroom he whispered, "Mel daddy is home..." The bed was empty, and he quickly thought to himself it he had seen her red Lexus Coup when he parked, he didn't. "Fucken Sirus and his bullshit."

Quickly he dialed Melinda's phone and it went straight to voicemail. Hanging up he dialed Sirus phone and on the second ring she answered. "Who is this?" K-2 frowned.

"This is detective Krystal Walker. Whom am I speaking too?" K-2 paused and thought.

"What you doing answering my brothers phone?"

"Sir... he needs a lawyer... Bad!" The female detective said. "Were gonna charge him with murder."

"Wait is my wife there? Let me speak to her please... what the hell happened?"

The detective pause made K-2's stomach spill to the floor. "Sir... Is there a tattoo of a baby dragon on her lower back?"

K-2 dropped his phone and ran towards his car. He never stopped he just drove, through light and stop signs with one thing on his mind... Melinda... his ghetto queen!

Twenty-five minutes was what he turned a hour drive into and he pulled in beside the cherry red Lexus. There was a scream fighting to free itself, begging K-2 to let it out before it consumed him from the inside. But his gangster was Playing boyish games with his mind. Telling him to control what was a natural emotion... sorrow.

Kendell K-2 Woods for the first time in years felt out of control of a situation. Last night he was a king, this morning as the sun peeked through the greyish blue horizon of the north west neighborhood.

"Nope!" Somebody said as clear as day as he jumped from his own car. "Uh-uh... nope!" It said again as he felt what he thought was rain drops on his face. Unconsciously his hand wiped the water away

"Sorry son..." A uniformed officer tried to stop the raging bull that plunged towards the apartment. He was to late K-2 had somehow changed inside, and only the sight he saw coming out of 23A could have stopped him.

"Noooo!" That voice screamed again and K-2 heard it but still hadn't recognized it as his own. Later he would swear god wanted him crazy and to pay for all the shit he and his team had done. Just when he reached the stretcher Melinda's hand fell from under the sheet. She wore the ring he had just gotten her for Christmas.

"I didn't do it Kendell… I swear… I didn't do it K-2…" Sirus cried and for the first time K-2 realized Sirus was in the patrol car on the other side of Melinda's Lexus.

K-2 dropped to his knees and finally recognize that screaming voice. It was Kendell Woods the child…

Chapter 14

The entire room was silent and still. Talisha and Blaque sat like little girls waiting for a reaction. They had no idea how Angelita would react to the news. Talisha had no choice but to admit what she had done. Not by choice, but because Blaque had refused to be transport with next shipment. She was afraid of the king team.

"Estupido Talisha!" Angelita whispered. Everyone who knew Angelita knew her whispers meant danger.

"But mama he killed…"

"Silencio idiota!" Angelita quickly crossed the room without warning she slapped Talisha hard enough to knock her to the floor. "if you weren't my own daughter I'd have you turned into a whore… Get up!"

"Mama I'm sorry." She rubbed her face.

"You are not… selfish little bitch… Get up!" Angelita walked to the window. "I know who you are! I also know why you do what you do. If you were not such a spoil bitch you'd see you are next in line to what we've built. But like your father your pussy is your main concern… Puta… Kendell was your Talib stupidio and every move you've made has pulled him away. Think Talisha…" Angelita turned aggressively. "Six million dollars a year on their own. From a few thousand dollars' worth of product. Is there a man worth throwing that away!" She looked at Blaque. "Can we fix this? Is Tavious in a position to help fix this?"

"Si mama, he can do the deal for them. But Sirus is familia to them all. The question is if they believe he did it of that Talisha…" Blaque looked at her best friend. "Sorry chica… but the truth is only if they believe him or not."

"Blaque come…" Angelita held out her hand. "Let's talk strategy." Angelita rolled her eyes at her daughter. "Get up! Act like a Boss Bitch!"

"Baby you hungry?" Tandeka whispered from the doorway of Kendell's room. "Baby."

"No mom" K-2 answered sitting on his bed.

"Well I got some fish and potatoes cooked up with cornbread when you get hungry." Tandeka turned to go back downstairs.

"Mommy…" K02 wiped a tear from his face and made Tandeka's heart mourn for her son's loss. "Sirus didn't do it… You do know that don't you?"

"Oh baby." Tandeka rushed to her son's side. "It's alright to cry." She cried and unleashed k-2's pain once and for all. Kendell cried in her arms for both Melinda and Sirus.

"He didn't do it…" K-2 cried. Tay turned and went back downstairs, neither Tandeka of K-2 noticed he had come into their home.

"They'll be coming down in a minute." Tay whispered shooting pass Karen to keep her from seeing his own tears. Quickly he hit the basement and the hidden safe he and the team kept emergency money in. Tay counted thirty-five thousand out and shoved it in the large pocket on his leather bomber and then another ten thousand for their trip this weekend.

"Tavious… boy get up here and get off that that game." Tandeka yelled down the stairs. "That boy of yours."

"Hey mom." Tay kissed Tan on the cheek as he came from the basement.

"What the lawyer say?" she asked.

"Girl he wanted thirty grand, plus five more on the table for appeals just in case… They talking death penalty.

"Please god no…" Tandeka flopped into the chair. She couldn't help but sob again.

"He ain't do it!" Tay said. "Fuck that!"

"Tavious!"

"Sorry… but…" Tay walked upstairs to be with K-2.

"They all believe he was set up." Tandeka said.

"By who? Who would do it… I mean they found sperm… his sperm in her stomach, her vagina… girl inside her ass. How is the question? And all he keeps saying is they had sex and he fell out."

"He told K-2 and Tay something else but they won't say what he told them, but whatever it is, they believe him." Tandeka said. "This is gonna turn bad Kay."

"Pretty Boy." Tay closed the door. "He was her cousin."

"Is Sirus sure/"

"Of course." Tay whispered. "K-2." He locked eyes with his big brother. "This is gonna end our relationship with the girls... we gonna need another connect."

"Tay we're done. Sixteen million between five is enough. After this we are no longer involved in the business. Look at this." K-2 pushed up the screen on his computer. "Edward Hall Institution for Boys. They have a ninety eight percent graduation fate who goes on to HBCUs around the country."

"This says Carolina." Tay whispered.

"Yeah... you can finish school down south and me I'm going to Harvard."

"What about Man Down and Zahir. They not school niggas. Naw they live by the gun K-2. We can't just leave them here."

"We're not. I spoke to both of them. Zahir wants to move his moms up north with his grandmother and make some shit called HAJJ or something like that. Man Down just wants to go back to Florida where his dad's family is."

"And Sirus? What about him Kendell?" Qwen cried from his brother's door. "My son! What about him?"

"First we get him out of jail, then we get him into school too. Aunt Qwen ain't nothing change. He's my right-hand man til I'm dead."

"What about..." Qwen cried and fell into both boy's arms.

"Who the fuck is it?" The ex pimp yelled from the patched up lazy boy.

"You second chance at life mutha fucka. Open the door." Taum barked.

"oh yeah, I thought y'all wouldn't be here until later tonight." He snatched open the door to find the two large white men smiling.

"That's how life is… unexpecting… well? Fredderick smiled.

"Oh shit! My bad come in. Ummm excuse the mess, the bitch ain't cleaned a pimp shit in weeks."

"Pimp huh? Yeah whatever you say. Ready to get this cash… Pimp?" Taum laughed.

"Ummm yeah." Pretty boy smiled. "Let me grab my coat."

"Fur?" Taum smiled as Pretty Boy pulled on the matted piece of shit.

"Sort of… let's go!"

The ride took the down Van Buren and up to 32nd Avenue. "Make a right player." Pretty Boy pointed. Taum drove another fifteen minutes to Peoria Road.

"There!." Pretty Boy pointed.

Both Taum and Fredderick smiled as they watched Cash dumping trash in a can wearing nothing but jeans and a tank top.

"What about my money player."

"There they go right there just like I promised."

"Yeah, here they go." Fredderick said and turned with the silenced .22 long smith and wessen. He fired six shots into the man's chest.

"Thank you partner, he was getting on my nerves with that player shit."

"Mine too!" Fredderick laughed. "I'll call K-2."

"I got it mom." Tay shouted running down the stairs. In his hand he held a Glock 35. Tay looked at Tay looked at Karen's closed bedroom door. "Shit!" He whispered snatching the door open. Instinct made him level the Glock at Blaque's head. "Hands… Hands… Bitch hands…" Tay roughly whispered as Blaque pushed pass him. She knew in her heart Tavious wouldn't shoot her. She just prayed no one else was there.

"Put that away Tavious. You wouldn't hurt me, and you know it." Blaque smiled dropping her clutch bag on the sectional sofa. Instantly she turned and dropped her snow-white mink to the floor. "Now take me upstairs and shoot me Jefe."

Tay looked with mixed emotions while Blaque stood naked in knee high black timberland pumps and diamond choker.

"Tay-Tay who is it?" Karen asked coming down the stairs. She froze at the sight of the beautiful woman standing inches from her son naked and unashamed. "Girl!"

"Who is this Tavious? Already you turn on my love for you!" Blaque began to cry snatching up her coat. "No matter what Tavious I love you for real and still I put my life in jeopardy for you. This is how you'll do me? Cabron! I would make you my Jefe. El cabeza de familia. But nooo you must cheat with, with, carbon!" Blaque yelled and began to cry.

"Girl please, my son ain't old enough to be your nothing, and what is this carbon shit. What language is that?" Karen smiled. "And damn she fine Tay-Tay." Karen took Blaque's hand. "Come on in the kitchen ummm."

"Blaque… and Tavious is my man. Young or not."

"O.k. but you better put on some clothes before I want you." Karen joked. "Come on. Tay get her some of that new shit you brought me."

"But where is my clothes?" Blaque wiped a tear from her eyes. Karen turned to see Tay shaking his head no.

"Boy what's up?" Karen squinted. "Y'all been doing it in my house?"

"Mom!"

"Oh yes." Blaque smiled. "He's really a fast learned and good too. He will be my husband no matter what you say. Now that's out the way let's talk."

Chapter 15

La Primera Guerra Mundial

Two Days Later…

"I'm hungry mommy." Cash whispered.

"Me too bitch. Let's hit Buffalo Wings." K.O. said standing.

"Hell no bitch, we rich now!" Money laughed. "Let's go high class style. I won't Cantainess or The Steakhouse. Besides I want to wear some of those fine clothes Talisha make a bitch buy in them stores."

"Sure, why not… I'll call Tah and see if she wants to bounce too." K.O. said. "Cash pull that winter silk pant set for me."

"The green or the blood red?"

"Do you got to ask bitch? Blood for life hoe."

"Not hoe…" Cash joked in her Asian voice. "Me rich respectable Blood Bitch now. I suckie dickie now when me want."

"I know that's right bitch!" Money hi fived her twin. "Besides pussy taste better."

The women all dressed up and exited to meet Talisha downtown at the Rooftop Steakhouse for dinner.

"I'll drive mommy." Cash bounced to the driver side. K.O. tossed the keys to the new BMW across the roof of the fire red G5xi sedan.

"The driver Man." Zahir laughed.

"Why not K.O.?"

"One of the sisters K-2 said. Some shit about a sister for a brother. You know that symbolic shit he on." Zahir continued to laugh as he pulled right beside the BMW.

K.O. and Cash climbed into the car in the front seats. Money opened the back door and noticed the Econoline van pulling up fast.

"Oh shit!" She yelled and tried to pull her purse open for her gun. But it was too late.

"What?" K.O. yelled trying to jump back out of the car. The heels slowed her down one step. The van skidded to a halt and Cash looked up into the smiling Man Down.

Both twins cried out the words together, "God no!"

"This for Melinda bitch!" Man Down laughed loudly.

"Stop… wait!" K.O. yelled as both barrels of the 20-gauge double barrel tore Cash's head from her body. Her hands tightly gripped the steering wheel and held on in the death grip until the coroner removed her body.

The screams of Money could be heard for blocks as she went mentally insane instantly. K.O. had to hold her down on the ground so the medics could give her a second sedative.

It was ruled a gangland murder. The headlines read the next day in the Phoenix News:

Blood in Blood out!

"No!" Blaque whispered liking over at Tay who slept quietly beside her. "I'll be right there… of course all fifty at ten… yes… three days." Blaque listened a moment . "As you wish Angelita. I'll fly home today. The money will be shipped by overnight mail… Fed-Ex… yes." She hung up and climbed from the bed. Running to the shower Blaque knew shit had hit the fan and to be here puts her in danger, but more than that it put Tavious in danger and she could not let that be. Not now.

"Blaque?" Tay whispered.

"I must leave Tay." Blaque climbed from the shower. "Tay." Blaque took his face in her hand. "Do not disregard any of my calls. Listen to me my Jefe… not one… promise me!"

"Yeah sure…"

"Dammit Tavious promise me. I cannot lose you now! Did you know Tay?" she rushed to dress. She moved urgently.

"Of course I did… but…"

"Shhhh…" Tay put a finger to Blaque's lips. He turned and rushed into the hallway to find K-2 and Jack standing there. Each held Glocks. "Don't!"

"She's one of them Tay." K-2 smiled as Blaque walked out of the bathroom. "Is Talisha in town?"

"No Kendell she is not." Blaque whispered. "Am I to die now Kendell."

"No!" Tay barked. "She's my woman K-2!"

"Melinda was mine!" K-2 growled.

"Then you know what this will do to me... what I'll have to do to you if I live."

K-2 stared at Blaque with such hatred in his eyes as she stepped back. He slowly turned to Tay. "I love you Tay like my own brother..." He paused to look back at Blaque. "So, I'll die before I kill your women of let anyone kill your woman. But the rest will die and it's up to her to stay out the way!"

"Tavious my calls... promise... if they come I'll call... remember you promised." Blaque whispered kissing Tay softly. She hesitated a moment and looked into a fury she knew meant death. "Kendell trust me. I am not like..."

"Blaque get the fuck away from me bitch!" He growled.

"Trust me Kendell... Trust me Kendell..." She kept repeating as she ran for the door.

"Tay what's wrong with that crazy Mexican girl of yours." Karen yelled as she, Tandeka and Qwen came inside the house. "That crazy bitch just..." All three women froze seeing K-2, Jack and Tay who was naked standing there holding guns.

"Uh-uh what the fuck is this shit?" Qwen barked. "Jack you better talk to me now!"

"And Karen pack your clothes y'all gotta go on vacation for a while." K-2 whispered. "Mom I got your shit in the car."

"I got your Qwen. K-2 rented a house up in Boston for six months. This shit ain't good. Let's go y'all." Jack said.

"Look at this bitch." Man Down growled standing in Blaque's path. "Bitch I can do you right here." He grinned looking around.

"Very smart! Kill me in the middle of an international airport with thousands of witnesses. No wonder they call you Man… Down."

"Bitch!" Man Down took a step towards her fist clenched.

"Naw son… she's right. You'll get a chance again" Zahir smiled. "Let's get out of here." He winked at Balque and smirked.

"Tell K.O. I wanted to do her ass but K-2 insisted it e one of the gooks. The bitch had the nerve to call on god…" Man imitated Cash's voice. "No god help my gook ass… bitch died begging." He laughed and spit in Blaque's face. "See you soon bitch!"

Blaque wiped the saliva from her face along with tears of anger. "You will be dealt with one day Man down… I promise, if not for the disrespect, for my sister Cash." Blaque whispered and then continued to the planes waiting area. Fifteen minutes later she boarded first class back to Phoenix for the funeral of one Boss Blood Bitch.

"How has this happened?" Selina Monteza growled. "The plan was perfecto. What has started these killings?"

"It was me Abuelita." Talisha whispered walking into the room. "Me and my jealous rage."

"Jealous? Of who? For what baby bird? We give you everything. Even the empire we're building. Jealous of what?"

"Of something I will never possess. His power, his loyalty, his heart." Talisha began to cry.

"Well he has made us look weak. To send a team of killers into our home. To kill one of ours is unforgivable." Selina growled again.

"No mama... He has only revenged the death of his lover. It is Talisha who has transgressed. Even after we instructed her not to. Kendell is a good earner and very possible her... Never mind,,, but it is she who almost destroyed what we've tried to build." Angelita said.

"Then it is she who will clean this up! Selina said. "And baby bird remember, no one is above the Monteza clan. We have always put familia first... and also we clean our own house."

"Yes Abuelita.. Si. I will fix this."

"Yes, you will baby bird." Selina turned and left the ranch home quickly.

"I will send you to papa! He will protect you!" Angelita mumbled. She and she lone knew of her mother's treachery and the dangerous position Talisha was in.

"No mama! I can fix this... he loves me." She whispered. "He loves me mama... I know this is true." Talisha began to cry as she whispered. "I love him more."

"Oh no babe." Angelita held her arms open for her love sick spoiled daughter.

"He loves me mama... he does... he loves me mama." Talisha cried into her mother's chest. "He loves me mama."

"The question is do you trust her?"

"I love her…" Tay smiled. "I guess I knew that from the start."

"Naw Tay… K-2 asked you do you trust her. It's a big difference."

"I ain't got no choice Zah… she's my… yeah I trust her!" Tay nodded.

"Well I don't! Those bitches proved what I've been saying all along." Man Down said,. "Never trust a hoe… Never!" he stared at Tay.

"She's not like them Man. You don't know her like I do."

"Answer this then… the night they killed Mel, did she or did she not leave the club with them. That bitch Talisha made her little woo woo sound and they all bounced… One unit nigga. Remember that day when Chunky pulled up with Sirus. Did she or did she not have a gun in her hand, ready to kill with those bitches. Tay don't be no fool! The bitch is just like them." Man Down snapped.

Tay sat there in an unsure daze. Man was right she was there with that gun. The only reason she didn't do nothing was because he had the drop on her. And Melinda she admitted to knowing about and there was no way in hell he'd tell that to the team. Blaque loved him for sure. He felt it in his heart, that was no lie.

"She's my woman Man… you're my brother! I will not choose between the two. I would rather die.

"You don't have to Tay… she'll make that call for you." K-2 whispered. "Let's just hope she's…" K-2 looked away. There was no need to finish the thought that sat in everybody's mind anyway.

"I not crazy K.O." Money repeated again. "You'll see I not crazy girl." She giggled as Talisha and Blaque help dress her while K.O. stood guard in the psychological unit of Phoenix Memorial Hospital. The doctors all agreed that Monica Paciala suffered from a term called psychosis and was severely psychotic and dangerous. Her release would only come from a judge after mental stabilization from treatment and medication.

"I not crazy bitch K.O." She giggled and Blaque heard it for sure... this was not Money.

"I don't know y'all... Money just don't seem..." Blaque whispered.

"Shut up and hurry up! I'm on parole bitch, if we get caught in I'm back in county!" K.O. whispered. "Fuck them shoes, let's go!"

All three women looked at the orderly on the floor moaning. The knot on his head from the slap jack was slightly bleeding and he was waking. But the restraints would hold long enough for them to escape.

"We're ready!" Talisha smiled.

"I not one crazy bitch." Money repeated as they headed for the emergency fire stairs.

"Thanks Benny." K.O. whispered dropping the envelope in the maintenance bucket as he held the door open. Once it closed the alarm would reset, so he quickly headed for the elevator thirty feet down the corridor.

Four flights of stairs the women ran and stopped, they knew once they opened the door leading to the street all hell would break loose. The response would be quick and tactical. One fact the world did know about Phoenix

Memorial was that it housed the mentally insane criminals also, so response would be immediately.

"Money the car is to the right on the corner. Are you ready?" Talisha asked pulling on her clown mask.

"I Boss Blood Bitch, I not crazy whore like Benny say, see…" She pressed twenty dollars into K.O.'s hand. "I make him pay for pussy still." She giggled and Blaque quickly spoke up.

"Hell no y'all… Talisha… Estar loco de atar. She's crazy y'all!" Blaque almost begged looking at Talisha.

Without warning Money slammed the door open and ran to the left away from the car screaming. "I coming soon Cashmere. He will pay for what he has done. It's his fault I am crazy."

"Shit bitch I'm out of here!" K.O. growled.

"¡ Dios nos coja confesarnos... oh Dios... ¡ Dios Santo!" Talisha whispered following K.O. to her car.

"Yes…" Blaque cried, turning left and dropping her mask to the pavement. "God help us all!" she paid no attention to the calls or car horn from Talisha and K.O. as she walked away. "Santo Dios" she cried.

Three weeks later…

"Count Jo-Jo." Zahir mumbled keeping his eyes darting from car to car while the trappers moved up and down making sales.

"Seventy-three for the week and straight for the weekend. Want me to bag it?"

"Naw! Just a random count nigga here!" Zahir handed Jo-Jo a clean G-pack. "For doing such a good job. You've been straight every week nigga. Pay just went up!"

"That's what I'm talking about!" Jo-Jo said, and his attention shot up the block. "Marky got the white Chevy, it's been waiting for five minutes."

They both watched Marky approach the car, but just as he reached the rear fender it pulled off.

"That's the first time you seen that car Jo-Jo?"

"Naw it was here yesterday too. I thought they got mad because nobody served them half way up the block." Jo-Jo answered. "Hey Tank, do this look like a hang out. If you ain't trapping bounce!" he yelled.

"Next time that car shows up get the plates!" Zahir dapped him. "Keep up the good work my nigga!" Zahir jumped in his own ride and circled the hood looking for signs of the Chevy.

"Damn sexy!" Black Boy smiled leaning into the Chevy.

"What, you act like you ain't never seen a pussy before." She cooed.

"Not one so pretty. Goddamn what are you anyway, Chinese?"

"Naw fool…" She giggled dipping her fingers between her pussy lips and into her mouth. "I'm Korean boy… You buku?"

"What's buku and yeah if that means I can take you home."

"Let's see... most black buku dang." Money reached out and put her pussy soaked hand down Black's jeans. "Damn right you buku. Really buku boy" she smiled. "Never had black boy before. Do buku hurt like first time?"

"Only if you want it too. Wait you smoke rock? That's what you want?"

"What is this rock?" she smiled instantly.

"Crack ma... coke..." He held up a fifty piece.

"No do drugs. Want to go home with the... ummm how do Chris Rock say... ummm... yeah that it... want you to knock bottom out pussy. So I can please unfaithful husband."

"Shiddd I can do that!" Black smiled with his hard on still in her hand.

Money had to admit he could do it and after he would die. She had been watching the strips and houses for two weeks now. And she had made the choice it would have to be rugby street where Black lived with his little sister of Ashley street. But that boy who ran the strip down there would never approach her car to see what she had to offer. So Rugby street it was

"A dead sister and brother or a dead mother and son, neither made a difference to her or Cash." She thought and smiled. "You buku" she smiled as Black climbed in. "But do you taste my honey juices?" She slipped her fingers back into her pussy, then put them to his lips. His tongue licked them instantly. "How taste?"

"Like honey." Black Boy laughed as the white Chevy pulled away.

"Blaque."

"K-2" she sadly smiled. Blaque turned to Tay. "I missed you Tavious."

"I can't tell!" He stood and kissed her cheek. "No calls, no visits."

"We have a situation in Phoenix."

"Talisha?" K-2 whispered.

"No, its Money... she's... how can I say this. She's insane and we kind of helped her escape the hospital, but now we can't find her."

"Good!" Man Down barked coming into the room. "Maybe the hoe bitch killed her own good ass and saved me the trouble."

"Man don't!'' K-2 smiled.

"No, it's alright Kendell. The child amongst men is expected to whine and whimper sometimes." Blaque shot back.

"Bitch!" Man Down snapped.

"Puta!" she snapped back. "I am ready for you this time. Try to spit on my again pene menuda... pequeño pija... very little cock!" she rolled her eyes.

"Stop!" Tay yelled. "He is my brother and she is my woman and that is that! Now what we got?"

"Fifty kilos... same... ten apiece." Blaque said still angry. "Small dick, so Menuda you can fuck a fly." She rolled her eyes.

"Ask Cash how small this dick is whore!" Man Down yelled using his finger to indicate gun. He laughed and walked out of the living room repeating Cash last words. "oh god nooo!"

K-2 and Tay caught Blaque as she attacked. K-2 held her in his arms a foot off the ground as Man Down continued to drive her wild.

"Ohhh please god save a gook bitch... Noooo..."

"Odiar Man Down a muerte... Puta." She spit. "Bastard!" Blaque reached as if she could grab the man who had already vanished. "Alright!" she straightened her hair. "Let me down Kendell." She calmly said. "I am fine."

As soon as he sat her feet on the ground Blaque took off running behind Man Down. K-2 and Tay caught her just as she leapt on Man Down who played Madden. "Bastardo!" She cried trying to hit him. Man Down only laughed and taunted her.

"Ohh no... Ohhh god save me. Ohhh lord!..."

"Stop Man! For real!" K-2 barked hiding a smile.

"I can't... she's one of them and don't like her!"

Jen heard the front door open and knew she was caught. "Shit!" she whispered and rushed into the basement closet. Her eyes fell on the small chest on the floor and knew her brother would open the closet to grab re-up and stash count. "Dumb bitch!" Jen thought and made a dash for the garage door. "He'd never go out there." She thought in flight. When she heard the woman's voice she smiled. She had this experience before. Watching Black gut one of them bitches and it turned her on. Jen smiled remembering how big he was and how it looked sliding inside of her best friend Carol. Neither knew she watched from the garage which sat next to the foot of his queen size bed. Jen's hand had somehow made it inside of her pants already.

"Boy you very large... buku..." She said and came into view. "I need you fuck me crazy like porno movies."

Jen smiled when she noticed the Chinese girl holding her brother's hade dick in her hand She led him to the bed and sat in front of him and almost swallowed the whole thing. "Oh my god… how…" Jen thought covering her mouth in surprise.

"Damn!" Black moaned dropping his pants. In one swift move he had the Chinese girl sitting on his face while he laid on his back. She never choked or stopped sucking what Jen knew to be a ruler in length dick. Her brother was much bigger than her boyfriend Tavious and Tavious had trouble getting inside her pussy every time.

She remembered how she screamed each time he slid into her stomach and how she choked trying to deep throat him like he asked. Even when he came in her mouth she couldn't hold it all. So how can this Chinese who seem so small think she's gonna take Black.

"I cum… I cum… ewww shit nigga I cummmmm." She screamed slamming her small ass down on her brother's face. Jen's finger worked feverishly on her own clit.

"Mmmm shit!" Black groaned and bucked but Jen didn't see one squirt of cum shoot in the air. All she saw was Black's dick disappear down her throat.

"How the… mmmm shit…" Jen thought as she felt the first wave building inside her small body. "Hurry up boy!" she continued to think while masturbating. "Put that dick in me." Jen smiled as she imagined Black's twelve inches going inside her. Even though she knew she could never take it, she had no problem with the fantasy. "Fuck me… fuck me…" She moaned quietly as she watched her brother slid to a holt inside Chinese girl.

"Ohhhh god so buku… fuck me nigga!" The Chinese girl screamed and sent Jen over the edge.

Black fucked her for dear life trying to make her scream, but only managed to give her two orgasms which made him cum inside of her body.

"Goodness… I'mmm… Mmmm…" Jen hit the floor this time as her legs gave out on the second explosion. She never believed a woman could take that much and not scream.

"I got surprise for you buku nigga." Money giggle strangely. "Close your eyes." She whispered.

Jen heard them and rushed to watch. Her heart leapt into her throat and she wanted to scream, but to do so meant she would die too.

"Ready big black nigga dick." Money giggled and for the first time Jen heard the insanity in her giggle. "Open eyes."

(Bam!)

Jennifer's hands slapped her mouth as she backed away from the garage door. She turned and ran behind the cabinet to hide. She had to get help. There was no mistaken the sound of the basement steps creaks and groans. The crazy Chinese woman was going upstairs. This was Jen's chance. Slowly she crept to the door leading into the basement. It was still cracked because Jen knew to closes it meant the squeaks would for warn the crazy woman. She listened, and more terror filled her heart as she heard the crazy woman humming right above them in the kitchen. "The back door." Jen thought and instantly realized she had left her own keys upstairs. "Get Black Boy's… Hurry!" she thought and silently cross to where his pants laid. Her eyes fell on his gun and Jen grabbed it first then the keys. "Hurry." She told herself as she heard the crazy woman move to the living room stairs and go up.

"I'm sorry Black." She cried, and she couldn't help it as her eyes met his cold dead stare. "I'm gonna get help." Jen crept to the door and unlocked the dead bolt and slipped into the freezing cold.

"What?" Tay yelled jumping to his feet. "Stay right there Jennifer."

"What is it now?" Man Down shook his head.

"Money just killed Black Boy… She's in their house waiting for some reason."

"For one of us to show up." K-2 said. "Where is Jen?"

"Limekiln and Upsal." Tay said throwing on his leather bomber. "She had to sneak out the back door."

"Zahir, Man."

"We got that bitch!" Man Down grinned. "How you want this bitch?"

"Try to get that bitch alive. But…" K-2 said. "Let's go Tay!"

Ding Dong… Ding Dong… Ding Dong. The doorbell rang. Money stood in the dining room naked looking at the front door. She knew it could be one of them coming to collect as usual. Even though it was kind of early. She had to decide. Quickly she tipped toed to the steel door and smiled as she looked out the peephole.

"Man Down." She thought and placed the Glock inches from the door. Then it dawned on her. "Steel door bitch." She giggled hideously at the fact she would stare into his scared eyes as he died.

Ding Dong… Ding Dong… Ding Dong, the doorbell ranged again

"Open up Black Boy!" he yelled. "It's me Man."

His voice alone sent such rage through her body. Money reached for the door knob and snatched it open just as the butt of the AR-15 slammed into her skull.

Talisha and K.O. ran through Sky Harbor Airport to catch the flight to Kennedy Airport and then the Red Eye into Philadelphia International. Both women were surprised when they heard the news of Money being in Philly and that she had killed one of the team's crew.

The call Talisha made to Kendell went unanswered and her little brother hung up in her ear. Blaque had said Tay only called to let her know to stay clear of his house for now and he would deliver the half million in the morning. But both she and Talisha knew it meant sure death for Money either way.

Talisha and K.O. just made the flight and now all they could do is wait.

"Please Tavious… baby please…" Blaque begged in tears. "She is mentally ill. Let the authorities deal with her. Please do not kill her again.

"She's safe" Tay lied. "I'll call you in the morning. "He hung up the phone and entered the basement of Zahir's mom's old house. Just in time to see Benny's fat ass cumming in Money's asshole. Tay had to admit, the bitch was a pro. Not once did she beg for mercy and each man who fucked her, she told them she needed her money.

"This bitch ain't crazy, she faking it!" Man Down laughed holding the motorcycle chains they had around the bitch waist and neck.

"O.k. if she ain't crazy put your dick in her mouth" Zahir laughed.

"Hell no! That bitch hates me!"

With that Money looked back over her shoulder. "I not crazy. And you still gonna die… Man Down." She looked at Benny. "Give me my money boy." Money laughed out and proved herself wrong.

"I found ten more!" K-2shouted coming down stairs. "Who first?"

Money screamed and charged K-2 only to catch a vicious right hand he threw with bad intentions.

"Man go find your uncle and his two boyfriends." K-2 grimace rubbing his hands together. "Condoms."

"Oh god Blaque please tell me she's still alive!" K.O. yelled rushing from the terminal.

"I don't know, Tay won't answer my calls."

"Take me to Tandeka's house!" Talisha insisted.

"No!" Blaque quickly said. "I told you not to come here. They are really ready to finish this, and you are very close to death now as it is!"

"Then take me to a hotel!"

"Yeah" K-2 answered his cell phone. For the first time today, Money was moaning. Somehow Pony Boy and Kool Aid both had monster meat inside of both Money's holes. Zahir had a towel tied into her mouth from behind to keep her from biting Pony Boy again.

"Mmmmmmm… Mmmmmmm… Mmmmmmm…"

"I don't do fish." Bo Pete laughed. "But she kind of cute. Reminds me of Jet Li." He giggled as Kool Aid pulled from her ass and came in her hair.

"I might go back for this fish." Kool Aid laughed.

"Sorry but I ain't sharing after tonight bitch!" Bo Pete laughed and slid behind Money. "This may hurt a little."

"Urrrrrrrr!" She moaned, and they watched him rip flesh.

Chapter 16

"Room service." Tay whispered.

"It's about time. I ordered almost thirty…" Talisha stood in the door frozen. She feared for her life instantly.

"Talisha!" K-2 shoved her to the floor. Quickly Man Down and Zahir grabbed her from the floor and slung her to the bed. K-2 pointed to the bathroom where he heard the shower running and Zahir and Man Down charged inside. They heard a scuffle, and someone hit the floor. There was no doubt in Talisha's mind who it was.

"Stupid bitch!" Zahir yelled. And both men dragged K.O. from the bathroom dripping we and unconscious.

"Let's do these bitches and be gone!" Man Down smirked.

"is that how this ends Rey, you kill your true Reina?" Talisha whispered. "Did you come to me…" She paused to let her words register. "To kill the only woman who can be your mate."

"Talisha stop playing. I will not kill you, my love for Tut will not allow that. But these bitches…" He smiled.

"And money? Where is she?"

"She was crazy as a fruit fly. We put her in a Mental Institution somewhere. You'll never find her so don't try." He lied. "My reason for coming here is to end this shit If not for me then for Tut and Angelita." K-2 moved to the bed and sat down. "Listen I wanted all of you dead. But that won't help Sirus. They are talking the death penalty Tah… He won't tell them what you did he'll die first, but if he dies, so will she." K-2 looked at the still unconscious K.O. "But still what you all did to Melinda I cannot forgive. She was my Reina, not you!" He nodded to Zahir who quickly restrained K.O. hand's behind her back. Man Down pulled his pants down while Tay opened the door.

"Don't!" Talisha whispered as all twenty men entered smiling.

"Not you my Queen." K-2 smiled as Man Down spread K.O.'s legs. "You belong to me now."

K.O.'s eyes opened just as Man Down rammed into her hairy pussy. "Ohhhh!" She screamed and struggled as the men all undressed.

"You must watch!" K-2 ordered Talisha.

Blaque and Talisha sat silently by the tub while K.O. soaked her sexually ravaged body. There was no need for words. Not a tear would she show as she gritted her teeth and bared the pain. Six hours they raped her, everywhere.

Suddenly the phone rang in Talisha's hand. She looked at the caller I.D, it read Kendell Woods. She looked to Blaque first, then to K.O. "Oh shit!" Talisha murmured looking at the screen.

"Answer it" Blaque whispered. "He's ready to talk."

"Hello Kendell… Alright, Alright… K-2." She looked up in frustration. "Yes of course I will… Yes, alone if you insist." Talisha hung up the phone. "He wants me to come to him."

"Where?" Blaque asked.

"Zahir has a car downstairs waiting." Talisha smiled seeing K.O. smile. "What girl?"

K.O. looked up and surprised both women. "At least they made me cum." And she began to laugh hysterically and instant tears.

"Go!" Blaque whispered as she undressed to climb in the tub with K.O. "I'll take care of K.O., you go… and Tah…" Blaque pauses. "This is no time to fight for the power. Submit for now!"

With that Talisha turned and rushed from the suite to meet the man who proved to be more than her match, he proved to be her superior.

"Zahir." Talisha whispered suspiciously.

"Naw ma, dead ain't what we want for you… yet. You and this nigga got some kind of bond and Tay insist that nothing happens to you either. But ma let me give you some advice." Zahir held the door open. "Tay may be your half-brother, but he don't know you. K-2 may love you…" Zahir smiled. "Yeah it's obvious ma, but he to really don't know you and its really his loyalty to Tut that kept us off you so far, not love! But if you don't make this right ma everything goes to shit!" Zahir closed the door and ran around to deliver her to K-2.

Forty minutes later they pulled in front of the manor.

"Kendell does know I still own this building right?"

"Technically yes…" Zahir grinned but physically its ours until the fire department gets here."

Talisha smiled and made a note to fully insure the property and to stock it with fictitious valuables.

"You know the way." Zahir smiled and Talisha looked unsure. "Who him?" Zahir grinned seeing Man Down in the manor's doorway. "Don't worry ma… like I said, dead is dead. Here, Phoenix of that fancy ass Ritz hotel. You're safe with us. For now!"

"Zahir can I ask you something… Please!" Talisha whispered. "Did he tell you he loved me?"

"Naw ma K-2 don't do things like expressing, he's mote of a show me kind of nigga. And his actions express nothing but love for you, but I got to admit…" Zahir smiled seeing Talisha tighten up when Man Down headed their way. "You sure almost pushed his buttons"

"And what about me? Do you see it in me? Do I love him?" Talisha continued to watch Man Down.

"No doubt ma, you're just selfish and spoiled rotten!" Zahir laughed. "Now go get your shit right with my man upstairs."

The door suddenly snatched open. "Get out bit… I mean Talisha." Man Down growled. The look in his face told her that one day he'd have to disappear the hard way.

Talisha rushed upstairs wearing the long sable the color of her hair and dew drop diamond earrings.

"That bitch a dime plus." Man Down smiled. "K-2 got the cream dog."

"So why do you treat them like shit son?" Zahir laughed.

"They gotta fear one of us nigga. Them two bitches can bring us to our knees. Shiddd I almost broke when Blaque cried last week. Naw nigga no matter how much I like them bitches I gotta keep K-2 and Tay on their toes."

"And what about me? I think I'm in love with that big bitch." Zahir laughed.

"Love? Nigga please! You like me, we love money!"

At the top of the stairs Talisha realized she was not alone. Somehow men were positioned in ways that made them blend into the hidden spaces of darkness.

"Go inside." She heard the scary mumble of the big figure stand a few feet away. No matter how hard she tried she could not make out his face. Quickly she pushed into the apartment where her father died, her fear so deep she breathed as if she had run up the two flights of stairs.

"Kendell." She cried dashing into his arms. Talisha fear was bone deep as she shook in his arms.

"Relax." K-2 whispered and held her to his body. At that moment so many things flashed through his mind. Melinda, King Tut, his brother Sirus, even the twins and K.O. "Tah this has to end! Today… right now!"

"Yes… yes Kendell… please Kendell forgive me… I'm ready to be anything you need me to be. I swear I'm sorry… I'm sorry.. Kendell…"

"Wait Talisha," K-2 held her at arm's length. "I want you to be only Talisha. Nothing more, nothing less. But it's the bullshit I need you to step away from." K-2 paused. "Do you realize how badly we disgraces Tut and his memory. He wanted nothing more than us to be a family. Tah I don't even remember how things got this bad."

"I do!" She pushed back into his arms. "It all happened that day you sat at that damn piano. I fell in love with you. Don't ask me how or why. I just did Kendell." She began to cry. "I wanted to prove I was your equal, when I should have been proving I was your mate." Talisha held on tight this time. "Don't!" She moaned as K-2 tried to push her away softly again. "No Kendell don't… ever… please! I surrender!"

With that she was in his arms heading where ever he wanted to take her. They both knew he was king!

Chapter 17

Peace in the Kingdom is only a Mirage

July 3rd, 2012

"So how was the fight?" Man Down asked putting Tay in his super head lock as usual.

"Boring nigga… Ouch mutha fucka!" Tay growled struggling as usual. "Alright Man I tap out nigga!" He laughed.

"Thought so!" Man gave an extra squeeze.

"Get off my man!" Blaque giggled as she attacked Man Down. With little effort he held her on his back laughing.

"Tay get your crazy lady off me." He yelled as the whites looked on in wonderment at the colored people.

"I'm a show you crazy muscle head." Blaque giggled wrapping her legs around his waist from his back. "Now carry me to the car."

"Whatever you say college girl." Man Down laughed. Once in the car Tay got serious. "Did the shipment make it?"

"Why wouldn't it?" Man asked. Studying Tay's face Man knew something wasn't right. "What's up Tay?"

"I told him not to worry…" Blaque interrupted. "She's loyal to us."

"To you and Tah maybe. She hates us!" Tay whispered.

"Who now? Surly not our guest…" Man asked and realized he said to much. Blaque looked at both men but knew not to ask again, she was lost for now. But one day the team would let her go.

"He's worried about K.O.!" Blaque said nonchalantly.

"What? She was talking crazy Blaque and then the bitch just up and disappear. Why shouldn't I be worried?"

"Because I have told you, she is loyal to Talisha and me."

"What she say Tay?" Man whispered pulling into the rush hour traffic.

"The bitch talking about revenging old shit… Cash and Money" Tay said. "Talking about the rape and her virginity. Especially your crazy ass." Tay laughed. "She hates you the most Man."

The car went silent for a moment than Man Down spoke with a sureness and confidence both Tay and Blaque knew he earned. He directed his statement toward Blaque.

"I swear Blaque I never really hated none of y'all with the exception of Chunky's scandalous ass and I was right. For the sake of my own mental wellness I had to drop that bully shit I used to keep y'all at bay. I actually love you…" He paused to lush. "But I swear on my swear on my own sweet grandmoms grave, if that bitch…"

"She won't Man Down. I promise… she was only blowing off steam. She still misses the twins and now that me and Talisha… well… she's just emotionally drained that's all. Give up a little more time with her." Blaque seemed to beg. "Besides, I think she likes you, that's why she talks about you like that."

"Hey punk!" Tay jabbed Man in the side.

"Sorry chump!" Man Down laughed. "I'm taking your woman Tiny."

The trio talked and laughed all the way uptown, neither worried about tomorrow, none taking notice of the black Tahoe behind them as they exited the freeway.

"How much you got this time Jennifer?" Talisha asked rubbing her temple.

"Five sixty, just like last time." Jen said rubbing her swollen belly. "Mmm girl this baby is greedy." She reached for the last slice of broccoli and pineapple pizza. "Oops!" Jen giggled after biting into the slice. "Did you want that?"

"I guess not bitch!" Talisha laughed. "Eight slices girl and I only ate two. Whoever that baby daddy is betted be glad you getting money."

"That's that crazy ass man down right there." Jen said. Both women heard the bass of his system as he pulled into the driveway behind Tandeka's old home. Now that peace had come K-2 brought his mom a home closer to his father in Norristown, Qwen and Jack insisted on a home up there to be closer to Sirus who just received a life sentence and now celled with K-Dog. Karen of course had to be her own crazy self. Instead of a home in Norristown she chose to stay in Boston with some friend as she called him.

"I got five sixty too." Talisha smiled. "And I'm keeping the change."

"What change?" K-2 asked coming into the dining room.

"We counted it four times and it keeps coming out two over." Talisha smiled.

"Not by my count." Jen rubbed her belly.

"Shiddd by your count you only ate two slices of pizza and I ate six." Talisha joked. "Kendell make sure this girl's baby daddy is…" Talisha whole body jumped as the shots rang out.

"Tay I want somebody." Blaque whispered in his ear as Man pulled behind the garage.

"I heard that." Man Down yelled. "Me to Blaque." He winked in the mirror at her.

"Boy I'm telling you if…" Tay stopped mid-sentence as the Tahoe skid to a stop. He only had time to react as the semi-automatic gunshots roared. Tay felt something slam into his shoulder, sending him down on top Blaque's body. He never saw what happened to Man. So bad he tried to get up, but Blaque held him to the ground as she fired at the fleeing Tahoe. Without looking she knew Man Down was dead, His gun was silent, so there could be no other explanation.

"It was K.O!" Tay grunted as Blaque pressed the towel into his shoulder. "Our eyes locked as she shot me. K-2 she was smiling. The bitch was smiling!"

"Shhhh!" Blaque cried as K-2 swung the Volvo around Ogantz Avenue doing close to seventy.

"Where's Man?" Tay whispered in pain. "K-2 why did you leave Man?"

"Quiet Tavious!" K-2 used his real name for the first time since he was born.

"Ohhhhh noooo Man!" Tay cried now for the first time. The pain from the .44 in his shoulder couldn't compare to the loss of another brother. The sound seems not to be able to come from his mouth as he tried to get it out. His mouth opened to scream but only tears rushed from his eyes and blood from his shoulder. Tay never knew when it happened, but he realized he was no longer in the car.

The lights all around him were bright and voices spoke about him while one talked at him.

"What's your name son?... Who did this to you?... Your friend is dead... Talk to us son... Are you in a gang?... Who brought you here?"

All Tay remember after that was Blaque's voice saying, "I brought him here sir... My name is Blaque Gomeza... I'm a..." He heard no more until...

Four days later...

"Tavious baby" she whispered. "Tavious, boy you better wake up" Karen cried.

"Mom?" He whispered, and she screamed. Blaque woke instantly. She'd been there the whole week waiting. "Ouuuch" Tay smiled.

"Tay" Blaque whispered. Stepping to the side of the bed, and bending she kissed him fully.

"Hey baby" he moaned. "This shit hurts!"

"Tay-Tay" Karen whispered. "Man Down..." she tried to explain. But her own tears and sorrow filled her chest. Quickly he turned his head and tears rolled down his face.

"The police have arrested her at the hotel." Blaque said. "She tried to get us to help her escape."

Tay instantly turned towards Blaque. "How did they find her there?" He knew Zahir and K-2 would be waiting there to kill her first. "What about Zahir?"

"He was too late and Kendell was..." Blaque lied.

"Stop it!" Tay snapped. "Don't lie to me!"

"Tell him!" K-2 barked from the door. "Tell him the truth Blaque!"

"We couldn't let..." she began to cry. "Don't do this."

"No tell him how she contacted y'all and one of you called the police and lied to me and Zahir by telling us she was at the airport waiting on a flight to Canada." K-2 harshly said stepping into the room. "No matter how much we try to trust y'all... They lied to save her life Tay. Not that I blame them, but they could've trusted us... me... at least me. I would not have let Zahir go off half-crazy like he is now." K-2 eyes fell on Blaque. "Right now, he's on the hunt to kill one of you. That's right and I can't stop him of do I blame him. You and Talisha have single handedly destroyed everything... EVERY GODDAMN THING!"

"K..."

"Naw Tay don't worry. Unlike them I'll keep it one hundred. Won't nothing happed to her while I'm alive, I promise. But after this I'm done. Jen is boxing up Zahir's, Sirus and yours. She'll get a half for her to start her life over somewhere. Enough a piece with the exception of Man Down's mother. She gets five to move away from here. I'll be back to discuss the exact amount. But first I gotta get this lying ass woman of yours safe, mom." K-2 kissed Karen on the forehead. "Let's go Blaque."

"No!" Blaque snapped.

"What?" K-2 frowned. "Didn't you hear me. Zahir is out to murder and if I don't find him first and talk some sense into him… YOU"LL DIE!"

"And I said no! I will not leave Tavious side. Go hide Talisha, Kendell please. Zahir will not hurt me."

"He sure won't!" Karen butted in. "You go Kendell. I'll watch her."

"K-2 go ahead. Please find him. Bring him here to us man." Tay moaned out. "Nurse!" K-2 yelled and turned back to Tay. "Tay he aint right, right now. Keep her here! For real Tay… KEEP HER HERE!" K-w2 was gone.

"Alright boss." Zahir frowned looking at the screen of his laptop. "Drive Jo-Jo…" He ordered the frighten corner controller. "Take me to this bitch." Zahir smiled watching the red dot that represented K-2's Volvo V8 turbo. "Left nigga and slow down. No closer than two blocks. What I told you? If he sees me you die."

Zahir knew K-2 would eventually come to see Tay and he did. That's when he had Jo-Jo bitch ass put the Lo-Jack home system 3625 PGS under the frame.

"Best damn fifty-five hundred I spent! Make a right chump." Zahir kept watch on K-2 from two city blocks behind.

"Go back to the house of correction. Listen up for your name and give me your number as you step up to the bus." The sheriff yelled. "Gale Blunt."

"Yeah… 26351-622" she answered.

"Kimberly Orton" he yelled.

"Yeah 26363-622" K.O. answered.

The sheriff cuffed the two women together sent them on the old blue school bus converted into a prison transport bus.

"So, you the bitch who took out Man Down?" Gale smiled. "They said you was fine as hell, but they never told me you looked like Britney Grinder sexy ass."

"And what's it to you bitch?" K.O. took a defensive position next to Gale.

"Slow your roll girlfriend. I just know them niggas from back when were kids together. Shiddd bitch if you took out Man Down I ain't no match for you. No with my hands. I just want to have some fun with a bad bitch. Anyway, them niggas ain't did shit for me but put dicks in my mouth and pussy."

"Yea well they did the same to me!" K.O. frowned.

"I heard the judge set your bail at twenty million… Damn!"

"I don't need no bail. Bitch I'm gone beat this shit!" K.O. smiled. "Aint no body see me do shit! No weapon, nothing but my prints on a car." K.O. laughed.

"And a dead body bitch. You in Pennsylvania that's at least three and a half to seven."

"That's it? Shiddd, I can do that on my knuckles pretty! Gal huh?" K.O. leaned in. Her free hand on Gale's chin. "Three to seven? You sure?"

"Yea." Gale smiled and closed her eyes while K.O. hissed her and became wet. "Girl you on my block and my cellmate just went home. Why don't you move down with me? I got a tv shot, and I know the law."

"Do you know how to eat pussy?" K.O. winked and licked her lips.

"Not yet…but…" Gale giggled. "You gonna teach me."

"Get out Jo-Jo!" Zahir growled. He held a stack in his left hand. "Yo Jo-Jo!" He pulled his 40 caliber. "chose!"

"I'll take the cash nigga!"

"Then keep your mouth shut!" Zahir winked. "Bounce."

"No problem Zah. None at all boss."

Zahir sat behind the large green dumpster only fifty yards away from the front door of an apartment inside of the new Kormen Capital Duplex Suites on Rising Sun Avenue.

"So, this is where you got that bitch?" He smiled and turned the radio on by hand. Slowly he turned to WDAS 105.8 backwards twice.

Two days later…

Talisha stood by Blaque as K-2 helped Tay dress in the proposition denim short set. The Tod loafers made the perfect shoe for the look Blaque wanted for him. It was called the preppy look. Most of the black college guys from Morehouse wore this same look.

"I feel stupid." Tay whispered.

"You look guape." Blaque smiled.

"Si el hombre más apuesto hermano." Talisha said.

"What about me?" K-2 frowned.

"las mismas caras de siempre." Talisha yawned.

"No… you are very handsome also." Blaque giggled. The nurse entered with Karen and a wheelchair as Tay stood from the bed. His arm still in a full sling.

"Y'all got my baby ready to go? Because I fixed all that food last night for him and I need some sleep." Karen looked at Talisha and K-w. "Blaque baby what does, ummm… Su grande tata... su largo... echa de memos para me... dejar reventado me por favor.. mean?"

"Did she say tata?" Blaque giggled.

"Yes girl… all goddamn night. See at first I kind of thought they was…" Karen grinded her hips as if she was fucking. "You know banging. So, I got out my dildo, but then she got to moaning loud and shit. I ain't know whether to masturbate of call for help."

"Mom stope it!" Tay burst out laughing as Talisha turned deep purple and K-2 turned away smiling.

"For real… Ohhh tata por favor dejar reventade me… over and over and then Kendell started with his shit. Who's your Rey… Say it, say it, say it!" Karen said with a straight face. "And I thought you and Tay was something with that Dar una paliza a chocho... comer el cono... comer el cono bastado! Shit I got to get me some!" Karen teased. "Y'all got a bitch horny."

Tay and Blaque now looked embarrassed and it was K-2 turn to laugh.

The poor Spanish nurse was on the empty bed in stitches turning blue. Karen had stopped her from breathing with her jokes.

It was time to ho and they rolled Tay out in the wheelchair. K-2 left to get the car while the women sat with Tay in the lobby.

"There's the Volvo." Talisha smiled. "My man and his simple car. I insisted on a Benz, but he says this city is a magnet attracted to glamour. What that mean. I have no idea."

"It means everybody watches the money." Blaque laughed.

"So what good is money if you can't flaunt it?" Talisha asked.

"See this watch? It's a $38,000 ross and bell. But a nigga on the street would think it is worthless, but it is the best money can buy." Tay explained. "Say they rob me, nine out of ten times I'll still have my watch after they run off with two grand out my pocket. Bling is for the broke niggas, comfort is niggas like up. Get it?"

"Bitch listen to my babe! He's smart." Blaque laughed. They all loaded into the Volvo ad headed to the smile house.

"Zahir what are you doing? This shit ain't cool!" He whispered to himself. Quietly he sat on the bed and stared at one of the only pictures that existed of the entire King Team. Tay, Sirus, King Tut, K-2 and himself all standing in front of Tandeka's crib. He smiled remembering that Labor Day weekend. That was the week Tut made them bosses. "Dammit Zahir." He wiped away a tear from his face. "Don't get soft now… This bitch is directly the cause of everything. Now Man Down is dead." Zahir spoke to the photograph. "We played fair Tut for real man she came and destroyed it all Jefe with her shit. Why you have to go and get killed without knowing your true daughter. For god sake Tut, she's no good… I'm sorry boss…" Zahir looked up as he heard a car outside the apartment. Quietly Zahir picked up his H.K. assault weapon and laid the picture on the bed. "Sorry Tut" he whispered and walked into the living room walk-in closet.

"Take my baby into the bedroom… The one on the right, not mine or the sex fanatics. He need his rest. And you Blaque keep your hands away from his grande too." Karen laughed. "I'ma heat up that chicken and greens I cooked last night. Y'all kids need some weight on them bones." She rushed into the kitchen behind the loveseat where K-2 and Talisha flopped.

"Rub my feet Kendell." Talisha moaned. "I think I now understand why Tay say comfort is for us and Bling is for the broke niggas. Ouch Kendell, these cost fifteen hundred and got my feet feeling so dolorido Tata."

"Hey, don't y'all start that cono and chocho and all that grande stuff in there." Karen laughed.

"Well it is Karen!" Talisha joked. "He can't help it if he was born with a deformity. It is deformado and I love it."

"Kendell can you help me open this jar please?" Karen asked. "And it better not be out. Y'all sex crazy kids with all that money. Now I see how those white kids always seem to be in trouble. Y'all got too much shit!" Karen mumbled as K-2 walked into the kitchen.

"Please god forgive me." Zahire silently prayed peeking through the vertical slits in the closet fan door. Quietly he eased them open and stepped out. His eyes darted towards the bedroom behind him where Blaque just took Tay and back to Talisha who sat with her eyes closed.

"Zahir don't do this man." K-2 whispered. "I love her dog... Please Zahir! I can't take that again man."

"It's her fault K-2. Listen man why can't you and Tay see what those bitches are up too. First Sirus and Melinda. Now Man Down homie! Who next?"

"Listen homie its over! No more killing... No more funerals. Zahir I'm tired of crying and not sleeping. We can get out and just live. Live for Sirus and Melinda. Make it all be for something Zahir. Man its done, don't do this shit homie... I beg you Zah please!"

"What about Sirus man? Life nigga without parole!" Zahir eyes darted to the kitchen where he saw Karen standing in the doorway.

"Don't do it baby" Karen whispered.

"Man Down died loving these two bitches. They set him up! They even help the bitch to escape." Zahir was now crying.

"No Zahir, we loved him too" Talisha whispered.

"Shut up bitch." He raised the H.K.

"Zahir look at me. Not her dog. We sis shit to man. K.O. was a virgin, we raped the bitch with twenty niggas for hours. Nigga we blew Cash head completely off and drove her sister Money insane. Man as we speak we got that crazy bitch in Manchester Canada in a mental hell hole under a false name. Zahir we all did shit and we all knew the consequences could mean death one day. So did Man Down." K-2 begged.

"K-2 I'm tripping! You're right, we all knew the consequences could be death…" Everything went into slow motion with those words. K-2 first warning was the look of rage in Zahir's eyes as they glanced over. Tay read Kendell's eyes to late. "And so… Did… She!" The H.K. raised as Kendell Woods Jr dove on top of Talisha to shield her small body from the 5.56mm that flew with certain death her way.

Tavious raised his Glock and fired one shot, twenty-two shots to late as the assault rifle let loose sure death on three people he loved. Neither he or Blaque knew who screamed first or the loudest, all they knew was that everybody they loved was dead. EVERYBODY!

The neighbors who called the police will dream of the cries of anguish forever, o much pain rolled into one drawn out scream from two lovers.

Chapter 18

¡ Viva los Reyes! – The King is Dead

Angelita sat facing her father Don Monteza on his private jet. They taxied into Philadelphia international airport. She knew her mother had only days to live. If he asked the question she knew he would. Angelita could lie and protect mama, but she knew he already knows and to lie would be to kill herself. Now they came to retrieve the body of the only person papa really loved, his own Talisha.

Don Monteza turned away from his only child and asked what she feared to hear him ask for over fifteen hundred miles. His eyes blood shot red from crying.

"Who is at fault here Angelita." He quietly growled. "You will tell me what I already know child." And again, her father began to cry.

"Mama father." Angelita cried also. "And I papa." she finished.

"For this she will die! I gave life after the bull-fighter. I set her up in Miami away from me and my anger. Angelita I warned you away from her ice-cold heart… But how does a child avoid its mama? And now you let her take!" he screamed. "My only joy, Talisha, my little bird…" Don Monteza cried openly in the cabin of his private jet.

Peaceful Mourning Cemetery filled with twenty-five white limousines and hundreds of white rentals. Everyone who mourned the fallen brothers came as requested wearing White. The city stood still for two men most never even know. The news coverage had the deaths as a tragic teen shooting where four lost their lives. What about the other three, what were they to do now?

Legally Tavious Tay-Tay Lewis was now the ward of Tandeka Woods, but how could a woman raise a grown man who's seen more and done things only a grown man could do. No… Tay was now almost on his own… Almost.

"Tavious" she cried beside her man. His only answer was to put his hand on hers in silence. Blaque realized all his words were gone and all his tears cried out. She could only hope he still held love in his heart, a love meant only for her. Blaque laid her head on his shoulder and continued to cry, she would cry if he couldn't. For Talisha, for Kendell, for Man Down and Sirus. She'd cry for Karen, for Money and Cash. She'd cry for Chunky and also Black Boy who she barely knew. But most of all, she'd cry for Tavious her King….

Epilogue

"Jennifer this is called an epidural, it's sort of a pain killer. It's actually a spinal anesthetic to help with the pain. I'll apply it to your lower spine.."

"Ohhhhh!" Jen cried out in pain. The labor came on as they left the cemetery this morning. Only she and the driver knew she was taken to Chestnut Hill hospital to deliver his child. He didn't know in his time of grief he would become the father of a proud baby girl.

"Ohhhh goddd." Jen cried out as the long needle penetrated her lower spinal cord.

"Jennifer I'm going to need you to push when the next labor contraction hits." Dr Martinez whispered. Instantly Jen screamed as so did the doctor. "Push."

For the second time in less than two weeks Don Monteza's private jet landed at the Philadelphia international airport. And again, he sat facing Angelita Monteza.

There were no words spoken between them, for he still wanted revenge for the death of his only reason to be who he has become. But he knew not to speak would send the wrong message to Angelita about the actions he was about to take.

"You will bring me both!" he whispered.

"Yes papa." Angelita replied "Both papa."

"Remember she lives only for you… The bitch is no good. But for a child's sake she lives."

"Yes papa… Thank you." Angelita kissed his hand.

"Both… Now go!" he ordered.

"Tay" Blaque whispered.

He looked up with empty eyes and almost broke her heart.

"The hospital just called and said Jen is having the baby. I want to go… Be with her since she's now all alone." Blaque whispered.

Tay could see the hurt in her eyes. He felt her pain and wanted to hold her so bad. But he himself felt empty, void of an extra emotion at that moment. Even the news of his child being born held no excitement for him at that moment. Only he, Karen and Jen knew he was the father and it was his mother who looked forward to the child, not him or Jennifer. But now who would they have. Jen alone in this world without even Karen. No, he could not let that happen for his mother's sake.

"I'm going to baby." He tried to smile and only managed a half smile. "You drive beautiful."

"Thank you Tavious." Blaque almost burst in tears.

"Doctor that's two heart beats!" The nurse urgently said.

"What? Wait two… Ohhhh!" Jen moaned deeply. "How could my baby have two hearts?"

"No Jennifer... It's not one big baby... It's two babies."

"But... Ohhhh!... You said a girl... one girl... Ohhhh shit! That drug ain't working... Ohhhh!"

"Doctor... we have a drop in pressure... she's flatlining." The nurse yelled rushing for the crash cart.

"Shit, scalpel." Dr Martinez screamed dragging the table closer. "Scalpel dammit!" Quickly he made the incision and removed a baby girl.

"She's gone doctor..." The nurse whispered as he removed a baby boy.

"Clear! Dammit clear!" He screamed looking at this child on his table dead. The electric charge entered her body causing it to lift from the table. "Clear!" He hit it again, and again and again. "CLEAR DAMMIT!"

"She's gone doctor... doctor... Donald stop! She's gone!"

"Kimberly Orton legal visit." The prison guard yelled from the front gate at his desk.

"That's me." K.O. growled walking up. Three weeks inside and everybody knew not to fuck with the bitch name K.O. on C-2.

"Big time..." The guard smiled. "It's the DEA and ATF, damn sucks to be you! By the way a friend of a friend said Blaque wanted you comfortable. So, holla at me when you get back."

"Yeah I'll do that." K.O. winked and left to go see who wanted what. Her lawyer was moving fast. And now that three and a half to seven looked a whole lot shorter.

"Ms. Orton." The tall white man smiled. "First let me say I am a big fan of yours and wish you'd come back to the ring. I'm special agent Wilkerson and this is special agent Carmen Diaz... DEA!"

Quickly K.O. eye fucked Diaz and knew she was interested in her.

"K.O. let's talk about the Monteza Cartel and what really happened to a Ms. Melinda Clark and Sirus." Diaz quickly said avoiding eye contact. "Don't worry he's already on board."

"What do you mean dead? Who..." Don Monteza growled more with his eyes than with his powerful voice.

"No papa... she died in child birth. Martinez said he did everything to save her. Her heart just stopped." Angelita whispered.

"Dios tenga en su Gloria." Don Monteza crossed his heart "This one is so cute." He kissed the baby on the forehead. "Hello Talisha." He smiled, and baby talked.

"And his name father?" Angelita smiled.

"What else... Tavious Kaytue Lewis" the Don culled his newborn Talisha.

"What do you mean gone?" Blaque exploded. "The grandparents... they took them..." The nurse flinched.

Blaque saw what no women would want to see in her man eyes, the truth. She knew by his sadden reaction of sorrow.

He was the father! And there was something else… He now held rage inside like you hold down vomit. Sooner or later it had to come out.

"Tavious." She moaned now really afraid it was too much, He just shook violently where he stood.

www.ingramcontent.com/pod-product-compliance
Lightning Source LLC
Chambersburg PA
CBHW021518240626
47154CB00002B/686

* 9 7 8 0 6 9 2 1 0 8 2 2 2 *